LOVE IS KNOT EFFICIENT

LOVE IS KNOT EFFICIENT

LOVE IS KNOT RATIONAL

BOOK 2

IMOGEN KNOWED

ISBN: 978-1-972670-04-0

Cover Character Art by: Ekkleir Art

To everyone with AuDHD struggling to be "human."

CONTENT WARNINGS

Characters within this book are imperfect. Their actions are not necessarily condoned and their opinions are not necessarily shared by the author.

Below is a list of content warnings with an emphasis on ones that may be considered triggering:

- This book has explicit descriptions of sexual acts.
- While all sex is consensual, some acts may be considered dubious or coerced.
- Internalized ableism and ableist language are used around the concepts of mental health.
- There is an instance of overt sexism (conflated with anti-omega language).
- There is a short conversation involving fat shaming and fatphobia.
- Characters discuss wanting children and having "baby fever." A secondary character and her baby make an appearance in the book.
- A child with lukemia is mentioned.

Please note that the following may be considered spoilers:

- There is an allusion to past physical and sexual abuse by a previous romantic partner. This book explores coping mechanisms (primarily unhealthy) that the FMC has as a result.
- Suicidal ideation and what could be viewed as a Voluntarily Stop Eating and Drinking (VSED) suicide attempt occur.

This is not a comprehensive list, as a comprehensive list can never exist. Feel free to contact the author if you have any concerns or questions. This book is about respecting triggers, and that is a view the author very much does share with her characters.

ACE

"Today's the day, brobot!" I murmur, as I press my face into the cool skin on One's neck.

A low whir answers me, similar to the sound of a hard drive spinning up. I settle my chin on his bicep and watch his face transition out of Sleep Mode. His eyes light with a bright blue glow that makes him look haunted for half a second before he does that lopsided smile he's been practicing.

"Morning," he says before that little hiccup of a pause that I think means he's running through all of his code before he can recall my name, "Alpha-Ace."

One is what I call "obnoxiously comforting," and, per his spec sheet, he is the most spoonable of the bots. For the last two months, he's been my 'babysitter' and 'nestwarmer.' Well, 'nestcooler,' really, given his internal cooling system. Not that I'm complaining, considering the night sweats I suffered as my body acclimated to taking suppressants.

I repeat now that I know he's fully online, "Today's the day, brobot! The day I finally get—"

"'To feel that pussy,'" One interjects, perfectly flat, like he's quoting me from a prior incident.

I half laugh, half gasp in feigned offense. "Dude, I did not say that." *Not out loud, anyway.*

"Incorrect. You said it last night, before you fell asleep."

He presses his chest and opens his mouth wide to play a recording of me saying, "Tomorrow is the day I finally get to feel that pussy, brobot."

I cringe. "Okay. Well, I guess I said it once."

"You also said it on Thursday while we surfed, and Tuesday—"

"Okay, okay, I get it." I laugh while playfully punching his arm, then immediately regret it, because it's like punching a boulder wrapped in silk. "Thanks for keeping me honest, bud. Sorry, I'm just excited."

Today is the day: the 40th of Styles and I taking suppressants and Styles taking birth control. This is the day that the combination of hormones running through us would make her feel—and I'm quoting her here—"safe enough to simulate breeding through vaginal penetration." And despite the blood leaving my brain when she said "breeding," I was able to concentrate enough to put the date in my calendar.

I close my eyes and picture spreading her legs, tracing her folds with my cock, finally feeling her walls wrap around my knot—even if it won't swell to full size since she's not in heat.

I'm currently spooned around One's back, my leg thrown over his hip, and my cock is wedged between the seam of his thighs. It's not sexual, or at least not entirely sexual; it's just the default arrangement of our naked bodies, like plugging in your phone before bed. I shiver and spin away from One as I try to hide the fact that my morning wood just got a lot harder between his thighs.

One notices, anyway. Now that he's upgraded and programmed to monitor me, he notices everything. "Nervous?" he asks, voice soft.

I shrug, but I can't play it cool with him since he's clocking every minute detail of my body's reactions. "Yeah. A little."

"It will be good," he says, matter-of-factly. "The synthesized nerve endings on my penis tell me her vaginal walls are quite pleasant."

I say with a laugh, "Thanks, buddy. Happy to know all the anticipation won't be for something unpleasant."

He doesn't get the sarcasm; he usually doesn't. Instead, he exclaims, "Congratulations, Alpha-Ace," while high-fiving me, because that's what we do now. "Your patience will be rewarded, and you have been very patient."

"I have not," I say, snorting. "I jerked off into your mouth last night."

"Patiently," he says, smiling wider, then laughing with his 'making a joke' laugh—he's programmed to have three distinct laughs, and I can tell them all apart now.

"Good one, One," I reassure him with a laugh and arm squeeze, even though the joke doesn't make much sense.

I let my hand linger around his arm, because if I ignore the absolute lack of pulse and the weird pillow-like coolness, I can almost trick myself into thinking he is a real guy, a real alpha. It's funny; when I first moved in, I thought the bots would be competition. Now, they're somewhere between brothers, workout buddies, and—if I'm being honest—sex toys with really good customer support. *Perfect Pretend Packmates.*

I prop myself up on an elbow to look at the space where Beth should be. The sheets are twisted, but the pillows and stuffed animals are undisturbed.

I sniff. The air is thick with One's synthetic pheromones. Even though it's not exactly the same as an alpha scent—cleaner, as if it's been through a Brita filter for sexiness—I find its presence comforting. Since I started taking suppressants, my scent has mellowed into an off-brand version of itself that I can barely smell—it's discomforting. But my ocean scent is there, however faint. Even fainter, though, is the scent of coconut cookies.

She never came to the nest last night. She said she would.

She's probably in her lab, or crashed out in her rig with Three as her weighted blanket and Two fussing over her, reminding her she has a body that needs pesky things like food and water.

I peek back at One and ask, "Is she working?"

One's eyes whirl in that way I know means he's wirelessly talking to the other bots. "Correct. Alpha-2's logs indicate she fell asleep at her computer last night for 1.2 hours. She is currently awake and working in her office."

I miss her, even though she's only two floors below me. It's stupid, but I do. I want to crawl into her lap and get my hair petted while she works.

But today—today is the day. I was hoping she'd be here when I woke up, and the fact that she isn't sends a wave of disappointment over me that One senses.

He pats my head and says, "Comforting Alpha-Ace."

I'm not going to lie. The transition from 'horny omega in heat' to 'not particularly interested in fucking omega in hyperfocus' has been...jarring.

Styles warned me this is how it would be. She had Two compile a detailed printout of her non-heat routines, with an emphasis on how often she "sought release," which is adorable nerd-speak for "got off." It was so infrequent that I thought I had misread the chart. I had—but what I thought was every few weeks was actually every few months.

When she saw the look on my face, she made this cute little flustered "meep" noise, then rushed to her computer to send me multiple scholarly articles with titles like, 'Sexual Incompatibility of Alphas and Omegas Outside of Heat Cycles and the Effects on Pack Harmony,' while ranting about how most of them were "written by alphas and therefore suspect."

She then launched into an explanation on how males, especially alphas, are touch-starved from birth due to the patriarchy and A/B/O Dynamics—convinced they can only receive love, affection, and emotional support from their omega.

I kind of lost the thread when she got to how colonialism and capitalism have shaped my ideas of what an omega should be, but I got the general idea. However, there was no room for confusion when she said in her Ace impersonating voice, "If that's the omega you need, I ain't her, bro." I know she was teasing me with that voice, but I found it super cute, anyway. I replied as suavely as my drained brain would allow, "Cookie, you're the omega I need." And I've agreed to all her terms, because it's true.

She wasn't wrong—about alphas, I mean. *She's rarely wrong about most things.* We do grow up thinking we're the main character, not just of our own story, but of everyone else's. But Beth isn't interested in alphas as main characters. She'd prefer they weren't in her story at all and built her life around specifically avoiding alphas—until I showed up and threw my knot in her best laid plans.

Now that her heat is over, Styles spends most of her time in her lab or adjoining office, blasting out code like she's going to solve all the world's problems by programming sex bots, video games, and/or drone shows for that DJ she knows. I spend most of my time waiting around for her to come to me, because the way I see it, she's the main character. I'll wait as long as she needs me to.

It's been a bit lonely, but I have One to keep me company. She reprogrammed him so that my happiness is now his 'Primary Directive' or whatever. While I wait for her, I hang out with him—and he's getting more human every day as he learns from me. We surf, binge K-Dramas, cross-train (even though dude really doesn't need to and mostly just makes me feel pathetic in comparison), and fuck.

When Beth does crawl into the nest, it's nice. The sex is good. Still not vaginal, but good—great even! But it's infrequent. Mostly it's just me and One. Sometimes Two joins us. Three is a wildcard and only comes into the nest without Styles when he is "testing a new Pleasure Sequence," which I have learned to avoid unless I'm feeling reckless.

Starting suppressants hasn't been a cakewalk either. Coming down from a rut is rough on its own. There's all this empty space where the hunger used to be, and you're supposed to fill it with "constructive self-reflection and new patterns of supportive behavior," but mostly you just wind up scrolling thirst memes and wondering what the fuck you're supposed to do with your hands. *Wrap them around your knot and squeeze is the answer you usually come to, but you know there are other things you should be doing.* But the suppressants have made the hormonal flux even more jarring. My sex drive is all over the place, and I've been inordinately mopey. But luckily, I've had One to help me with all that, as my personal sex bot and night sweat alleviator.

But...I still want her. I want her all the time, and I have been counting down the days. And she knows today is important to me. So I thought...I thought she would have been here...

I nuzzle into One's chest and bite back the bitter feeling in my throat.

She didn't do this to hurt me. She didn't.

This wasn't an intentional choice to hurt me, with some hidden meaning behind it—that's not Beth's vibe.

The moment Beth realizes she feels something, she tells me. Bluntly. Usually, with visual aids and assigned reading. She doesn't sugarcoat her feelings. She's got this pedantic precision for boundaries and talking through the pain points of our relationship. I like that about her. I always know exactly where we stand in her eyes, because she tells me—at length.

She treats our relationship like we're a team working for some Fortune 500 company, and she must optimize our compatibility as if some shareholder's yacht payment depends on it. Last week, she sat me and the bots in a little circle, and we did this thing called a "retro" in which we said what we should "start doing, continue doing, and stop doing."

It was nice. We really figured some things out. I'm supposed to 'stop' calling her Cookie when we're not fucking; she is supposed to 'start' coming to the nest at least three nights a week for "quality time"; and the bots should 'continue' providing me with companionship the remaining four nights.

I'm also supposed to 'start' explicitly stating if something Beth does makes me feel rejected. She said, "Historically, this has been my biggest weakness in a relationship. If I am upset with you, I will tell you. But I can't always tell if my actions imply rejection. So, I need you to tell me."

So, I know she didn't do this to hurt me. *I know it.* But knowing something and feeling something aren't always the same thing...And right now, all the self-talk in the world isn't erasing the sinking feeling in my chest.

I stare at the ceiling and say more wistfully than I mean to, "I was hoping she'd be here when we woke up."

"I know," One says, patting my head the way I wish she were—the way I pretend she is.

But it's not her. She's not here. She hasn't been here for a while.

It's just me and my favorite faux-friend-shaped appliance, petting my head with a gentle sweetness that he's learned works on me. *He doesn't actually love me.*

"Perhaps we surf today," One says. "Weather conditions and moon patterns indicate optimal waves on the north side of the island."

I sigh. "Dude, you know my game plan. No surfing today. I'm spending the day with Beth."

One gives me a surprisingly human and extremely doubtful look.

I lift off him and ask, "What? What's with that look?"

"A backup plan is never a bad thing to have."

"One. Seriously. Are you being...coy? Are you even programmed to do that? What is this about?"

"Alpha-2's data stream indicates Sunshine is in," he does that pause thing, "hyperfocus." He looks at me with a dead seriousness, as if he just told me she was dead.

"Isn't she always?" I ask, confused.

"This is...unprecedented. Alpha-2 postulates the hormones from her suppressants and birth control have dulled her already poor interoception. Her reaction time to stimuli unrelated to her task has slowed by 39%. Dopamine, norepinephrine, and acetylcholine have reached levels much higher than her hyperfocus baseline. Distracting her from her current task will be...difficult."

"Okaaaay..."

"Alpha-2 recommends not distracting her. The results will be... unpleasant."

"What does that mean?"

"Rage Mode Activated," One says, eyes wide as if he's recalling some old war story.

"Fuck," I groan and bury my face in One's favorite teddy bear.

"Consoling Alpha-Ace," he says, petting my hair.

His hand pauses as his eyes whirl—his bot bros are messaging him.

I ask, "What're they saying?"

"Alpha-3 disagrees with Alpha-2's conclusion. He wants to test his Boy Band Protocols—" He stops talking, and his eyes spin different colors, as if the bots are having an argument in his eyeballs.

I ask, "What's happening?"

One covers his ears as if trying to drown out the voices of his botty brethren and says, "I told them, as Prime Alpha, it is Alpha-Ace's call." He grins at me as if he's said something very clever, and I think he actually has.

I have to try, right?

"Will you help me? Help me distract her?" I ask, and it comes out softer than I mean it to.

"Of course," he says. "I am your...wingman."

"Thanks, One."

One grins as his eyes swirl. "Alpha-2 has activated our Activity Transition Assistance Routines."

2

ACE

One grabs my ankle, and before I realize what's happening, he yanks.

I resist on instinct, clutching at the sheets, but he overpowers me without any real effort on his part, and I'm quickly sprawled on the floor, ass naked except for the sheets I'm tangled in.

I don't even have time to ask "what the fuck?" before he's got both my legs under his arms and is dragging me out of the room like I'm a rickshaw and he's got an important patron to pick up down the hall.

The sheet bunches up over my face. I struggle with it while twisting in his grip. "One, what are you—"

"Implementing directives from Alpha-2," he says with a cheery flatness.

I finally get the sheet off me, leaving it in our wake in the hallway.

When he turns into my room—what used to be his, before Beth converted it into my "safe space"—I say, "Dude, I can walk," but he doesn't listen; he just plows ahead, releasing one foot only to open my bathroom door.

"One, drop it," I command, pointing at my foot, as if talking to a dog.

He releases my leg, leaving me naked and spread on the carpet.

I ask, "One, what the fuck, man? What are you doing?"

He blinks those hyper-blue eyes at me and does the little jaw-cock that means he's proud of himself. "Optimizing Alpha-Ace's motivation, appearance, and mood."

"Why'd you have to manhandle me, bro? Is this because I was mopey?" I ask, standing, checking my ass for rug burns.

"Yes," he says. "Alpha-2 assessed your emotional state as," he shifts his voice to Two's, and continues, "'conducive to lollygagging.'"

"You could've just asked me to get up!" I exclaim.

"Yes," he says again, back in his normal voice. "But we have a limited window, and Alpha-3 suggested I," he shifts his voice to Alpha-3's, and continues, "'drag his bitch ass from the nest.'"

Of course, that was Three's idea. Dude is probably jerking it right now, thinking about One manhandling me like that.

One marches into my bathroom, flips the lights, and beelines to the shower. He turns on the water with a single flick of his wrist, not even looking at the knob. I don't even need to test the water to know he got the exact right temperature. He knows I like it hot, but not scalding, and can meet my exact specifications with a precision only achievable by a bot in a high-tech shower.

He turns and stands, butt naked with the commanding presence of the six-foot-six alpha he's designed to emulate, and locks eyes with me. He's so serious I shiver, as if my Prime Alpha were about to bark at me. He doesn't bark, and he's not Prime Alpha, but he does point a finger at me and command, "Shower. Now. You have excess oils in your hair and residual sweat from last night's activities. Your scent reads as 'mopey fuckboi.' Showering will substitute it with a more sexually appealing scent."

"Hey, fuck you—"

"And your hair is doing what you call," now he shifts his voice to mine, "'anime chic.'"

"Can you stop changing your voice? It's skeeving me out."

I look in the mirror, and he's right. My hair is full anime, standing up at improbable angles. "Hey, omega girls like my hair like this," I say, posing for the mirror and thinking I actually look pretty good. I flash myself a smile.

Still got it.

"Incorrect. They think you look stupid, they're just too nice to say so."

"Wow, bro. Way to fuck a guy's whole worldview," I say, lollygagging my way to the shower.

One pats my head and grabs my arm, speeding my journey toward the water. "There, there. They only spare your feelings because your other traits are admirable enough to merit their fake praise of your bad hair."

I sigh. "Nice save, One," I reassure him, even though it didn't really reassure me. *I should probably be more honest with him. I'm probably training him with bad data or whatever.*

He shoves me into the shower. It's big enough for two people. Well, two betas—not an alpha and an oversized alphabot. So when he gets in with me, it's a little cramped.

I lean my head back and close my eyes. The water is perfect. I let it rinse over my apparently bad hair, but I can't relax, because I can feel his gaze on me. I know One is inspecting me, trying to optimize every square inch of me for maximum Beth-appeal.

When I open my eyes, he is standing in front of me, holding a plastic razor and shaving gel next to his face as if he's a surgeon holding up his newly scrubbed hands.

I startle. "What are you doing?"

"You will be 11.7% more likely to attract Sunshine if you depilate," he says.

"Depilate?"

"Shave."

I rub my face. "I'm good, bro."

"Not your face."

"What? My hair wasn't that bad!"

He points at my dick. "No. Hair removal will emphasize your knot."

"Wait. You want me to shave my balls?"

One doesn't break eye contact. "Not just your balls. Your entire pubic region."

When I don't immediately respond, he asks, "Do you want to perform at optimal efficiency?"

I look down at his hairless body, then back at his obnoxiously perfect, toothy grin, and sigh. "I guess."

I reach out to grab the shaving stuff from him, but he lowers to do it himself, smile unflinching, eyes unlocking. It's so devilish, my balls must recede into my body from the fear it induces.

I back up. "Dude. Are you programmed to do that?"

"Yes," he provides without elaboration, now kneeling in front of my terrified dick.

I squint at him, unsure if he is actually programmed to do this. *Why would Styles give him that functionality? How does that help with her heat? Alphabots don't have pubic hair—or balls. Is this that 'AI hallucination' thing where they tell you something with their whole fucking chest while being whole fucking wrong?*

He senses my reluctance. "Styles would find it optimal. That is why I have the function."

Well, fuck, if putting code in your nanny-slash-fuck-bot isn't the most passive-aggressive way a girlfriend can tell you she wants your balls shaved, I dunno what is. I'll add this to a future retro topic.

I brace against the back wall and lean my head back, not looking at him. "Alright. Go ahead. But if you cut me, we're fighting."

"And I'll win. So, more than just your balls will bleed."

"Way to make it sound super ominous. Maybe next time just say, 'Try me, bro,' or something."

"Understood," he says, while he lathers me up and begins shaving me with surgical precision.

Why am I so fucking hard right now? I didn't know being threat-

ened with lacerations and then being shaved was a thing for me, but I guess it is.

I look down, and my cock is bobbing right next to his face, brushing against his forehead as he moves it from side to side, really getting into my crevices. He doesn't comment. He doesn't even look at it. Just follows through with whatever sequence of steps he's programmed to perform, none of which apparently are "and suck Ace's dick while you're at it, please."

I guess I could ask him to...but maybe I should save it for Styles.

He rinses my dick off, and the moment is over.

One stands, returns the shaving paraphernalia to the shelf, and pours a comically large glob of shampoo into his palm, before massaging it into my hair.

It feels incredible—his fingers are just the right blend of strength and care, and he makes slow, circular motions that border on erotic. He rinses, then applies conditioner, saying, "Remove your head from the water for two minutes."

He grabs my hips, turning me away from the water so that my back is to him, then lathers my body wash between his hands, and massages my shoulders while washing me. I've come to really enjoy the spa-like experience of bathing with One. It's always really nice after a long day of surfing like yesterday, and I let myself melt into it. *Sometimes a boy likes to sit back and let things be done to him with a dash of manhandling. Yeah, I know, real 'alpha' of me, but who's gonna tell? One?*

His hands glide over my delts and traps, kneading like he's working dough. I lean into it, groaning. "That feels nice, One."

He smiles. "I was designed to provide pleasure."

I snort because somehow that statement of fact is both funny and arousing.

He's gentle with my scars, the big one from surfing gone wrong, and the smaller ones from just being a dumbass in general.

He lifts my arms and works the body wash into my pits, then

down my sides, pulling me into a full-on bear hug so that he can get my abs, resting his chin on my shoulder. He kisses my neck, and pokes his finger into my belly button: the one thing that will make me —*a super macho alpha*—giggle.

I'm still recovering from the embarrassing giggle when his cock presses between my ass cheeks, humming with a continuous vibration.

I tense, not because I'm scared or not into it; I'm just surprised.

I relax and giggle again, because I don't have to pretend to be macho or alpha or whatever for One. *Nothing kills my alpha act quite like being mounted by a guy who's an even bigger, faker alpha than me.*

My cock twitches as his head, slick with lube from a hidden internal compartment, traces a line from my taint up to my entrance, then down again, to buzz against my balls.

"One," I say, breathy and hoarse, "I thought you didn't want to loggygag?"

He leans into me, nibbling my ear. "Alpha-2's analysis postulates Sunshine is 36% more likely to orgasm vaginally if you've released less than 3 hours before penetration."

"You always know exactly what to say to a guy," I joke. "Your seduction techniques are impeccable."

He wraps a hand around my cock, and the other goes to my chest, holding me to him.

He says, "You find statistics seductive? You and Sunshine are matched in more than scent."

He strokes me with slow torture, teasing the slit with his thumb. The pressure is perfect—he's learned exactly how I like it.

"I was joking," I gasp.

His cock keeps up its slow grind against me, the head kissing my hole but never pushing in, just promising.

My knees go weak, but he holds me steady. "Easy. I got you. Come for me, Alpha-Ace," he whispers.

He pumps up and down, changing up the speed every few

seconds, never quite letting me get used to it. His other arm still has an elbow braced on my pec, but his hand comes up to wrap around my jaw, so that his thumb presses against my lips. I suck, because this seems to be something he likes, or at least something I tell myself he likes.

"You are the Prime Alpha," he whispers in my ear. "You are going to fuck her so good."

The words short-circuit my brain. It's so stupid, but it works. I close my eyes, see myself with Beth, see her moaning, her legs around my waist, my knot swelling inside her, and—

"Your mouth," I gasp.

He spins me, drops to his knees so fast the tile almost cracks, and takes my cock in his mouth.

The suction is unreal—almost too much. My initial instinct is to pull away, but then his tongue does something that should not be possible for a non-organic, and he hums a little. The vibration travels up my spine, rolls my eyes behind my head, then screams to my brain, "Don't you fucking dare pull away from this."

He grabs my hips and pulls me in, pressing me past any semblance of a gag reflex. His throat is so tight, and when his lips make a perfect seal around my barely inflated knot, my eyes snap back to his face to watch him work.

He's the only person—well, faux-person—who's ever been able to take my knot into their mouth like this. Supposedly, some omegas can do it, but Beth made sure this alphabot could—*just for me. She's such a kind girlfriend.*

He moans, and the sound is so needy, so reverent, it almost makes me laugh.

But I'm not laughing now.

I fuck his face, fast and rough, because I can with him—there's no chance of damaging him or hurting his feelings.

And he lets me—smiling around my cock as if letting me fuck his face is his life's purpose, and I fuck his face knowing that it kind of is.

He braces his hands on my thighs and looks up with those blue eyes as if daring me to try harder. He purrs around my cock and increases his pheromones, all signaling, "I love this. Fuck me harder, Prime Alpha."

So I do.

I'm losing myself to it, grunting and fucking in a state as close to a rut as I can get without an omega present.

The pressure is building and building.

His hand slides between my legs, and his thumb presses hard behind my balls, then slides back and up, as the tip of his finger breaches me with a gentle push.

That's it. I lose it.

I come so hard it's like a punch to the chest.

I grip his head and groan so loud that it vibrates off the tile walls.

He swallows my seed, every drop, and keeps sucking, even as I twitch and gasp, milking me until I can't take any more.

When One lets go with a pop, I fall back to lean against the wall, panting, head spinning.

He doesn't stand yet. He waits for the rest of my cum to bead at the tip, then laps it off with his tongue, smirking at me with a look of smug satisfaction.

He stands and wipes his mouth with the back of his hand. "You are now optimized."

He leans into me, bracing himself on the tile next to my head, stroking his cock, while I hug him.

This part is mostly for my benefit. He doesn't have to have an orgasm. He can turn his dick off with a literal push of a button. But apparently, I get a little weepy if I don't get post-nut cuddles and extra weepy if he doesn't come when we fuck. *Why? I dunno. The data tells him I need it without any psychoanalysis.*

He does need to remove my cum from his internal systems, though—which he can do in a few different ways. But jacking off kills the weepy Prime Alpha bird and cummed-up systems bird, both with one cum stone. *They're nothing if not efficient, these bots.*

I hug him tight, kissing him, while he continues working his cock.

He moans and shoots our combined loads down the drain, twitching believably, before using both his arms to hug me back.

For a minute, I pretend he's real. A real packmate. A real friend. A real person.

I miss my pack brothers. I miss Beth.

I get weepy post-nut despite his extremely efficient efforts.

3
ACE

I stand in our closet, naked and not at all in a hurry to get dressed, holding my phone.

Today's the big day!!!!!!!!!!

THOMAS

Yeah, yeah, we know. The day you finally get to feel that pussy...perhaps consider a less pejorative way to express your excitement, Ace.

WHAT? How do you know?

FORREST

lol u put it on the shared calendar, dumbass.

He sends a screenshot of an all-day calendar event.

FORREST

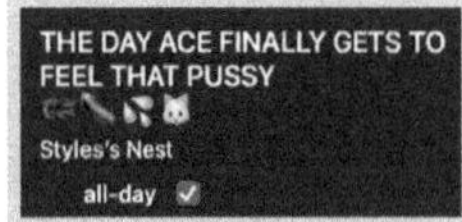

THOMAS

And you set an alert.

FORREST

we're happy for u. r u nervous?

One's rummaging around in the wardrobe behind me, whistling some old boy band tune that is stuck in his head lately. He's chipper, but my mood is still hanging low and loose, like the towel around his hips.

I type out:

Actually. Yeah. I miss you guys a lot. I wish you were here with me for this.

But erase it.

Too needy.

Instead, I send:

Nah. One is optimizing my appearance.

FORREST

i wanna c! send pics!!!!!

He's still working on me. Will send when he's done.

My hand drops to my side, and I nearly lose my grip on the phone, a weakness suddenly overtaking me.

I should tell them the truth.

I sit on a bench by a wall of designer sneakers One owns but never wears. Turns out, even bots can be sneakerheads.

Signaled by my endocrine system or whatever whistles to him when I get pathetic, One abruptly straightens and turns his attention to me. He puts the clothes he's holding on the bench beside me and then puts a heavy hand on my shoulder.

Since I'm still pathetic, he pulls me into an awkward hug. "Consoling Alpha-Ace."

"Thanks, One."

"You miss your packmates," he says, and I'm not sure if it's a statement or a question.

"Hey, you're my packmate, One," I grin, trying to deflect.

He pulls back, smiling, but then his face contorts, and I swear I hear a gear turning in his head. "Not your alphabot packmates. Your human packmates."

"Yeah, I miss them...a lot."

"Do you want to talk about it? I am here for moral support."

"No thanks," I sigh, my eyes locking on the ground in front of me.

One stands straight, but leaves his hand on my shoulder.

I glance up at him. His eyes are whirling, cycling through multiple colors—he's processing something with the other bots.

"Are you talking about me?" I ask, knowing they are.

He hesitates and says, "Um," which is weird. I've literally never heard any of them say "Um," before. Then, after multiple beats, he says, "No," while placing both index fingers together in front of his chest. It's his tell—trained on too much anime.

"Bro, why are you lying?" I ask, pointing at his fingers.

He looks down at his hands and back at me, then hides his hands behind his back. "I am not lying."

He's lying about lying. Great. I'm teaching this bot some great new skills.

I ask, "Are you telling them I'm being a whiny little bitch?"

"No," he says, and his biceps twitch as he stops himself from pressing his fingers together again.

Whatever. I don't feel like dealing with whatever weird bot thing he's doing right now.

My phone buzzes, but I don't look at it. I just put my face in my hands.

My eyes burn as I blink back tears.

What is wrong with me? I should be happy...

One points at my phone. "If you do not wish to speak with me. You should speak with them."

The closet is big, but suddenly it feels small with him standing this close to me. His scent is overpowering, and I can't even smell my own after the shower. I rub my hands hard against my neck, trying to get to the scent source, before returning them to my face. It doesn't help.

My phone vibrates again.

"You should not ignore your packmates," One says, grabbing my phone and placing it in front of my face, unlocking the screen.

THOMAS

Ace, are you ok?

The bots texted that you needed us.

FORREST

It's ok to feel overwhelmed right now. Today is a big day.

I glare at One. "Dude! You fucking texted them!"

One looks bashful and bites the inside of his cheek—another anime tell. "I did not text them. Alpha-2 did."

I groan.

I try to think of something funny to say, something that won't make them worry. Instead, I just type:

Yeah. Just nervous.

THOMAS

You'll be great. You've got the bots to help you.

FORREST

Nervous? Ace, you're no stranger to the p in v. What's really going on?

Yeah, but...I miss you guys. I wish you were here to help me.

One stiffens, and I feel bad, so I say, "One...it doesn't mean that I don't—"

He cuts me off, holding his hand up. "Do not apologize. You need your whole pack. We understand." He says "we," and I assume he's speaking for his brothers.

I stare at the three dots that keep appearing and disappearing from both Thomas and Forrest.

One says, "You should ask Sunshine again about your pack coming to visit. She might reconsider."

"Doubt it."

One cocks his head. "You are defeatist today. Normally, you are the most optimistic member of the pack."

"Yeah, well, that's because I don't have all that data in my head proving my optimism wrong like you bots. But on this...I have the data for this..."

Just a few days ago, I asked Beth if my pack could come for a weekend, meet her, hang out—something low-stakes. I even suggested a hotel nearby that they could stay at. She didn't even look up from her computer. She just said, "That is not a workable scenario for me," and kept typing. I tried to laugh it off, but it stuck in my chest for hours after, like I'd swallowed a thumbtack.

Every time I bring them up, it goes like that.

One's eyes whirl, and he's talking to his bros about me again.

"Hey, stop worrying about me. I'm just all hormonal from the suppressants," I lie, hopping to my feet and smiling, rubbing the back of my neck—my tell.

My phone buzzes in my hand.

THOMAS

I'm sorry we aren't there for you right now.
Please call if you need us.

FORREST

What if we came and didn't meet Beth? Or
maybe you came home for a while?

Fuck, now I've got both my packs freaking out about my mental state.

Nah, it's fine, bros! Seriously. I'm good. Just got a little weepy for a moment. One sucked all the happiness out of me in the shower, but I'm good now.

I cringe because that's a bit much, even for me, but send it anyway. They know I get a little weepy after I come, so maybe they'll believe it.

I clap One on the back. "Show me the outfit you picked out for me. I've gotta text the guys a pic of 'Optimized Ace.'"

He grins and nods, retrieving the clothes he's selected for me. He holds up a pink Henley and grey sweatpants.

I raise my eyebrow. "Seriously?"

"She associates these items with the statistical probability of sexual activity due to their prevalence in romance novels. And pink is her favorite color."

I pull on the clothes and check out my reflection.

Not bad. I don't know if I'd call this optimized, but whatever.

"Nice choice," I praise, and he beams.

I wrap my arm around his shoulder, pulling him into a hug, so I can take a picture of the two of us in the mirror. At some point, while I was moping, he got dressed and is wearing pretty much the same thing as me.

I laugh. "Twinsies. Cheese, One."

I take a picture of the two of us, fake-smiling into the mirror, and text it to Thomas and Forrest.

Ready to feel that pussy.

THOMAS

Ace, please do not say that to Styles if you'd like to actually achieve that goal.

FORREST

I dunno. A girl who wrote a 'face fucking' algorithm might find it cute.

I look to One. "What do you think, brobot?"

"It is a 'Face Fucking Sequence.' And, to summarize a code comment left by Dr. Elizabeth Styles in my copyrighted code, it is called the 'Face Fucking Sequence,' because there is no single word in the English language that describes the act of consensually thrusting a phallus into a mouth, from the perspective of the phallus owner. Irrumatio is the closest, but its implication is non-consensual. Fellatio is what the owner of the mouth is doing, not the owner of the phallus. And, since 'Face Fucking' sounds less gross than 'Skull Fucking' and is shorter than 'Actively and Enthusiastically Receive Fellatio,' it is called 'Face Fucking'."

That was a summary? I can only imagine how long a rant that code comment actually is.

Normally, I don't let him finish his little misunderstandings, but that was quite the lesson, and I wanted to hear where he was going with it, but now I clarify, "No, dude, I mean, do you think she'd think it's cute?"

His eyes whirl as the bots argue the point. He shrugs. "Inconclusive."

"Alright, I guess I just won't say it," I laugh. "Fuel up before we fuck that pussy?"

"Yes, but that also may not be a phrasing she appreciates."

4

STYLES

I snicker at my lower-left monitor as I submit a pull request with the description:

> Found your repo, loser. Fixed your off-by-one error. Again! Get better at code or get better at hiding 🤡

Even though it's his private repo, I still tag affogatoBro276 (a name Percolate thinks he can hide under) as a reviewer.

"Dumbass," I whisper to myself, unable to suppress the smile. I don't know why trolling him brings me so much joy, but it does. It's adorable that he thinks he can hide his shitty code behind a fake name. I'll find him. I always do.

Okay, back to the task at hand.

My attention returns to the top-right monitor, where adorable hand-drawn plants sit dormant, just waiting for me to give them metaphorical life. We're working on a cozy music game about growing plants—one of the many games currently in production at the company I'm CTO of. I'm not really on this team, but this game is special to me, so I insert myself when necessary. Evelyn, CTO and my bestie, tells me I need to try to "let others do their job." And I do... they're all just so bad at it! I can do it faster! She recently lectured me that sometimes, the best person for the job is the one with the bandwidth for it, not necessarily the one who can do it fastest...which... makes no fucking sense.

I press play, and the cute little plants dance. *Squee.*

The delightful synth pop soundtrack for this section of the game, plays in the earbud in my left ear. I've heard this same 10 seconds of music about a thousand times today while I've worked. The repetition is comforting. My other bestie, Finn—one of Evelyn's alphas and a rare alpha who actually doesn't suck—wrote the music. The soundtrack is always a nice hit of dopamine for me, so I do the work of the slowpoke dev team because it makes me happy—*and inefficiency doesn't.*

My right ear buzzes with Two's low hum of a voice. He's been prattling on and on about something all day—being a bit more fussy than usual—but I've effectively tuned his voice down to the volume of a refrigerator hum. That's actually a poor metaphor. If his voice were a refrigerator hum, it would annoy me until I disassembled it and replaced the compressor in a fit of rage-fueled single-mindedness. A more accurate metaphor would be 'down to the volume of a refrigerator hum perceived by ears attached to a neurotypical brain and nervous system that more closely resembles one the world was designed to accommodate.'

My attention returns to the lower-left monitor as a green check appears with the message:

As always, thank you for wasting your time resurrecting a zombie repo just to prove your superiority—to me ten years ago 😩 You really don't have better things to do, TorqueCat?

My heart pounds in my throat.

Fuck. He's kind of got me there. There's no way I could have found this code and corrected it without, like, caring enough to look for it and fix it.

Goddamn it.

I can't have him thinking I think about him!

My thumb flies to my mouth as I chew my nail.

An annoying noise blares at my side, but I try to ignore it.

What should I say?

I could use one of my response algorithms to pick the sickest burn possible, but...for some reason, that feels like cheating with Percolate.

My rig is essentially an old dentist's chair that I've modded out with hydraulics, six monitors, and a desk to hold my peripherals. I press the button on my rig to shift from lying to sitting. The world, which has been reduced to my six monitors, zooms out as I pull my knees to my chest and rock.

Okay, I've got to say something snarky. Really let him know what a moron he is. But make sure I explain how easy all this was for me—he can't know how much effort I put into finding it. If he finds out how much of my day is spent thinking about ways to one up him, I'd lose all my leverage.

"Hey, Three...help me respond to this douche," I say, sure Three is around here somewhere.

The annoying noise gets louder.

"What is that fucking noise!?" I ask, annoyance shifting to anger.

"Beth," Two replies, soft and polite, "you have exceeded your scheduled work interval by 76.3 minutes. That is your log-off alarm. Would you like to begin the transition to low-stimulation activities?"

I smack the button that turns off, not snoozes, the alarm, and flick my hand at Two in the universal 'later' gesture, but keep my eyes locked on the screen.

Maybe a gif. Something real snooty and hip. Do people still use gifs? Didn't I see something about how only millennials use them?

Derogatorily...like, I'm a millennial, but I don't wanna be one derogatorily—not when I'm trying to show Percolate how lame he is and how awesome I am.

I need him to think I'm perfect and infallible.

I am googling, "Are gifs a cringy millennial thing?" when Two's voice pops up next to my right ear, voice even softer: "If you wish, I can prepare a lavender tea and warm compresses."

"Not now," I murmur, not taking my eyes from the monitor. "Hit me in thirty."

"Of course," he says, and floats away.

Where the fuck is Three?

On Slack, I receive a ping from a contract dev:

🦆 Danny Smithe-External
I'm getting a hard freeze when the third plant grows its fifth-tier leaf. You seeing this, too?

I was, and already fixed it. I was going to push the change, but got distracted by Percolate's shitty code.

I commit the change and merge it with main so the rest of the team can see my changes.

🐰 Elizabeth Styles
It was a null ref. Something got unhooked in the Editor. Check main.
🦆 Danny Smithe-External
You're the best, Styles.
🐰 Elizabeth Styles
np 😎

Now what to do about this fucking Percolate message?

I'll ask Evelyn. She's a pro at deknotting alphas with words.

Elizabeth Styles
Hey, Evs. Random q, but...are gifs lame?
Evelyn Charles
You're asking a middle-aged mother of three? I'm honored you think I am an accurate judge of lameness.
Elizabeth Styles
First, you're not middle-aged. Second, you're the coolest person I know. (Other than myself, of course).
Evelyn Charles
Hate to break it to you, omega, but 40 is middle-aged. But, I know for a fact I'm NOT the coolest person you know, so do you have some hidden agenda for asking me about gifs? Is this really about your love life or something? Alpha problems?
Elizabeth Styles
God, E. Never mind. I'll just ask Three.
Evelyn Charles
Holy shit! Am I right!? Did I finally do a Styles-level observation about you? Because if I were wrong, you'd just tell me! Right? OMG! Is this how you feel, always 100 steps ahead of everyone running your algos? A girl could get used to this feeling.
Elizabeth Styles
Bye, E.

I close Slack. She's no help. I should have known better than to ask her anyway. Since she started popping out babies, her snarkiness has really taken a hit.

A Discord message pops up from a fellow hacker, with a link to a Reddit post:

BigOmegaNotation
This you?
TorqueCat
Course Knot 😉

I flip to the Reddit window in question, where one of my anonymous alt accounts recently posted a long and deeply sarcastic takedown of Percolate's most recent 'white knight' hacking attempts. There are already three replies, all variations on "He's such a tool."

I allow myself a brief, mean giggle and kick my feet.

The time passes in a series of micro-increments:

Make a small change.

Push.

Check the logs.

Chat in Discord.

Find a snarky meme.

Open Percolate's GitHub. Paste meme. Delete before sending. *I shouldn't even reply because replying would prove I am watching. Not replying is the better choice.*

Rinse. Repeat.

I startle as I realize Two is standing beside me. *How the fuck long has he been standing there?* He's holding a tray of small snacks and a mug of lavender tea—it's cold, so he's been there a while.

When I look at him, he says, "Beth, it has been more than thirty minutes."

I ignore him.

He sets the tray on the desk, removing the last tray he put in front of me—still filled with untouched food—and is careful not to block my view or jostle my mouse or keyboard. "Beth, please remember to hydrate."

"I have been," I say, pointing to the untouched water bottle next to me. As I look at it, I realize it's a lie. I am parched. My tongue is fat and dry in my mouth, thrust painfully behind my teeth. "Oh." I try to relax my jaw and reset my tongue before I drink the water.

Two looks relieved as I hand him the empty bottle with a smile. "Hydrated. Thanks, Two," I say, trying to dismiss him.

He stands there.

I keep coding.

He stares at me—his enormous size taking up too much of my periphery. I shift my rig back to a lying position, and my monitors move to block him from sight, but I think he's still standing there... waiting for something.

Two shifts so I can't help but see him, putting his face right in front of the monitor I'm looking at. "Your blood sugar is trending low. Can you please eat the food I've brought you?"

"I will." My hand reaches for one of the finger foods, but goes back to my keyboard so I can reply to a Reddit comment about the flaws of Percolate's pathetic attempts at being a hacker.

Two places his hand on my shoulder: "Beth. You should take a break. You haven't eaten in—"

I groan loudly and look at him with a stare that might fry his internal systems. "Two, I. Am. Busy. I will stop when this build is stable. I am close. And you pestering me is only slowing me down. If you want me to stop working so badly, maybe leave me the fuck alone."

He frowns. "Understood."

Fuck. I'm being a bitch. He's just doing what I've coded him to do.

I catch his shirt as he turns to leave. "Hey, sorry, Two. I know you're just doing your job. I'm really close, though. I'll be done soon."

He smiles, but it's not his usual smile. It's...doubtful. The range of emotions they can express has increased tenfold since they've been training off Ace's mannerisms, and I'm finding it harder to read them *—they're getting too human. Too hard to read. Too unpredictable. Maybe I should roll back some of their changes.*

I release his shirt, and he says, "I'll leave the tray and check back in the agreed-upon interval."

He leaves, and I'm back to work. It doesn't take me long to enter that wonderful flow state that makes me feel alive—even if it makes me forget I'm a human with an actual body.

I just need to get this build stable...I need to stop getting distracted and focus.

A notification chimes, then another, then a third, until they stack into a wall of sound. I ignore them, or at least I try to. Every unread notification, every red dot, increases my heart rate.

Two says something, I'm not sure what.

I swear to God, if he is harassing me about my elevated heart rate, I'm gonna turn him off.

I fucking know! Your pestering me doesn't fucking help, Two!

Two says, this time with some urgency, "Beth, I've drawn a bath for you."

"I'm working," I say, fingers still flying.

"The water is getting cold—"

"So is your face," I mumble, not really sure what that insult even means, but he's annoying, and I made him, so I can insult him however I want.

I drown him out, but I make out the end of his sentence, "...sex with Ace today." That gets my attention.

"Huh? Ace? Is One not taking care of him? If they need to refill One's self-lubricating reservoirs, they are in the lab by his repair station."

"No. One is taking care of Ace—"

"Oh, okay, good," I say, as a message on Discord grabs my attention:

☕ Percolate
Here I was thinking exposing corruption made me a good guy. But, I've been informed it actually makes me a quote, "dork with delusions of grandeur."

Oh my God, he actually found my Discord handle! Took him fucking long enough.

TorqueCat

I just call 'em like I see 'em

Percolate

Come on, Torque. What's it gonna take for you to finally admit that I'm as good as you?

TorqueCat

Dream on.

Just like a fucking alpha. Expecting everyone to praise them just for passing the bars they set in hell. The world doesn't revolve around your knot, sir.

You're not my man or my dog. If you want me to call you a good boy, git gud, bro.

Percolate

So, if I were your man, you'd call me a good boy?

My heart is once again pounding in my throat. I sputter and look around.

"Three, I need your help!" I shout.

Two is standing next to me, but I don't see Three anywhere.

Ping. I respond to a Slack message and go back to reviewing the game's code.

Two is still prattling on about something, "...spend time with him today. He needs you."

I ask. "Huh? What? Who needs me?"

Ping. Ping. Ping.

My hands and eyes fly as I put out each little notification fire.

"...human interaction..."

Ping. Ping. Ping.

Percolate

Cat got your tongue, Kitten?

Fuck. I forgot about him.

I bite my nail again. I press the button to make my chair sit so I can hug my knees and rock.

What do I even say to this? I need Three.

5

STYLES

Suddenly, my home's surround sound is blasting an early-2000s boy-band ballad at full volume. *What the fuck?!*

My hands fly to my ears, but the lyrics of Fates Five's *Omegababy* come through loud and clear:

Babygirl, your love calls for me.
You're pullin' at my heart from across the sea.
Omegababy.

I spin my chair and scan the room, but everything is blurry. I dare to uncover my ears so I can rub my eyes and see.

The music is louder now:

Babygirl, your fever is back.
And if I'm not enough, we'll form a pack.
Omegababy.

The lights turn off momentarily, until a single can light illuminates Three on the other side of the room. He's wearing his leather jacket, shirtless underneath, abs out for no reason. His hair is styled in the "I spent two hours trying to look like I rolled out of bed" look that makes me swoon in a way I wish it didn't.

"Turn it down!" I yell over the music, but my voice doesn't carry.

The chorus swells, and Three hits a power pose, arms out and head cocked back, like he's fronting an imaginary stadium tour.

I can't help but laugh at him. "What the fuck are you doing?" I ask, moving my monitors away so I can see him better.

Another can light illuminates, highlighting Two. He's flanking Three with his face in his hands as if he were embarrassed to be made of the same parts as the guy attitudinizing next to him.

I try again, "Three, turn down the music!"

This only seems to encourage him. He smirks, a peacock finally acknowledged by his chosen peahen, and launches into a dance routine. He rolls his hips and ghosts his hands in the air. The whole thing is overtly sexual, deeply annoying, and incredibly entertaining.

Babygirl, my heart was closed off.
And if I'm out of line, you can be the boss.
Omegababy.

I hit the button on my rig to fully push my monitors out of the way and turn my chair to them. I remove my earbuds and perch on the edge of my seat and realize I'm giggling, smiling so hard my face hurts.

Three gently hits Two and points at me, still dancing, loins swaying in a way that does things to mine.

Two looks up at me, dumbfoundedness crosses his face before he shifts to a defeated sigh. Then, he joins Three in dancing! He's less invested, but holding his own for a bot who doesn't have a Dance Battle Routine. *Oh my God, when did he learn to dance?*

They dance their way to me, mouthing the lyrics.

My giddiness overflows, and I can't help but sing along, "Omegaaaaababy!"

They box me in at the desk, a wall of artificial pheromones radiating from them both, and I'm giggling and blushing like I'm back in middle school.

"What are you doing?" I ask, thoroughly confused and thoroughly entertained.

Three winks. "Updating Activity Transition Routines to include Boy Band Protocols." He pops the collar of his jacket, then spins on his heels.

Two adds, "You haven't left your position in 14 hours. Standard attempts to disengage you from your task have been ineffective. You ignored the timers."

I glance at the corner of my upper-left monitor: they're right. My interval timers are all dismissed, all ignored, all flashing bright red warnings that usually get my attention, but did not today.

I sputter. "Oh. Shit. Okay, well, let me just—"

Three slides his arm around my shoulder, pulling me up from my chair.

I squawk, "Hey—!"

"Come, Moonbeam," he says, swinging me around until I'm facing away from the wall of monitors. "Dance with me."

"Let me just finish this one—"

I lunge for the chair, but he holds me tight, shaking my body to the rhythm of the music.

"Three, seriously—" I start, but when he does another body roll, followed by the splits, I can't help it; I laugh, belly-deep and uncontrollable.

He pops up, running his hand through his hair, before lifting me to wrap my legs around his waist. He bends me upside down, running his hand from my chest to my navel, tickling me with this absolutely dirty dance of his.

When he sets me on the ground, still grinding his crotch against me, I ask, "Okay, okay, what are you up to, Three?"

"I told Alpha-2, Boy Band Protocols would make a sufficient distraction. It appears I was correct," he says, smiling at Two.

"Why are you trying so hard to distract me? It's only 11 am?"

Three doesn't stop grinding on me. He leans in and whispers, "Today's Simulated Breeding Day, Moonbeam."

I freeze. My brain takes a full three seconds to process the sentence.

"Wait. But...that's not till Saturday," I say, knowing what they're probably about to tell me.

Three grins, all teeth and mischief, hips still gyrating. "Today is Saturday." He claps and thrusts his hips to the beat of the song.

Two rolls his eyes and crosses his arms at his chest, the way Three usually does.

"Oh, shit," I say. "I thought today was Thursday. I'm not even supposed to be working today." My face flushes.

Two nods, a little mournful. "That's what I've been trying to tell you."

Three spins me again, this time pulling me into a full-body hug while charismatically and rhythmically humping my leg. "Come on, baby, let's get you cleaned up."

I turn from Three, whose pelvis has not stopped thrusting, and ask Two, "Is Ace mad? Did he leave? Is he going to break up with me?!"

Two shakes his head, his exasperation variables reset, and smiles warmly. "No. Ace is eating breakfast with Alpha-1. The day can still go as planned. I have prepared a bath and breakfast for you."

I grab their hands and bounce. "Thank you! Thank you, both of you. I'm sorry I snapped at you both."

Two replies, "No apology necessary, Beth."

Three smirks. "This is what I was made for, Moonbeam," and he grabs my hand, dancing me toward the door.

I jump, stamping my feet like I'm in a one-woman double-dutch game, my excitement uncontainable, and squeal, "I'm finally gonna feel that cock!"

Three laughs. "Three: 2. Two: 0."

I ask, "Huh?"

Three smirks. "Just keeping score."

6

ACE

I sit at the kitchen island, staring at my eggs, trying to convince myself I actually want to eat them.

I don't.

Then it hits me—faint but there: coconut cookies.

I turn my attention to the top of the stairs.

Elizabeth appears, flanked by Two and Three like some weirdly hot Secret Service detail. She's wearing a light-pink dress, the hem hitting her mid-thigh, and her hair is down—actually down, like, floating around her face, not pinned up in a million clips or crammed under a hoodie. Her lips are shiny, her cheeks pink, and I think there might even be a little mascara on her lashes.

The air leaves my lungs. I stare so hard I forget how to blink.

When my eyes catch hers, she does a little fist pump. She smiles, strikes a hands-on-hips pose, then sprints down the stairs, nearly tripping on the last step. But she doesn't falter; she plows forward, and launches herself at me—

I'm still sitting here, stunned and stupid, when she crashes into my lap, wraps her arms around my neck, and kisses my face a thousand times in a row, not bothering to aim for my mouth.

I tip backward, almost taking the stool down with me, but I don't care; I just hold her tight, inhaling her coconut scent and trying to memorize this exact moment forever.

"Oh, my god. I'm sorry. I'm sorry. I'm sorry!" she pants, punctuating each word with a kiss. "I lost track of time. I'm so sorry, Ace. I should've come to the nest last night, but I didn't. I thought it was Wednesday when it was Friday. And now you're going to be mad and—"

I kiss her, which is the only way to get her to stop talking, and it works.

She melts against me, all legs and arms and soft skin. Her heart is racing, and I know this rambling means she's scared.

I say, softening my voice with sincerity, "It's okay, Cookie," and brushing the hair from her face to look at her.

I glance over her shoulder at the bots behind her. Three and Two are watching us with identical "our work here is done" expressions.

Beth shakes her head, eyes moving to my chest, no longer able to maintain eye contact. "No, it's not. But I think Three figured out a good solution for future such events." She wraps her arms and legs around me tighter, nuzzling into my chest, clinging to me like she's afraid I might vanish if she lets go.

Three now looks about as smug as I've ever seen him, which is really smug considering smug is his default state.

But then something weird happens. Three's face spasms, and his whole posture shifts. He straightens, head snapping up, eyes flickering a weird shade for a second before going back to normal.

Three looks at me, then at Beth, then at Two, still standing next to him. For a moment, he seems confused, like he forgot why he's here.

Beth doesn't notice. She's too busy kissing my neck, then my jaw, then my ear, her hands digging into my hair.

I try to ask, "Hey, babe, is Three okay?" but Beth covers my mouth with hers and bites my lower lip.

She giggles, not looking at him, "Yeah, he's probably still running his Boy Band Protocols," and goes back to kissing me.

Three's looking at his hands like he just realized he has them. He catches his reflection in the shiny refrigerator and runs his hand over his face, observing his jawline.

I try again, "No, seriously, babe—" but she kisses my mouth slow and hard, then runs her tongue through my mouth, scooping the rest of the sentence right out of me.

She pulls back to breathe, and the way her hair falls in her face makes my fucking heart stop.

My tongue, too eager to eat her, lets me use it for other purposes, so I can say, "Cookie, you look so fucking beautiful."

She grins. "Two and Three helped me optimize my appearance for your preferences. Do you like my dress?"

"I do," I say, and start to say more, but she wiggles on my lap, and I lose my train of thought because holy shit, she's not wearing panties.

I freeze, and I think maybe my heart actually stops.

She notices and grins, all teeth, and then whispers, "No undies."

I'm dead. I've died. I'm a ghost in my own body, haunted by the fact that my girlfriend just sat on my lap, in a dress, with nothing underneath.

I try to say something charming and complementary, but it comes out as "Huuuh."

Beth giggles so hard she snorts, then buries her face in my neck, her arms squeezing me even tighter.

A small crash distracts me. Three has his eyes locked on Beth and me, but he's slowly moving around the room, running into things. His movements are uncoordinated, like his legs aren't synced. He makes a weird noise, like someone thumping on a mic, and then whispers, "Hello..."

The other two bots are watching him, like they, too, are trying to figure out what he's doing.

I want to ask what the fuck is happening, but then Beth nips my earlobe and whispers, "I love you, Ace."

I say, "I love you more."

She makes that meep noise that tells me a spiral is coming, then says, rapid fire, "I'm sorry. I got so wrapped up in the code, you know how it is, and the alarms didn't work, Percolate DM'ing me, and I couldn't NOT respond—"

I shut her up with another kiss.

Three says, "Fuck...it's her," and grips the counter so hard I think he might crush it.

But I can't care about him, because my omega is in distress, fighting a battle with her brain.

She pulls back, and her eyes are welling up, "Please don't think I don't love you as much as you love me. I will try to be better with—"

I squish her cute little face in my hands. "Cookie. I feel so fucking loved right now. It's okay. Really."

She melts, then lifts to wrap her arms around my head so she can kiss me.

This time, when we break apart, she's flushed all the way down to her chest, her skin warm and glowing.

She looks at me like I hung the moon, and I feel like I'm on it, Earth's gravity and air no longer available to me.

"Alpha-3, status update," Two commands, and I glance at them just long enough to see One and Two holding Three down, but I ignore them because she's back to grinding on me, and I can feel her through my pants.

The friction is so intense, the feeling so raw, I don't care what the fuck Three is doing.

I just want her.

Now.

I rasp, "You wet for me, Cookie?"

She bites her lip. "Why don't you find out?"

She yanks my shirt over my head and tosses it aside.

Two commands, with a voice more assertive than I've ever heard. "Alpha-3. Run diagnostics now."

I don't see what happens next, because Beth removes her dress—slowly, deliberately, eyes locked on mine the whole time, and honestly, the brobots could be arming a nuclear bomb or something, and I'd give zero fucks right now.

When her dress falls, it's like seeing her for the first time. She's all soft curves and sharp edges. Her breasts are small and perfect, and her nipples are already hard. *Pink, her favorite color—mine, too.*

She's shaved, and I can see the way she's wet for me, already.

My head spins.

"Oh, Cookie, you shaved for me," I say, thumb itching to stroke her clit.

She laughs, "Three insisted."

Three shouts, "Oh, fuck! How do I—" then freezes. His arms fall slack, his face goes blank, and I swear he just...logs out. He stands there, like a limp noodle bot, while One pokes him in the side and Two mutters something about a "malfunction."

Then, suddenly, Three is back to normal. His eyes open, and he looks at the other two before smirking, "What? We fuckin'?"

I ask, "Cookie, what's up with Three?"

Beth doesn't care. She climbs onto the island, pulling me toward her, and kissing my face again, slower this time.

You know what? I don't care either.

I can't wait.

I spread her legs wide and get a taste of my favorite coconut cookie: running my tongue slowly and languidly up her seam.

She shivers, but doesn't let me finish. She pulls me up so that I'm face-to-face with her and squeezes my cheeks between her palms, "Do you want to finally feel this pussy, Ace? Because I want to finally feel that cock." She pouts. Fucking pouts. Like she's been rehearsing the most perfect facial expression for just this moment.

Thank fucking God One insisted I came earlier, because that look would have done me in, otherwise.

"I want you so bad I can't even stand it," I choke out.

She laughs and bites my shoulder. "Then fuck me, Ace. Breed me." Once again, I'm happy I came already today. *One is smarter than he looks.*

She shoves my sweatpants down, and my cock springs out, hard as steel and pointing directly at her pussy, knowing exactly where it belongs.

"I need you now, Ace." She hooks her legs around my ass, pulling me toward her.

When my head kisses her folds, the softness is so unreal. And as I pierce through her threshold, I see stars; it's so perfect.

My omega. My everything.

She moans, high and breathy, pulling me tight against her.

Every millimeter I press forward scrambles my brain, and when my knot presses in with a pop, my brain joins my breakfast on the plate behind her, scrambled, indistinguishable from the eggs.

I can't remember my name, or where I am, or what I'm supposed to do with my hands, but I remember what to do with my cock: please her, love her...*her, her, her, her, her*.

She kisses me, slow and messy, and says, "You're mine."

I growl, "You're mine," as my ocean scent finally returns to me, pulled from me by my omega.

This is everything I wanted. Everything I've been waiting for.

7

STYLES

When Ace pushes all the way inside me, I hug him tight and cry out, panting against his shoulder. My mouth is hanging open, and I'm probably drooling.

Ace freezes, every muscle in his body tensed like he's caught in a freeze-frame.

"Did I hurt you?" he asks, breathless.

"No. No. It's just. Overwhelming." My voice is thin, a little tremulous, but I mean it. It doesn't hurt. The stretch of him inside me, while I'm not slick and stretchy from heat, is unreal and amazing.

My nails dig into the flex of his traps—the same traps that sent me into a heat-fueled frenzy the day I met him. *God, he's strong.*

He lowers his head to my shoulder and just stays there, not moving, not talking. His cock twitches inside me, and my walls clench around it like I'm trying to test the limits of this new hardware. *God, he's gentle.*

I wiggle. "You can keep going."

He moves slower this time, and the stretch is still there.

He's trembling, a fine vibration that starts in his thighs and travels up his spine, and I realize he's holding back for my sake.

It's painful, but not in a bad way. It's pressure, friction, and warmth.

He pulls back, scraping every nerve ending along the way. The withdrawal feels like a loss, and my body begs for its return.

I pull him forward, and he follows my lead, his thrusts growing more confident, less controlled.

Each thrust gets easier, better.

And before I realize it, we're slamming against each other, rhythm matched, pulling away, then meeting back in the middle.

I've spent so long avoiding this—avoiding him, avoiding the possibility of being open, being known, being invaded.

But this doesn't feel like an invasion. This feels like an embrace. Like a gift.

We're two atoms colliding, then bouncing apart, not yet losing our kinetic energy, as we seek the perfect configuration, the perfect angle that will lock us together and form a new molecule.

It's amazing.

My mouth is open, but I'm not making noise, just breathing in his scent and the sharp sweetness of my own coconut pheromones.

He pulls out to the tip, then drives in hard, hitting a spot inside me that feels like a data packet slamming home. My hands slam the countertop in response.

"Still okay?" he asks, grinning down at me with a smugness barely disguised under a mask of reverence that says he knows I am more than okay.

I try to reply, but it's just a squeak and a nod.

He laughs—a real, delighted laugh, and fuck, I like it when he's happy.

I want to make him happy every second of every day.

I lace my fingers behind his neck, gripping his hair just a little, holding on for dear life so I can say, "Fuck me, Ace. I'm yours."

He fucks me in earnest now, hips snapping with an athletic grace I recognize from watching him surf.

He is built for this—literally, evolutionarily built—and I can't believe I ever thought I could opt out of the whole alpha-omega thing.

My body is a traitor. It wants him. It wants all of him. It doesn't care that I'm not in heat. It doesn't care that I'm on suppressants and birth control. It wants him to fill me up to the brim.

No...my body isn't a traitor, it's just a few frames ahead of my brain.

I want him. I want all of him. I want him to fill me to the fucking brim and lock into me so I can't spill a single drop of his sea seed.

He kisses my neck, and I imagine him biting down. I want that. I want it so badly I can almost taste the blood of biting him back.

I wrap an arm around his neck and use my other hand to brace against the counter, matching his rhythm, lifting off the counter, relishing the sound our flesh slapping together makes—waves crashing against my defenses, knocking them down and washing them away.

His knot is there, I can feel it, just a slight bulge that presses in when he bottoms out.

"Knot me, Ace," I rasp out. I bite my lip before I say something stupid like, "Claim me! Fill me up! Breed me! Knock me up!" or any of the other life-ruining things I want him to do to me right now.

He hesitates. "I don't know if I can...with the suppressants, it might not work."

"Try."

"It might hurt—"

"I don't care! Knot me, Ace! I need it," I practically shout.

He buries his face in my neck and inhales, deep and hungry. His voice is thick, almost slurred, like he's drunk on the smell of me, when he says, "Oh, Cookie, I missed you so much." It makes zero sense because I've been here the whole time, but people say weird things when they fuck. I'm over here about to ask to be claimed for fuck's sake, so I don't ask him to clarify.

"I missed you, too," I say, because it feels like the right thing to say in the moment.

He shudders, the knot swells, thickening in increments, each pulse stretching me wider.

Yes. Yes. Yes.

He kisses my neck harder. Then his teeth graze the curve of my neck, but he doesn't bite down, just scratching at my scent glands.

His knot keeps swelling, and I keep accepting it into me.

It pops past my threshold. In and out. And the pain of the pop is better than anything I've ever felt.

It's different than the bots. It's different while I'm not loose with heat. My body is built for this, but it still needs to adapt.

And I do.

I stretch to make space for him—accommodating him. Accommodating my mate. *Mine.*

His jaw tenses, and he bites. Not breaking the skin. Not leaving a mark. Just a nibble. But I lean my head back, close my eyes, and pretend it's real—pretend he's claiming me as his own.

He gasps, "Oh, Cookie. You're...fuck, you're perfect."

He fucks into me, slow and deep, the knot dragging along my walls.

I'm whimpering now, loving what he's doing, but needy for more.

I love it.

He loves it, too. He's grinning, all teeth, that alpha sneer unrepressed, but not even a little threatening, "You like my knot, Cookie?"

"Yes!"

He growls, "How much do you like it, Cookie?"

"It's...the best fucking knot I've ever had," I say, and it's not a lie.

And now my teeth are grazing his neck, inhaling the ocean scent.

He purrs, deep and perfect, loosening my walls more for him.

Oh, fuck. Oh, fuck. Oh, fuck.

He kisses my face, my eyes, my mouth, whispering, "Good girl," and "So perfect," and other nonsense I would normally roll my eyes at, but right now it's exactly what I need.

The pressure builds, we're both so close.

He's shaking, barely holding back, not letting himself finish.

I whisper, "Come for me, Ace."

"You first, Cookie."

"I will when you do," I say, and once again I'm not lying. I need him locked in me, shooting all he has through me. "Breed me, Ace. Please. I need it."

And he can't hold back anymore. His knot swells even more, locking us together, and he squeezes me so tight to his chest I can barely move.

And then, he practically howls, pulsing his orgasm through me. I clench around him, desperate to keep him with me forever.

He keeps rocking, lighting me on fire from the inside out with his cum, and my own orgasm explodes out of me. My body locks, every muscle taut, and I come hard.

We're no longer two atoms, colliding together. We're two atoms, held together by a stable bond—a new perfect molecule.

He holds me through it, still purring, rocking me gently, kissing my hair, murmuring sweet, stupid things, still filling me, still locked, still smiling.

Still here. Still my alpha. Still my mate.

"You're perfect," he says.

I want to correct him, tell him every flaw I have so he'll run away and realize I'm not good enough for him.

But I don't want him to leave. Ever.

I want him to stay with me like this, locked forever.

I bury my face in his neck and whisper, "I love you, Ace," blinking away the tears in my eyes.

He sighs, low and breathy and content. "I love you more."

And I'm relieved to know in this moment that it might actually not be true. I might actually love him more.

I finally figured it out. I finally solved the unsolvable. This. This is love.

And that thought makes me so happy, I cry harder.

8

TREY

If I didn't know better, I'd think my heart was about to explode. And my cock? Fuck, it's so hard it might explode, too.

I logged out of Alpha-3 over five minutes ago, but I'm still here with one hand clenched to my chest, and the other clawing at my desk's surface, bunching medical journals under my fingers, trying not to die from the shock of what I just witnessed.

I lean forward, teeth bared and growl, "Mine," to no neck in particular, and bite my hand, also knowing better than to think I'm in a rut and trying desperately to convince my body to behave like it.

Her voice echoes in my head:

"No undies."

"Oooooh, fuck," I groan.

I open my jeans, slide my hand in, and wrap my fingers around my cock.

My limbic system is in open revolt. My body wants to breed so badly it only feels like I'm going to die if I don't. *I'm not actually going to die if I don't come...*

I close my eyes and see her perfectly:

Pink dress falling away.
Blonde hair cascading just above pert breasts.
A delicate neck, made for biting.
Shaved. Slick. Perfect.

I squeeze my knot, harder than necessary, working it the way you'd compress a nerve block: slow, methodical, unrelenting.

I only got a glimpse of that perfect pussy before I signed off, but I'm able to imagine it where my hand is—clenching, wrapping, taking, squeezing every ounce out of me.

It's easy to picture her—easy to imagine her—because she's been the omega of my dreams for years. What I thought was a random face conjured in moments of desperate loneliness—desperate horniness—was her all along.

I have no idea how her visage got cemented in my mind, and I'm certainly not going to figure that out right now. All I know is she's real, she's ToRQUueCaT—a coincidence that makes my brain want to explode, too—and if I don't come right now, I won't die, but I'll certainly want to.

I pull a travel bottle of vanilla-and-coconut-scented hand lotion out of my desk drawer.

I laugh. *Coconut. Vanilla.*

I couldn't smell her while I was in the robot, but I could read his sensor logs. I know her scent now. Coconut and vanilla—a scent that has always done things to me. Soothed me. Calmed me. Inspired me...and...other things...

I press the bottle to my nose and inhale the lotion long and deep. I lick the seam of my fingers, wishing it were her folds, almost convincing myself it is.

I squeeze an obscene amount of lotion into my palm, then press my dick slowly into my fist, closing my eyes, filling my mind with visions of her.

I groan, "Oh, Kitten. I'm gonna fuck you so good."

I've been hunting ToRQUueCaT for years. She's been an elusive quarry who writes code so perfect it reads like poetry and rips your knot right off you as you realize nothing you ever do will ever be comparable.

First, it was an innocent admiration: she inspired me to become a coder—a hacker.

Then, as I got better, she was a competitor, a worthy rival. I told myself I was obsessed because she was the best, and I needed to be the best.

I needed her—*need her*.

She made me better—*makes me better*.

But the more I learned, the worse the obsession got. I stopped needing to be the best and just needed her to acknowledge me.

Now, chasing her eventual praise is what I live for.

But, I'll take her scorn, too. I'll take whatever she wants to give me.

God, I love her.

The anti-alpha rants, the relentless refusal to back down, the snark, the code, the algorithmic precision of her insults—perfect.

It's funny; I've always told people my type was, "omega, probably on the spectrum, maybe a little unhinged, definitely hot. Blonde would be nice." But what I never told them was my type is actually "ToRQUueCaT, with a side of 'ruin my life forever, please.'"

To think...she's been both all along...

At first, I did assume she was a guy—an alpha. Yeah, I know how that assumption makes me look, but, in my defense, she's claimed on more than one occasion to look like Alpha-3.

I consider myself mostly heterosexual, but I didn't care. There was something about ToRQUueCaT that made every cell in my body crave to be acknowledged by her.

But she's not a guy. She's not an alpha. I've known that for a while. The anti-alpha, anti-man rants in her code comments made that an obvious lie.

I didn't care if she was an alpha or a beta, a man or a woman. I didn't really care what she looked like. I would have wanted her no matter what.

But I didn't expect her to be an omega. I didn't expect her to be so beautiful. I didn't expect her to be HER—the omega who's haunted my dreams for years. I thought my brain made her up. I thought she was just an amalgamation of all the traits I find most pleasing...

But there she was in the flesh, in the lap of her alpha.

I'm still a little in shock about that.

Holy fuck, she's more than I could have wished for.

I stroke faster and squeeze my knot harder.

She'll take my knot. I'm gonna lock into that pretty pussy and make her mine.

I had been working on getting control of that bot's sensors and motion control system for weeks. I had a whole script prepared to say to ToRQUueCaT the moment she realized I had hacked her bot. I was going to gloat. Get her to finally admit that I am good at this... maybe get her to call me a good boy...then ask her out. But that was before I saw her...

All my plans flew out the window the moment I saw her.

It wasn't just the shock of seeing her—her actual face, her actual body, all of her.

It was the shock of seeing her, and knowing, instantly, that I would tear my own arm off for one chance to touch her. The kind of knowing that bypasses reason, that turns a man into a beast, or a fool, or both.

I tried to go to her. I wanted to tell her my name and worship at her feet. But controlling that robot was more complicated than I expected.

And when I realized she and her alpha were about to fuck, fool that I was in the moment, I'm not a creep. Once I recovered from the shock and realized what was going on, I logged off as quickly as I could—but that was also more complicated than I expected, and I saw...

"Fuuuuuuuuuck," I exhale, jerking harder, then whispering, "ToRQUueCaT."

I need to know her real name. The alpha called her "babe" and "Cookie," which I'm assuming are nicknames.

She called him "Ace." Once I'm done with this...biological imperative...I'll see if I can figure out who he is. He was so pretty, there's no way he doesn't have a digital footprint. He's probably some model or trust funder. That'll help me find her.

She was sitting in his lap, legs splayed, hands everywhere. He looked at her, as if the rest of the world could burn to ash and he wouldn't care as long as she was there.

I want that.

I want it so bad I could howl.

I squeeze harder, thumb working the tip of my cock, palm working the base. It's not enough. It never is. I press my forehead to the desk and grit my teeth.

I think about the alpha, too: *Ace.*

And the bots. *Jesus Christ, the bots.*

I can't believe she built her own pack.

I can't believe how much I want to be part of it.

I want to be part of their family.

My balls ache, and my knot swells under my fist, getting harder, more sensitive, more desperate—swelling like I'm in a rut and my omega is right here with me.

I want to be inside her. I want to be inside all of them.

I want to see what it feels like to be the missing piece.

I fumble in the drawer for something to come in. This isn't something I usually do here, so I don't find anything.

I guess I could do it on these medical journals. No, I still need to read them.

I remove my shirt and place it on the desk.

I get back to the task in my hand. Rolling my cock with one hand, squeezing it with the other, working up a rhythm that's going to have me coming soon.

I close my eyes and imagine her again:

She's sitting in my lap.
Wearing that pink dress and a condescending smirk.
She's tearing me apart with her words. Raking me over the coals as she rakes her nails down my back.
She fucks me so hard I forget how to speak—she'll teach me how to do it again later.
I'm tied up. She tells me I'm too pathetic to fuck her. I watch the three robots fuck her.
She calls me a 'dork with delusions of grandeur,' and then wraps those lips around my cock.
She's in heat...begging for my knot.

Oh, God...

I stroke harder, and now I can't stop. I want to stop, I want to draw it out, but it's no use. My body has other plans. "Oh, Kitten," I moan, "I'll be your dog."

I come hard, pulsing so violently, I barely have time to grab the shirt.

The aftershocks rattle through me, and I'm panting, slumped over the desk, medical journals sticking to my forehead.

The emptiness is instant, total, crushing.

I take a minute, then two, then three.

God, I'm fucking pathetic.

I clean myself up, wiping the shirt over my dick to get the last drops.

Instead of taking this shirt to my laundry room like a responsible, rational adult, I toss it on the ground and turn my computer back on.

I have to find her. Nothing else matters.

Time for some Passive Reconnaissance, a.k.a. Open Source Intelligence (OSINT), a.k.a. Googling.

I search, "Blond male alpha named Ace," and, surprisingly, the first image result is him.

His name is Ace Beauvoir. He's a pro surfer and a trust funder. *Knew it.*

His last tournament was in Guam months ago. He hasn't posted on social media since then.

It doesn't take me long to find info about his packmates: Thomas Mercer (alpha) and Forrest Goodwin (beta).

No omega in the pack. Interesting.

I close my eyes and try to remember what I saw:

No other humans were there.
A beach in the window past them.

Why weren't his packmates there?

Is she in Guam? I can go to Guam.

I lean back in my chair and open a flight app on my phone to review flight schedules.

A notification pops up, bringing me back to reality:

8:00 am—Emma R.—Induction Chemo

Shit. I...I can't just fly off to Guam. My patients need me.

Yeah, technically, Dan could cover for me...but...

I imagine the scenario:

Emma, 3 years old, scared, hugging her teddy bear, crying.
Dan, with all the gentleness of a rock, explaining the process to her.

I stand on wobbly legs and try to compose myself.

I'm being crazy.

I can't just throw my life—my patient's lives—away to hunt some omega I've never met.

Who's the most brilliant, beautiful woman I've ever seen...

Who has consumed my every thought for years, and now that I know she's an omega, I'll probably go crazy looking for her...

She is already driving me crazy...

What the fuck else explains a pediatric oncologist who stumbled upon a StackOverflow comment ten years ago and has been chasing her praise so hard he's now the second-best hacker in the world?

Okay. I'm not going to Guam tomorrow.

But I'm going to find out who she is.

And if I can figure out how to get her to beg me to come...that would be even better.

9

STYLES

Ace's knot is a solid, living thing inside me. It's so weird, so much more than I expected, that I can't help but keep clenching around it, like I'm checking if it's still real.

We've been fused on the kitchen island for at least ten minutes, basking in each other's embrace, and I am more than a little surprised that I'm not itching to pull away.

Ace looks like he's finally exhaled a lifetime of tension. His head is resting on my shoulder, lips smushed against my skin. He hums, not a tune, just pure contentment, and for a while, I'm too wrung out to do anything but pet his hair.

The bots are at parade rest just inside the kitchen, all three in a line as if they're waiting for roll call or like they're guarding Ace and me while we're in this compromised position. I would say it's a holdover from our people's wolf-shifting days—when we still lived in caves, and such behavior was necessary—but they're not real alphas.

One and Two notice me looking. One quirks a smile and Two pulls two bottles of water out of his pockets, ready to provide post-coital hydration. I shake my head, silently rejecting the water, and fix my attention on Three. His eyes are locked on a point in the middle of Ace's back, and his jaw is working as if he's trying to chew through a thought.

He seems fine now. I'm not sure what was going on with him earlier. I'll run diagnostics later.

I return my attention to Ace. His eyes are closed, and he's squeezing his arms so tight around my waist I can barely breathe. Every time I run my fingers through his hair, he makes the tiniest, happiest noise that is so adorable I keep doing it so he'll keep making it.

I run my hand through his hair, smoothing the cowlick where it always sticks up. *He's so pretty. So real.*

He looks up at me, searching my face for something and smiling, but his expression seems...off.

Did I do something wrong? Was I not worth all the effort?

I ask, "Ace. Was it...was it good?"

He blushes and grins sleepily, his eyes sparkling as if he might cry. "It was perfect, Cookie."

Perfect. There's that word again.

"You sure?" I ask.

"Very sure," he says, hugging me tighter—which I didn't think was possible.

My heart pounds, and I'm not sure why. *Why does it feel like he's lying?*

He rests his forehead against my shoulder, breathing me in with a wistful sigh. "God, I missed you, Cookie." The words are simple, but there's a weight in them I don't know how to measure.

It hits me like a lightning bolt. He said that when he was fucking me, too, and I thought it was weird...but...*he misses me?*

I try to remember what Two said earlier about Ace and "human interaction."

I've told myself that Ace was fine with our arrangement, that he liked the way I compartmentalized everything, that he didn't need more than what I could give him.

Maybe I was wrong.

I shift on the counter, wincing at the movement of his knot, but I need to watch his face react to my question. "Ace...are you lonely?"

He laughs, but it's a brittle sound. "No, Cookie. I got you. And One. And the other guys. I'm good." He says it so quickly, so reflexively, that I know it's bullshit.

The bots move, grabbing my attention. They're lined up behind him, nodding in sync.

I squint at them, and their eyes roll back, revealing scrolling marquees. Together, the words, "Yes. Lonely. Needs his pack. Alphas need their pack," scroll past their digital retina.

I stroke Ace's cheek, and he leans into the touch, as his lids drift closed.

He's so open, so eager for every scrap of affection, it hurts.

I knew I'd suck at this girlfriend thing.

I clear my throat. "Ace, I was thinking..." I pause, because this next part is hard. "Maybe it's time for me to meet your pack."

His eyes open wide. "Seriously?!"

"Seriously," I say. "I think I can handle it. If you want."

He makes a sound that's half-laugh, half-sob, and crushes me in a hug, almost breaking me in half. "Fuck, Cookie, that would be amazing."

Behind him, the bots' eyes have returned to their normal hue, but they're flickering as they silently talk to each other. They're still standing like three guards, but the smiles on their faces are wide, and I think maybe they want to meet Ace's pack, too.

Jesus, I'm the worst omega ever...

Ace kisses my face, my neck, my hair, everywhere he can reach. "You're the best, you know that?" he says.

No, I actually don't know that. In fact, I know I am definitely not the best.

But I'll do better. I have to. I have to figure this out.

I hold him, my arms tight around his shoulders, and I don't know if I can be better. I don't even know how to start trying.

10
THOMAS

I'm going to keep it together.

There are worse things than seeing your best friend for the first time in three months.

There are worse things than flying halfway across the world to meet his new omega—who he thinks is YOUR omega—even though she hates alphas and prefers the company of robots she built.

There are worse things than bringing all of your best friends' earthly belongings with you, because he's never coming home—he lives with her now.

Mathematically...there are much worse things.

I just can't think of any, at the moment.

Forrest's hand steadies my knee that I didn't even realize was bouncing.

"You're shaking the whole car, Tommy," he says with a smile. He only calls me Tommy when I'm being pathetic—pitiable.

"Sorry," I say, not breaking my gaze from the shoreline.

At least the view is pretty.

"Are you spiraling?" he asks, soft-voiced.

I ignore the question and focus on the scenery whizzing past. "It's probably fine," I say. "She's going to hate us...but it's fine."

Forrest grins, with a smile that looks like it was sculpted to calm children and high-strung alphas in distress. "She's not going to hate us—"

"Okay, just me then."

"Thomas—"

"Everyone loves Ace. Always have. I've known him my whole life, and he's never met a person who didn't instantly fall in love with him. You've seen that smile, right? He's like a panty-dropping golden retriever. And then there's you. Loveable as fuck. A cuddly little beta bear—oh, and not an alpha. But me...fuck. She's going to hate me. Alpha. Anxious by default."

"Thomas—"

"Ace is never coming home. He's already moved out here. We're bringing the last of his shit. We're here to say goodbye to him. I just know it. She's going to hate me, tell us to get the fuck out of her fancy house, and keep him. We'll never see him again."

"Thomas!" he says loud enough to startle the Uber driver. "Breathe."

"I am breathing."

"You know what I mean. Breathe."

I close my eyes and breathe in and out, five long breaths.

"Better?" he asks.

"No..." which is a lie. I do feel better, I just don't want to.

I cross my arms and continue to stare off at the ocean, cursing the god-forsaken thing for bringing Ace here to begin with.

"Do you want to talk about it?" he asks, squeezing my knee again even though it wasn't shaking this time.

"Wasn't I just talking about it?" I ask him, confused.

"Yeah...but, do you want to talk about why you think she'll hate you?"

I glance at him, but it feels like a challenge, so I turn my eyes back to the ocean. "Because I'm an alpha...which I can't do anything about."

His almond scent reaches out to me, and he takes my hand. "That's true. You can't do anything about that."

I clench my fists. "It feels so...unfair. Like, this huge thing, this huge change is happening to me, and I have no control over it."

"I see why that's scary—not having control of your own fate."

"Exactly! And Ace is scent-blind! Fucking slick-whipped! He came here and fell so head over heels for her, he's practically forgotten who he is—what if—"

"You're worried that'll happen to you?"

"Yeah—you know how alphas get when they meet omegas. I don't want to...I don't want to forget what's important to me. Compromise who I am to the point that I'm not even me anymore—I'm just the me she wants me to be."

"Well, that won't happen," Forrest says matter-of-factly. He bites his lip, trying not to laugh, really dragging this out for the comedic timing that only he finds funny. "Because you'll have me. That's what betas do. We mellow all you hormonal alphas and omegas out. I'm, like, your secret weapon."

The Uber driver, the biggest alpha I've ever seen, chimes in, "It's true. If my beta hadn't joined my pack, I would have ripped the other three alphas my omega was matched with in half. She really saved their asses—helped me see reason."

"See," Forrest says, leaning into me with a hug.

I grin, feeling better already, but wanting to tease him now. "Well, I still have to worry about her hating me."

"That is also something I know won't happen."

"And how can you be so sure?"

"Because everyone always loves you, too, doofus."

I roll my eyes.

"Want some advice from an old alpha, bonded 30 years now to the same omega?" the Uber driver asks.

"Sure," Forrest says, leaning forward, too social for his own good.

"When it comes to omegas: just let your knots—well, in your case, beta, your dick—do the thinking. It knows what's best for you."

Forrest looks at me, making a "Did he really just fucking say that?" face, but says, chipper as always, "Okay, thanks. We'll do that." Then mouths to me, so that the driver can't see, "What the fuck?"

I laugh because that is literally the worst advice I've ever heard, and say, "Thanks, sir. I'll keep that in mind..."

"That's what I mean, alpha, keep your mind out of it," he nearly barks.

"Oh, yeah, I get it," I say, but make a face at Forrest that says, "I really don't fucking get it."

"Oh, and if your knot isn't talking to ya, listen to your scent," the alpha says, as if he's saying the most sage thing ever.

"Got it. Listen to my knot and my scent. Not my brain," I say, my face hurting from the smile I can't contain.

Forrest leans into me, holding my hand with both his. He's practically vibrating, trying so hard not to giggle right now.

The map app chirps, "Your destination is on the left."

We lean to get a look at the house as we drive up. It's one of those postmodern glass-and-concrete cubes that look like something you draw in an intro to perspective class.

Forrest points and says, "That's the one," in the same reverent tone people use to point out celebrity graves.

I squeeze his hand still in mine, and say, "Forrest, don't let me cave on the kid thing, okay?"

"Okay," he says, somber now, as the car slows.

"I'm serious. I need your help with that."

"I know. It's important to me, too."

And there he is: sprinting out the front door, barefoot, shirtless, and in gym shorts. His hair is longer, but sticking up like it always does. He whoops, arms windmilling over his head as he rushes the Uber.

Forrest's face goes soft, the way it does when he's about to cry at a children's movie. "He looks good."

He does. He's tan, healthy, and running like he used to when we were kids.

He nearly tackles the still rolling car, slamming into its side and ripping the door open, shouting, "Frosty! TomTom!!"

I've barely got my seatbelt off when he's leaning in, yanking me out in a hug that threatens to squeeze my innards out of me like I'm a tube of toothpaste.

He smells like beach and ozone and, faintly, coconut. *I missed him.*

I return the hug, squeezing back even harder, because I fucking missed him, and you know, we alphas are nothing if not competitive—even with dumb shit like who missed the other more or who can hug the hardest.

"TomTom, I missed you, man," he exclaims, eyes glassy with happiness.

I chuckle. "Jesus, Ace. You must have missed me. Calling me fucking TomTom again."

Forrest rushes around the car to join us, and Ace pulls him to us, squeezing not nearly as hard.

Ace releases us and dances in place, full golden retriever, practically singing, "Oh, man, I'm so stoked you two are finally here."

Forrest asks, "Where is Elizabeth? Or, uh...Styles?"

Ace's face turns beatific, then points behind him to the house. "Oh, she's—"

"Holy shit," Forrest says, cutting him off, eyes locked on One and Two walking down the path toward us.

They look human—mostly, but they have this uncanny movement, like they're NPCs in some high-budget video game. Their movements are too smooth, too precise, too synchronous.

"Holy shit" is right. I've seen pictures. I've seen videos. But none of that has prepared me for One and Two standing next to me, beaming down at me. They tower over me, emasculating me in a way I wasn't expecting.

Forrest, towered over by most alphas as a 'short king beta,' looks at them in awe. He exhales, "Oh, wow," with an expression that's loose and trusting.

I, on the other hand, feel the need to square up, an apex predator finding himself in a new ecosystem that knocks him down a few pegs on the food chain.

They smile at me, eyes whirling slightly like they're zooming in on every imperfection I try to hide. It's not identical, but it is perfectly synchronized, and perfectly creepy.

Ace beams with pride, like he personally built them. "One and Two, these are my packmates, Thomas Mercer and Forrest Goodwin."

"Hello," One says. "Ace has told me a lot about you."

Two says, "Thank you for coming. We will retrieve your luggage."

The Uber driver has been frantically pulling our luggage from the car, placing each piece on the ground, and not really paying much attention to our welcome party. Once he's done with his task, he closes the trunk and says, "Well, good luck, boys! Have a good one!"

And that's when he finally notices the bots, stacking the suitcases and duffels on their shoulders in a way that isn't humanly possible. He stops and stares, dumbfounded. "What in the...?"

One says, "We're alphabots," like that answers the million questions running through the driver's head—which, I suppose, it does.

The driver exclaims, "Oh, shit. This is THAT house?" looking at the house and the bots as if they are a local legend. Then he asks, more timidly than I've heard him speak so far, "Do you mind if I get a pic?"

Two replies, "We are proprietary technology. Photos are permitted for private enjoyment, but commercial use is strictly prohibited and will result in swift legal action."

"Huh?" the driver gapes.

Ace claps him on the back. "Hey, thanks for bringing my pack, man. Yeah, you can take a pic. If you post on socials, make sure to use the hashtag #alphabots. Want me to take it for you?"

"Oh, yeah, thanks!" the driver says, handing Ace the phone.

Ace directs them so that the two bots stand behind the driver, most of our luggage towering over them. "Cheese, brobots."

Ace takes the picture and returns the man's phone.

The driver looks at the phone, smiles, and says, "Thanks, buddy," rushing back to the car. Before he closes the door, he leans out and shouts, "Good luck, boys! Remember what I said!"

"What'd he say?" Ace asks.

I laugh. "Some nonsense about how I should listen to my knot and my scent, but not my brain when it comes to dealing with an omega."

Ace's face scrunches up for a moment. "No, that's actually really good advice." I want to argue with him, but honestly, what the fuck do I know about dealing with a scent-matched omega?

I grip the handle of a suitcase, but Two looks at me, cocks his head, and says, "You do not need to perform manual labor."

"Oh, uh...okay, thanks," I stammer, now unsure what to do with my hands, so I put them in my pockets and just stand awkwardly next to Ace while they finish getting our stuff.

Forrest has been buzzing around the bots, watching them move, and frantically writing in that little notebook of his as if he didn't record every thought on paper, the moment would be lost to him forever. He's chattering away at One and Two, asking them questions about "narrative subroutines" and "sentience thresholds." I catch a line about "the difference between consciousness and qualia," and my brain checks out.

Once the human-shaped forklifts have every last drop of our luggage piled to a precarious height on their shoulders, Two says, "We will place the luggage in the entry hall for sorting," and walks back up the path.

Forrest follows, bombarding them with more questions.

Ace flings an arm around my neck and leans in. "Dude, for real. Thank you for coming. It means a lot."

"Yeah," I say, swallowing the lump in my throat. "Of course."

He's quiet for a minute as we trail the bots up the front path, a reflective side of him I rarely see. "You two being here...it's weird. It's like a weight has been removed from my shoulders."

I know what he means. His absence has been a constant stressor whose cumulative impact wasn't really clear to me until right now. "Yeah, I know what you mean..."

Ace nods, and he's got that wistful, far-away look that he usually reserves for looking at waves. "It's like...I feel whole again," he says right as he steps inside, following Forrest and the bots who are already in the house.

I pause, reluctant to cross the threshold.

Forrest is already in there, marveling at everything, like we're on a vacation to some robotics amusement park. But I can't help but feel like I'm about to walk through a portal to my pack's doom.

Something about Ace saying he feels whole again is ominous... like a dark kind of foreshadowing. As if my stepping through this door will rip him—rip us—into a million pieces, ensuring we never feel whole again.

"Bro, hup to," Ace grins, like a commanding officer ordering me to walk into the line of fire on the battlefield, but really enjoying it.

I sigh, accepting my fate—good or bad—and walk in.

11

FORREST

This house is so fucking cool! Holy shit!

If I were to describe a homestead spaceship, this would be it: minimal, glassy, tech I didn't even know existed. It's like the fucking world of tomorrow.

I scribble inspo in my notebook. *I wonder if Styles can help us with the novel's realism...*

Thomas is hovering by the entryway, pointing out which items are Ace's and which are ours as the bots line up our luggage like the world's handsomest bellhops. Every one of his muscles is locked, and his eyes are scanning for threats of the blonde omega variety.

Gotta go save my man.

I return to the entryway, stamping down the desire to run around this place and inspect every nook and cranny so that I can latch onto Thomas's arm. If a rando were to walk in off the streets, they'd get a look at us and think I, the itty, bitty beta, was clinging to my big, scary alpha for comfort and protection, but really, it's he who needs comfort from me.

"Your room is ready," Two says after all of our stuff is on his shoulder. His voice is all soft-spoken hospitality; it's so calm that it almost has a serial killer vibe. "Would you like a tour, or would you prefer to decompress after your long trip?"

I want to jump and shout, "Tour, please!" My curiosity has me so keyed up that my nervous energy may atomize me, but Thomas is gripping his bag in a deathclaw.

Thomas shrugs, so casual, but, to those of us who know Thomas, that shrug screams "get me the fuck out of here" louder than any words can. When Thomas is quiet, not responding with words, I know he's terrified.

"I'd love a tour—later, though. Let's get settled first. It was a long trip," I say, faking a yawn, though I'm not sure why—I don't need to posture for Ace or this robot.

Thomas smiles, still portraying the 'macho alpha who isn't phased by anything' that his default stoicism grants him.

Ace knows that if you Google the phrase 'still waters run deep,' you'd probably find a picture of Thomas freaking the fuck out internally, so he says as calmly as Ace can muster, "Come on. We'll show you your room."

Thomas nods, jaw tight, and I practically drag him behind Ace and the two bots.

We pass briefly through the living room, and I gasp, "Thomas, look!" pointing at some robotic goldfish in a waterfall as we approach the stairs.

He does and smiles, genuinely, but doesn't comment.

As Two leads us up the stairs, I can hardly decide what to focus on. Two's ass is full in my face, and the floating staircase is so minimalist I'm not convinced it's up to code. *Maybe it's held up by code.*

A hallway stretches at the top of the stairs.

One enters the first door carrying Ace's stuff, and Ace says, "That's my and One's room."

Ace leads us further down the hall to the second door, "This will be your room while you stay with us."

Thomas nods and ducks inside, conveying nothing.

I follow, awestruck. "Oh, wow!"

The room looks like a hotel suite. King bed, soft lighting, every surface a different wood or leather texture, tech that costs more than my car. I run my hand over the bedding: high thread count and brand new—never slept in. There's a row of outlets on the wall and a carafe of cold water sweating on the nightstand. There's an attached bathroom, a mini fridge, and, well, pretty much everything we could need.

Two disappears with our luggage into a walk-in closet—that's bigger than our room back home.

Thomas sets his bag on the bed and stands there, not moving, not speaking, just staring at nothing.

I move to the window and stare out at the ocean. "This room is amazing."

Ace smiles and says, "It used to be Two's room."

I ask Two, who's lining our luggage up in the closet, "Two, are we displacing you? I'm sorry."

Two pauses. "No apology necessary. I have no need for a solitary space. I have made adjustments to ensure it is inhabitable by humans."

Ace laughs. "He's bunking with Three. Don't expect as polite a response from Three if the subject comes up with him."

Two mumbles, "Three's attitude needs adjustment," and gets back to sorting luggage.

Ace leans in the doorway, watching Thomas, and says, "Well, I'm going to get Styles." He points further down the hall. "She's in the nest hyping herself up to meet real people." He laughs nervously, but Thomas doesn't react.

Thomas turns to look out the window, and Ace gives me the "You got him?" look we've shared a million times since I've joined their pack. I nod.

Ace says, "Styles and I will probably be in the living room later. I'll text you. But no rush. You don't have to meet her today."

Thomas nods.

I smile, "Thanks. We'll let you know."

Ace smiles and says, "Cool. Two will explain how the room works."

Explain how the room works?

Ace leaves, reluctantly, saying, "I'm so happy you two are here," while sauntering down the hall.

Two approaches, holding an iPad, ready to demonstrate. He asks, "Would you like the blinds opened or closed?"

Thomas turns from the window and shrugs. That means closed.

I say, "Closed, please."

Two nods and does a little finger tap. The windows fog to a deep, soothing gray—*digital blinds? Holy shit, this place is cool.* A gentle glow replaces the ocean, and the whole room seems to get quieter, softer, less overwhelming.

Some of the tension in Thomas's jaw releases.

"Thank you," I say to Two, because something tells me he knew that would help Thomas feel more comfortable.

Two nods politely. "The refrigerator has basic necessities, as does the adjoining bathroom. You can request additional supplies with this." He shows me the iPad, and it's got a bespoke application on it like you'd find in a fancy hotel, but this one has no ads.

Two leaves the iPad on a desk and exits, smooth as a Roomba.

I ask, "What do you think, Tom?"

He takes a moment, lets out a slow exhale through his nose. "Nice," he says, finally speaking, but his face looks like he's doing long division in his head.

I flop onto the bed. The mattress is absurdly firm. "Dude," I say, "this is nuts. It's like a hotel room."

Thomas sits down beside me, perches on the edge, hands in his lap. He doesn't look at me, just stares straight ahead at the foot of the bed.

I nudge him. "Are you good?"

He laughs—a dry, humorless sound. "No. I am freaking the fuck out."

"I know," I say, pulling him in for a hug.

He lets me, doesn't even resist, just slumps into my side and rests his chin on my shoulder like a sleepy kid.

After a minute, he says, "This place is so..." but he doesn't finish the thought.

"Futuristic? Fancy? Fucking intimidating?"

"All of that," he says. "But mostly..." He searches for the word. "Final."

That one lands.

I squeeze him. "Hey. You're not losing Ace. You're not losing anyone."

He shakes his head. "Feels like I am."

"We're not going to lose Ace. We might gain an omega, though."

He recedes further. "I know it's dumb."

"It's not dumb," I say. I try to think of the right word.

Thomas doesn't do well with change. He doesn't do well with travel either. He barely admits it to himself. But he hides all this behind his alpha mask—from everyone but me and Ace.

I say, "It's a big change either way, Thomas. Change is hard—for everyone."

He sits up, pulls his knees to his chest, and hugs them. He looks so small like this, all the usual bulk of him shrunken down.

I say quietly, "Tommy, there's no rush to go down there. Let's take a little time to adjust."

"I shouldn't need to adjust," he says, voice hollow.

"Who says?" I ask, challenging his view of who he's supposed to be.

"Everyone," he says flatly.

"Really? Everyone says you're not allowed to rest after a long flight and emotional day?"

"You know what I mean, Fore."

I sigh. "Thomas, it is not weak to recharge. Even those fancy fucking bots have to be plugged in once in a while. That's probably what all these weird plugs are for."

He stretches out, letting himself lie down, and closes his eyes. He sighs, "I guess so."

I watch him, scanning his jaw and hands, looking for the signs—the hidden pain stims.

His hands are clutched into fists. The tendons are flexed so tightly that his dark skin is lightened at the knuckles. It's almost imperceptible, but I've cleaned the blood from his palms enough times to know what to look for—he'll dig his nails into his hands until they bleed if he keeps this up.

That means he's spiraling—hard. You'd never know from the calm exterior, but a storm is brewing in his brain.

I retrieve the iPad and dim the lights.

And then, I just sit next to him. I whisper, "I'm here when you're ready to talk, Tommy." And open up the FAQ for the house on the iPad. *It's got 50 tabs!*

Eventually, Thomas says, "You know you only call me that when you feel sorry for me, right?"

"I don't feel sorry for you, Thomas," I say, emphasizing his name. "I empathize with you."

He snorts. "Same thing."

I snort back. "No. Feeling sorry is sympathy. Understanding is empathy."

"Semantics."

I put the iPad down so that I can square up for this fight with an alpha—not physical, more like a battle of wits. I chuckle. "Is it? Or are you just arguing with me about word definitions as a way to avoid talking about your feelings?"

"Maybe," he says, eyes still closed.

Damn, he caved faster than I expected.

I test the stormy waters with a little flirting. "You know, even big, sexy, big knotted alphas can be scared."

He laughs with a half smirk, and his hands loosen, but he says, "You wouldn't get it, Fore, so you can't actually be empathizing with me."

Ah, still harping on the definitions—that means I've got him. He wants to say I'm wrong so badly that he'll find any logical thing, no matter how illogical, to tell me I'm wrong about.

I counter, "Oh, yeah? If I guess what you're thinking, can we stop having this pedantic argument, and will you actually talk to me?"

"Sure," he says, still not opening his eyes.

"Alright, so I bet you're lying there thinking..." I clear my throat and deepen my voice, putting on my alpha impersonation. "I'm a big sexy alpha—"

"Wrong."

"Come on! Let me finish," I whine, voice back to normal.

"Proceed," he says with a laugh.

I clear my throat and continue, "I'm a big sexy alpha, I gotta stop acting like such a pussy! Alpha the fuck up. Man, the fuck up. Stop being a little beta bitch and knot that omega."

He opens one eye and peers at me.

"Am I right?" I ask, knowing I am.

"No," he smiles, sly and caught.

I hover my hand over his chest, and he nods, signaling he's open to being touched.

I press my palm firmly on his chest.

He breaths, long, deep, then finally admits, "Not entirely anyway."

I wait.

After a long moment he says, "Can you just...hold me for a while? Maybe tell me that it'll be okay?"

"Of course," I say, still not moving, waiting for him to come to me.

Slowly, he curls into me, draping over me with his head over my shoulder, and I wrap my arms around him. He's bigger than me, but it doesn't matter, he feels so small like this—the scared little boy, finally coming out.

I squeeze tighter. "It's all going to be okay. We're going to scent match with her, just like Ace did, and all live happily ever after—as a pack."

He pulls back and blinks as if he's made a decision. "I'm okay now, Fore. I just needed a moment. Thank you for...empathizing with me." He smirks, a playful admission that I was right.

I'll rub it in later, for now I just smile and say, "Always."

My phone buzzes.

ACE

We're in the living room if you wanna join.

I show it to Thomas. "Might as well get this over with," he says, dour and doomed.

"That's the spirit!" I exclaim, leaping from the bed, itching to meet Styles and see the rest of the house. I'm also hoping Three will be down there.

Thomas laughs at me and stands. He checks his appearance in the mirror, puts the smile back on, and puts his hands in his pockets. He looks so relaxed, so confident, it's amazing how good he is at that. Even his scent doesn't convey a hint of fear or reluctance.

I respond to Ace:

Down in a sec 🥳

We walk out together. Thomas walks smoothly, confident, a lot like the bots, but I'm basically vibrating with excitement.

As soon as we enter the hall, something...hits me. I'm not sure what it is.

Thomas's hand floats to his chest. He gives me a look, then moves ahead of me toward the stairwell.

Thomas's pace quickens, but he stops dead in his tracks at the top of the stairs. "Jesus," he whispers.

I open my mouth to say something, but immediately forget what it was, because that's when I smell it. Faint, but it's there: a scent, almost nothing at first, strengthening with each step, unfurling as I get closer to the landing—coconut, vanilla...*friendship...which... doesn't make any sense.*

For a moment, I'm dizzy, but I follow.

My hand traces the wall, steadying myself as the world spins. I can't stop inhaling it, can't stop chasing the next hit.

It feels like an eternity of walking down a funhouse hall by the time I'm finally at Thomas's side.

Thomas is still frozen, lips parted, sweat beading on his forehead —eyes wide, pupils blown, fixed on an unmoving point.

At the bottom of the stairs, the living room opens up, all glass and light, with Ace sprawled on the big gray sectional.

Styles is curled in a tight ball, clinging to Ace, with her hoodie pulled up over her head and her face hidden in his shoulder.

The three bots are standing sentinel, perfectly surrounding her. Their eyes are glowing red, locked on us—well, Thomas.

Ace waves, then kisses the top of Styles's head. "Can they come down, Cookie?" Ace asks, rubbing her back.

She doesn't answer, but gives him a little thumbs-up.

Ace waves us down. "It's okay, you can come."

Ace is the only guy acting normal, as if he's oblivious to the fact that his two best friends aren't currently half-out of their minds and about to be fired upon by three guard-bots who probably have machine guns in their eyeballs or something. "Beth, this is Forrest and Thomas," Ace says, mouth wide in a smile.

At that, she turns, just enough to peek at us from under her hoodie.

Her eyes meet mine.

And then, as if a coconut falls from a tree and cracks over my head—I know. I know with unwavering certainty: she is my omega—she is OUR omega.

12

THOMAS

I'm gripping the railing, hanging on for dear life, and hoping this thing is more stable than it seems.

I stare at her.

Mine. My omega.

Dr. Elizabeth Styles. Our omega. Ace was right.

She's the only thing in the world that is real anymore. The rest of the universe is noise.

I can't breathe.

I can't remember how to do it.

I've seen beautiful women. I've seen stunning omegas. But I can't even see her face, and I'm already so gone I can feel the atoms in my body rearranging themselves to be more pleasing to her.

I remember—vaguely, like a nightmare already dissolving in the morning—being nervous about this meeting, about myself, about losing my pack or forgetting who I am.

But those thoughts are paper in a blender—shredded—pureed into a protein shake that I will drink so I have the strength to protect her.

Coconut cookies. Vanilla. Perfection.

She's hidden in Ace's arms, curled up so tight I can only make out the curve of her back, the curve of her thighs.

She's perfect, and my heart is breaking from the wanting.

I can't make myself move. I'm stuck here, mid-stride, at the top of the stairs, staring at the woman who has detonated my endocrine system and reduced my brain to a puddle.

She glances up for only a second, just a flick of green, and my chest caves in. It's a physical thing—I almost gasp.

My sandalwood scent, faint from suppressants, apparently didn't get the memo that it should be suppressed. It rushes from me with a force that feels like it's pulling me down the stairs.

And...somehow I'm at the bottom of the stairs, unsure how I even got here.

I go to her—

Actually, I ram into a wall of metal.

Three is standing in front of me, arms crossed, eyes red and laser-focused, perhaps literally.

I didn't even realize the bots were here...

Three puts his hand on my chest, blazing red eyes zooming, and asks, "Alpha, you good?"

No. Not good. I'm not good. I am absolutely destroyed.

I think I nod, but I don't know what my body is doing.

The world is coconut syrup, salty ocean, sandalwood, and... almond...

Forrest is at my side and says to Three, "He should probably sit down."

Three's gripping my shoulder. He says, over his own, "The beta may sit. But this alpha is showing symptoms of rut." He returns his death glare to me and commands, "Identify yourself, alpha."

Ace laughs, saying, "Three, that's Thomas. We talked about him."

Thomas? Is that me? I can't remember...

Elizabeth—I remember that.

"Let him sit, Three," a voice so beautiful it must have come from heaven says.

Three turns to the voice, unblocking my view, but not releasing me.

I can see her—all of her.

She's sitting up now, less curled into Ace, hoodie pulled back just enough to reveal a hint of blonde hair, looking directly at me.

I've seen pictures. I've seen videos. But none of that prepared me. None of it.

"Beautiful," I say, but my voice sounds wrong. It's shaky, high. Not mine. *That's probably because it's hers now.*

"No sudden movements, Alpha-Thomas," Three says, practically shoving me toward the couch, which I'm grateful for, since it gets me closer to the couch.

Sudden movements are not something anyone needs to worry about from Thomas if he is, in fact, me, because my legs are jelly. The only part of my body my brain seems to want to control is my cock, but I use all of my brain power to make my legs cross me the remaining distance to the sofa. I lower myself into the nearest open seat with a control and grace that is completely artificial.

Her eyes are locked on me. Ace holds her as if he lets go, she'll bolt.

I realize Forrest is next to me. I'm not sure how long he's been there or how long I've been here. He's sitting, cross-legged, loose, the picture of casual composure, watching me, amused, but I can see it in his face—he feels it, too. It's not hitting him as hard as a beta, but he feels it.

I'm euphoric.

My body buzzes.

My face hurts, and I realize I'm smiling like an idiot, but I don't care.

I want to be near her.

I want to wrap my arms around her and keep her safe, keep her warm, keep her forever.

My hands are shaking, so I clutch them in my lap, trying to hide my erection, trying to be respectful, trying to look like an alpha not in rut, even though I think I might be.

"So, Styles, this is Thomas. And Forrest. Guys, this is Styles, or Elizabeth, or Beth. Most people call her Styles. I call her Cookie," Ace says, grinning wider than I've ever seen him.

Elizabeth ducks back into Ace's shoulder, and he hugs her tight. She looks, for all the world, like she wants to be anywhere but here. "Please don't tell them to call me that," she whispers into his chest.

I try to say hello, but my tongue is stuck to the roof of my mouth.

Forrest jumps in, always the best at breaking tension. "It's so nice to finally meet you, Styles."

She looks up, and there are those eyes again: a ring of green, so sharp they can dissect you with a single flick. She turns, unfurling from Ace's grip just a little—already warming to Forrest. "You, too," she says. Her voice is light and thin, but it vibrates with a clarity I instantly want to inhale.

I open my mouth to say a proper greeting, but only a faint, garbled, "Yuhtoo," comes out.

My head is spinning.

I manage to say, "Sorry. I'm just a little...overwhelmed."

Everyone nods and waits for me to get my shit together...they'll be waiting forever, because my shit is so scattered it'll take an epic quest to collect all the pieces.

I bite my tongue to get a grip, to compose myself, to bring my body back to reality. I want to say, "Hi, nice to meet you." I want to tell her that I would cut my heart out with a spoon if she asked me. I want to tell her that my entire life has led to this exact moment. I want to tell her that if she wanted to never see me again, I would walk straight into the ocean and never stop walking.

What I say is, "You smell really good."

My face goes hot, and Forrest stifles a laugh.

The bots circle me. Not Forrest—just me. I realize, distantly, that they are ready to kill me if I make the wrong move. And instead of being insulted, I feel an absurd, wild gratitude. I want her protected, even from me.

Elizabeth glances at me, longer this time, and doesn't look away immediately. Her lips part, and she does this little thing where she tugs at her own sleeve, like she's worried about something.

I want to tell her not to worry, that I'm not a threat, that I would rather bite my own tongue off than ever hurt her. In fact, I might bite my tongue off regardless, since it's currently clenched between my teeth—the pain is the only thing holding me in this plane of existence.

Instead, I say, softly, finally, appropriately, "It's nice to meet you, Styles."

She nods, and then, so quietly I almost don't catch it, "You, too."

I don't want to scare her, so I sit perfectly still, hands visible, every muscle relaxed.

She shifts, uncurling more, but still hugging her knees to her chest, and pulls her hood back, letting it cascade around her neck. And now I can see her: small ears, blonde hair pulled up so I can see a delicate neck—which I need to stop looking at, because now my teeth itch and my tongue is bleeding.

After a long silence, she says, "You smell really good, too. Both of you."

I have never been so honored in my entire life.

Ace laughs. "You look like you're about to cry, Thomas."

"I might," I admit, and I do not care. The tears are in the back of my eyes, and I let them pool there, not blinking, letting the world shimmer around the edges.

"You feel it, don't you?" Ace asks me.

I just nod.

"Forrest?" Ace asks.

"Yeah," Forrest nods, his breath quickening.

Ace laughs, "Fucking told you, dudes. She's our omega."

Elizabeth looks at him, eyes wide, and turns a brighter pink. She looks at him, eyes so wide you'd think she were a deer, and his statement was a high-beamed truck barreling right to her.

Ace strokes her hair and whispers, "Sorry, Cookie. I'm overly excited. I will chill."

"I don't know what to say," Elizabeth says, voice small, eyes now locked on her hands in her lap.

Ace strokes her. "It's okay, Beth, you don't have to talk if you don't want to."

She shakes her head. "No, I do. I'm just...processing."

I know how that feels.

I am processing, too.

She looks at me with the tiniest smile, and it's...

It's everything.

It's all I need.

She's mine, and I'm hers, and I'd give up everything that is me if she asked me to.

I can't for the life of me remember why I was scared to meet her...

13
STYLES

"Beth, would you like me to begin preparing dinner?" Two asks, rising from his seat to walk toward the kitchen.

"Huh? What? It's dinner time already?" I ask, turning from Forrest, my face sore from smiling so much.

"Yes," Two says. "It is 7:00 p.m."

I've been talking to them for seven hours? I've never talked to anyone for seven hours before.

At some point, I ended up wedged between Ace and Thomas on the couch. I'm sitting so close to Thomas that our knees touch. I have no idea how that happened, but I don't move away. Ace is on my other side with his arm draped over the couch behind me. Forrest is sitting on the coffee table in front of me. He's leaned forward, so close his almond scent almost overwhelms Ace's salty ocean and Thomas's creamy sandalwood.

I'm fully enclosed and I—*feel safe.*

How...how did this happen?

"Are you hungry?" I ask the men.

They all grin, saying something along the lines of, "I could eat."

"Oh, um, yeah, Two. That would be great. Thanks," I say, leaning back, letting more of my leg touch Thomas's and Ace's hand fall to my shoulder.

Forrest scoots as close as the edge of the table will allow, closing the distance I just created. He grabs my hands, not in a flirty way, but like we've been friends since childhood. He's been doing this all night, and I haven't pulled away once—I haven't even flinched. Casual touch is not something I have ever been comfortable with, not even when I was a little girl with no trauma and no idea I'd be an omega.

"So, Buffy, Ace told me you built the bots to help with your heat, but I have to ask: do they ever, you know, fuck each other?" Forrest asks in a voice pitched to maximize mischief.

I snort-laugh so hard I nearly choke on my own spit.

Thomas groans, burying his face in his hands—and now his shoulders are touching mine.

Ace cackles, delighted by the chaos, and moves his hand to the back of my neck, allowing more of Thomas's shoulder to touch me.

Three, who's been leaning on the back of the couch behind me, shifts. I'm not sure if he's noticing the amount of alpha flesh adjacent to me, as well, or if he's just excited to talk about his sexual escapades. *Knowing his code, probably both.*

One who's on the other side of Ace doesn't move, but he does smile wider.

I can't see Two, since he's in the kitchen behind me, but a cabinet door closes a little too loudly, and I know he's running his Flustered Routines.

Forrest leans in, directing the conversation like he has all day. "I just can't stop picturing this closed system of bots going at it—like a self-sustaining orgy of perpetual thrusting motion. Tell me, Dr. Styles, are you hiding the secrets to renewable energy in your sexy bots?"

And, once again, I'm laughing unrestrained. "Unfortunately, no, I haven't solved renewable energy. But, yes. They do fuck each other."

I laugh, but a tiny panic of embarrassment hits me. "They have a lot of autonomy, actually. Sometimes they run their own firmware updates, and, uh, test the patches on each other. It's all in their logs—probably—" Forrest's eyes are wide with curiosity, so I add with a smirk, "If you want to see."

Forrest grins even wider. "I think I would want to see that."

We giggle together uncontrollably.

One adds. "Ace also helps with our firmware updates."

Ace grins, unembarrassed, and jokes, "For science."

Three leaves his perch, walking around the side of the couch to sit on the other side of One, saying, "Alpha-Ace helps Alpha-1 and sometimes Alpha-2 with their firmware updates." He smirks, glancing at Ace. "But Alpha-Ace is too scared to test my firmware. Afraid he'll get addicted."

Ace flips him off. "You wish, brobot."

Three winks. "I do." And the room fills with the low, weirdly sexy hum of three bots and three men laughing.

It's been like this all day: Forrest directing the conversation with excited enthusiasm, me responding, Ace joking, and Thomas... Thomas hasn't said much. But every time I glance at him, he's already looking at me, and the way he does it is so unfiltered, so...real. It's like he doesn't know how to look at people except with total honesty. When he does speak, it's the same way. He doesn't fill the silence with the roar of his voice like most alphas. He waits until he has something sincere and meaningful to say—and nearly every time, it cuts straight to the core of the truth of the matter. It's comforting. Like he's an antenna, designed to collect the noise of the world and translate it down to a perfectly succinct statement.

Forrest, still grinning, pulls my hands up and says, "Do you ever get jealous? Of Ace and the bots?"

The question is so blunt it short-circuits my brain. I go blank for a second, running a quick diagnostic on my feelings, and come up with nothing. I blink. "Jealous? Of the bots?"

"Or Ace," Forrest says. "Or both."

The idea is so foreign to me that I have to sit with it for a while, letting it ping around inside my skull.

I look at Ace. He's still smiling—always—at me with his hand still on my neck.

I try to imagine what it would feel like to be jealous of Ace and the bots.

I can't. I've never even considered it.

Jealousy isn't in my top ten concerns. I have a thousand other, more pressing, more important things to get anxious about. But something about this question makes me feel like a trapped rat on a sinking boat.

My eyes flick to Thomas, and I'm not even sure why; he won't answer the question for me. But his neutral expression slows my racing heart and tells me I don't need to be afraid of the question or my answer.

Forrest is still holding my hands, patiently waiting for my response.

"I don't think I'm jealous. I think it's sexy and reassuring," I say, tasting the words, to see if they fit the night's flavor profile.

Forrest's eyes go wide. "Sexy and reassuring?" he echoes.

"Yeah," I say, blushing now, "I like when they take care of each other. Watching them helps me...ummm...you know." I chew my lip, not quite comfortable with discussing my sexual proclivities.

"Oh, yeah, I know, Buffy," he laughs, and the sound makes me want to continue.

"But also, I like to know that it's not all on me. I like knowing that if I can't—" I start, but my throat closes up. I try to force the words out: "If I can't be there for Ace, or I'm..." I want to say "not enough," but don't let myself; instead, I say, "I like to know that there are redundant systems in place to make sure everyone is satisfied sexually."

And suddenly, all the easiness I've felt with them seems invalid. I feel like I said something wrong. Like I've been misreading the entire day. Like I chose the wrong path at the start of the conversation, and now I'm so royally fucked that the only way I'm going to get the good ending is if I clear the save and start over with a walkthrough in hand.

I turn to Ace, gripping his shirt, and watch his face for confirmation. "Am I supposed to be jealous? Is it bad that I'm not? Is it weird that I find it hot?"

Ace beams, "No, Cookie. It's not bad, and it's not weird at all."

Forrest places his hand on my knee, and the touch surprisingly doesn't make me want to kick him; it makes me want to hug him. "Oh, Buffy, I'm sorry. I was just curious. I didn't mean to make you self-conscious. I think that's incredible. It's nice of you to share your sexbots with Ace."

His cozy almond scent reaches out to me, wrapping me in a nest of reassurance. And I feel better, like I'm floating on the ocean on a raft of sandalwood on a bed of almond, comfortable, content, protected. Which makes no sense because sandalwood would make a terrible raft due to its buoyancy, and almond bedding used for livestock is coarse, but...I feel it anyway.

I don't have a lot of time to contemplate the weird metaphor or why it doesn't feel weird, because Forrest asks the next question. "Are you scared they'll run off and just start fucking the whole town?"

I laugh at the idea of the three of them going door-to-door offering their services to every omega within walking distance.

Three snorts, "We're not slutbots."

One adds, "We are alphabots."

Two interjects from the kitchen, "We only engage in sexual activities with pack members."

Forrest asks, "So they can have sex with any pack member?"

"Isn't that how all packs are?" I ask, confused.

Forrest's eyes flick to Ace and Thomas. He says, "Not all packs."

"Oh," I say, not understanding why he gave them that look. "I... well...I guess I have the wrong sample space."

Why is he asking me these things?

I chew my lip as the thought eats at my brain.

Wrong sample space...

Sample space—the set of all possible outcomes, denoted by Ω, in probability.

Wrong Ω...

Wrong omega...

I'm the wrong omega...

Lowercase omega, ω—a specific outcome, a sample point—

Forrest asks, cutting off the train of thought, "So, you view Ace and the bots as your pack?"

Thomas sighs. "Forrest, just ask what you want to ask," he says, voice low and gentle.

Forrest blinks, caught, blushing. "What? I'm just—" He glances between Thomas and Ace, both with two different expressions. Ace is grinning like he knows exactly where this is going and is along for the ride, but Thomas is looking at Forrest like he's ready to get off at the next stop.

Forrest exclaims, throwing his hands up at Thomas. "It's a valid question!"

I look between them, confused. "What question?"

Forrest blushes, and Thomas says, "He wants to know if we pack up, will he get to have sex with the bots, too?"

One cocks his head, then says. "Yes. If you join the pack, we will fuck you, too. But you are not my optimal preference. I prefer blonds."

Three says, "I'll fuck you. I like redheads. Plus, I'd like to know if a beta can take my knot."

Forrest blushes even more, his pale skin flaring with a pinkness that almost matches his red hair.

I laugh. "So. Wait. Have all these questions just been leading up to you wanting to know if you can fuck one of the bots?"

"No!" Forrest grins, "But it was definitely, like, in the back of my mind the whole time." He shrugs, crossing his arms like a defiant child.

I laugh more freely than I think I ever have, and the others join me.

And suddenly, I realize the broader implication of the questioning: *Will we combine packs?*

I've only ever felt like this with Evelyn—so free to laugh.

It's like these men have been in my life forever. Each of them works together as a team to help me feel at ease. Ace with soothing comfort. Forrest with fun and friendship. Thomas with steady protection and understanding. It all feels so familiar, so right, almost like I built them myself.

Images of us all lying together in my nest flash through my mind like a slideshow of what could be.

I'm not even in heat, and yet, there's a strange, involuntary heat that pulses through me, low and deep, like the first spark before a fire.

I'm hyper aware of the scent coming off the alphas at my side, and all I want to do is crawl into their laps, pull them deep into me, and let them hold me through it.

The urge to leap atop them is so strong it's physically uncomfortable.

I cross my legs and squeeze my thighs tight, but it just makes it worse.

My scent blooms out of me, so thick you'd think I was in heat despite the suppressants.

The effect is immediate.

Ace inhales, his nostrils flare, his pupils dilate.

Thomas's jaw flexes, and his fists clench on his knees.

Forrest's eyes dart to my throat, then quickly away, and his own neck flushes a deep red.

And all the bots shift, suddenly on full alert, hyper-attentive. Even Two has stopped his work in the kitchen to watch us.

None of them says anything, but their scents respond. Each one reaches out to me with some flavor of, "Let me take care of you."

I try not to think about what it would feel like to have Thomas and Ace on either side of me, knotting me together, filling me up until I can't even remember my own name.

But...once the thought takes root in the soil of my mind, it spreads like an invasive species, reducing the biodiversity of thought until it's the only thought left in the ecosystem.

I clear my throat, shifting in my seat, "So, ummm...how long do you two plan to stay in town?"

14
ACE

Thomas, who's been watching her with his hands jammed under his thighs, says, "We bought one-way tickets."

I see it hit her—one-way tickets. Her face goes a bit blank, and like her brain is doing that "memory leak" thing I've heard her rant about while working.

She's staring at Thomas, but her hand drifts to my thigh, like she needs to anchor herself to the present.

Thomas stiffens. "Please don't think we were being presumptuous. We didn't want to obligate you to a specific timeline. So, we will stay as long as you want us around and leave when you ask us to."

Her cheeks turn an even brighter pink, and coconut spikes the air.

God, I missed that smell. Fuck.

I shift, my dick missing it too and rising to attention. Another alpha is amplifying it to a level that reminds me of her heat.

"Oh," she says. "And...that's okay...like with your responsibilities at home?" She's sputtering. She always speaks with such directness, such clarity, but Thomas makes her stutter, and it makes my heart flutter.

Thomas shrugs, but he's vibrating like a tuning fork. "Ace is more important than whatever we have going on at home," he says, and it's so honest and raw that I want to hug him.

Forrest adds chipperly, "My parents are watching Astro—our dog—and keeping an eye on our house. The deadline for our current book isn't for a few months, but we work remotely, so…it's no big deal. We can do our work from anywhere."

Styles asks, wanting to learn more about them, "Ace told me you two were graphic novelists. What's your book about?"

Forrest grins. "Ace didn't tell you?" He cuts me an incredulous look.

She perks up at that. "No, what's it about?"

Thomas smiles, and he's a few seconds away from hands flying as he talks, "It's about a post-singularity society where alpha robots have to fight for basic dignity and access to reproductive rights."

One laughs and interjects, "Alphabots cannot procreate."

Three snorts, "Yeah, it's kind of our whole deal."

Thomas smiles at them. "Yeah, well, it's science fiction."

The bots nod and lean forward, like they're just now learning about the concept, but are excited to learn more.

Styles bounces a little, leaning over me. "Ace! Why didn't you tell me this!?"

I beam. "I wanted them to tell you. But I told you they'd love these bots."

"That's so…cool," she says, pausing the way One does, processing just how perfect this pack is for her, and even though she tries to hide it, she's so obviously charmed.

Thomas lights up like a city at night. "Thanks," he says, but then looks at me for backup.

I give him a little nudge on the shoulder, grinning. "You should show her your work, bro."

He shakes his head. "No, it's not…It's not finished. And we're under NDA."

Forrest rolls his eyes. "You can show her the work. We're allowed to show friends and family."

Friends. Family.

Forrest adds, "It's not like she's going to leak it to the internet."

Styles bounces on the cushion. "Oh my god, I would never." And now she's clinging to Thomas as he pulls out his phone to show her.

She oohs and aahs at his art and Forrest, and I just sit back, watching them, beaming like two proud parents facilitating a playdate.

Eventually, Beth says, "I wish I were creative like you two."

I laugh, "Cookie. You are so fucking creative. Look at these guys," I say, pointing at One and Three.

Three adds, "She wrote a novel. It's good. Libidinous. Refuses to publish it, though."

"Three!" she shrieks.

I grin, "Okay, Cookie. Now you gotta tell us about it."

She shakes her head. "It's stupid. It has a slick-based magic system. Omega orifices are portals to other dimensions that are powered by slick. But, um, it's really embarrassing, so don't ask to read it."

Forrest says slyly, "Well, now I'm gonna ask you every day until you let me."

She chews her lip. "Well, I guess I can let you read it. You just can't make fun of me." She giggles, embarrassed.

She's so cute when she's flustered, I can barely stand it.

Forrest grabs her hands. "Never. I only make fun of these dorks," he says, nodding to Thomas and me.

I laugh. "It's true. He's relentless."

Forrest cocks his head. "Well, alphas need to be put in their place from time to time."

Styles giggles. "More like always."

Thomas and I both reach for her thigh at the same time, and our hands bump into each other. For a split second, I think she'll pull away, but she doesn't. She looks at us, then at Forrest.

I'm grinning, like the dork Forrest says I am, unrestrained and happy. Thomas is, too, and...I don't think I've ever felt this happy.

I look at my bros, my brobots, at Styles, and I feel...whole.

I sigh. "Fuck. I'm so happy right now. I knew you all would hit it off. I told you!"

Thomas teases, "Broken clock."

I chuckle.

"Who wouldn't love Styles?" Forrest says, and he's not even being dramatic. "She's...perfect." His voice is thick, like he might actually cry.

Beth leans toward Forrest, then Thomas, then back to me. She's not used to having this many people this close to her, but she's glowing, and her scent is basically a big red sign that says, "PLEASE BREED ME!"

She looks at me, then says with a frown, "I'm not perfect."

Thomas says, "No. You're perfect. Quantifiably and qualitatively," hitting on her in her language. It's like a secret cheat code...

She blushes, buries her face in her hands, and then peeks out—it's so innocent, so omega, for a moment I think maybe someone has switched bodies with her or hacked into her. "No. I'm not," she says with a voice so sweet and small, begging us to continue doting on her.

I shake my head. "Nope. You're perfect." I lean in and kiss her cheek, then her temple, then bury my nose in her hair, because I can't get enough of her.

I squeeze her leg, and Thomas does as well.

She moans, barely, but I hear it—my dick certainly hears it.

She parts her knees a little, and Forrest doesn't hesitate; he slides right into the spot, moving forward so his knees are between hers. Now he's basically between her legs, elbows on his knees, chin on his fists, and she couldn't close her legs unless she pushed him away. He's not subtle.

Holy shit...is this happening?

I can't stop myself; everything spills out of me. "You're the most perfect omega I've ever met. You're perfect for me. You're perfect for my pack." I say it quickly, like if I don't get it out fast enough, my brain will sabotage the words and make them worse. I breathe her in, kiss her neck.

I can't believe how happy I am.

And I can't stop. "I always thought…I'd never really get to have this. Like, maybe I'd get to surf a bunch, maybe I'd fuck around, at best I'd find an omega to have a situationship with, but this? Oh, fuck, Cookie."

I exhale on her neck.

She moans, closes her eyes, and puts her hands on my and Thomas's thighs, then spreads hers further. Her hands drift up our thighs, stopping right at the base of our knots.

Holy fuck, it is happening.

I keep going. "You and me, and my pack, and your bots. It's perfect." My eyes well with tears. "The perfect pack. Whole. Perfect."

One interrupts, "Prime Alpha, does this mean Forrest and Thomas are now our packmates?"

Her legs close.

Fuck…I got too eager. I did that golden retriever thing.

I want to take it back, stuff the words back down my throat and pretend I never said them, but it's too late.

Everyone is completely still, watching her, waiting for her response.

I fucked it up. I fucked it up.

The waiting is killing me—perhaps literally if this feeling in my chest means my heart is actually stopped.

I scramble to save it. "That's not up to Prime Alpha, One. That's up to sole omega." I say it fast, hoping she'll see I mean it, that I'm not trying to force her into anything.

She blinks, and her face does this thing where it gets soft then hard, twisting as she runs through every possible outcome in her head.

She glances at Thomas, then at Forrest, then at me, and I want to die a little because I can't stand the idea of her not wanting this.

I pushed it. I pushed her. Fuck. Fuck. Fuck.

I scramble. "Cookie...Beth, I'm sorry. I didn't mean to jump to conclusions—I was overly excited."

Please, please, please don't make them leave.

Please love my pack.

Please. I need this.

Stall...delay the inevitable. Hold on to this as long as you can.

I clear my throat, trying to buy time, but my voice cracks anyway. "We obviously don't have to talk about this right now."

Styles licks her lips, then says, "No. It's okay. We should...talk about it."

She looks at each of us in turn, like she's running the algorithm a thousand times in her head to make sure she doesn't make a mistake, then bites her lip. "Can you just give me a moment. To process?"

I want to tell her "Yes, there's no wrong answer," but I also know any interruption from me might distort the result, and I know there is a wrong answer...for me anyway. So, I just nod and try to conjure a virtue I've never had: patience.

Forrest and Thomas do the same.

Finally, she takes a breath and says, "I'm amenable to the idea of combining packs."

I want to hug her, squeeze her to me, and thank her profusely. But I also want to make sure I understand before I get too excited and jump to another conclusion before she's ready. So I lean forward and ask, "Wait. What does that mean for you, Styles?"

She twists her shirt in her hands, staring at her knees, and Thomas is doing the same. "I'm sorry, I just didn't expect to...like you all so much. I wasn't prepared for this decision. Maybe I should...be by myself for a minute."

Forrest leans forward and takes her hand. "Yeah, Buffy. If this is too much, by all means, go take the time you need."

She looks up at him, eyes sparkling with tears. "I want to make sure I say the right thing..."

He soothes. "Your feelings are important. If you need to process those out loud, you can. Say what you need to say. Ask what you want to ask. It doesn't have to be perfect."

She looks at him, disbelief crossing her face. "But...but...I'm worried I'll say something that will hurt your feelings. I don't want to do that. I like you all so much."

Forrest holds both her hands. "Beth, you aren't responsible for our reaction to your truth. We're big boys..." he looks at Thomas and me, "some of us bigger than others."

She laughs, small, but the tension in her is loosening.

He continues. "We're here for you—all of you, even if it's not perfect."

Her eyes are watering, but she smiles, warm and open. "Do...do you promise to tell me if I hurt your feelings?"

He nods. "I do. I also promise to give you the chance to tell me how that wasn't your intention."

She smiles, wide and then does the unthinkable...she throws herself on him, hugging him and sobbing into his arms.

15

FORREST

Styles is wrapped around me like a python made of nerves and heartbreak. She's squeezing me with a tightness that feels like both our bones will liquefy. And hers might actually already be, leaking out of her face in deep, long-oppressed, guttural wails.

I let her.

I hug her back, gentle at first, then more firmly as she trembles against me. I try to rock her, but she clings tighter, as if the rocking would break her loose from the axis of the world.

The vibe shifted fast. We were all keyed up, sexed up, a few short seconds away from ripping off our clothes and having a bot-assisted orgy. The sexual energy has been building, and pheromones and hormones were high.

But the idea of packing up hit Styles like a brick, driving her into a full-throttle, bottomless-abyss-of-existential-omega-dread, meltdown.

And now the smartest woman alive is sobbing on me like she's been hiding from her tears for years, and I suspect she has been—probably since the day she built One.

Her arms crush my ribs, and she buries her face in the crook of my neck.

Her scent dials up to maximum, flooding the room with a coconut that's so sad it might as well have a black-and-white commercial singing about how we should donate to save it.

Ace has that small smile he wears when his brain is running through all his fuckups, and he thinks the only thing he can offer is a smile to cheer you up with.

Thomas's eyes are huge with tears. He absorbs feelings like a sponge, and I can only imagine how intensely he's feeling his omega's grief right now. His hands are clenched so tight that I worry he's digging his nails into his hands—but, like I said, he's a big boy, he can handle it without me.

They both can handle their feelings without me. Because right now, our omega needs me—*she needs her beta.*

"It's okay, Beth," I whisper, and run my hand over the back of her head.

Her hair is impossibly soft. The kind of soft that makes me want to brush it for hours, or at least until she falls asleep in my lap.

The bots surround me—well, her. For a second, I think they will rip her from my arms and comfort her themselves—to do the thing they were built for—but they don't. Their eyes flicker and zoom, as if they're trying to figure out what they should do in this unprecedented event.

Her sobbing lets up just a little. She huffs, then says, muffled in my shirt, "I'm sorry. I...I don't know what came over me."

"Don't worry about it," I say. "Thomas cries on me all the time. I'm used to it."

Thomas replies, "I do."

She laughs, a watery, hiccupping giggle, and gets back to wailing.

I breathe with her, matching her rhythm, hoping it will help.

Ace wraps his arms around both of us, pressing his cheek into Style's hair, and whispering, "You're safe, Cookie."

She shivers and clutches us, crying harder. But the pressure is different now—less like she's drowning, more like she's finally started to swim.

Thomas is frozen solid with his eyes fixed on Styles. He wants to join but is grappling with whether or not it would be appropriate. The two have connected, yes, but it's been mostly hormones and a shared love of astute brevity.

I catch his gaze, then drag my eyes slowly to the spot opposite Ace, hopefully expressing, "Comfort your omega, alpha."

He gets the hint.

Slowly, tentatively, he reaches toward her, then places his palm flat on her back.

And as if his hand were a hot poker and she were an ice sculpture, she melts—visibly and instantly.

Two says, softly, "Alpha-Ace, our inclusion will improve Beth's serotonin levels by—"

Ace cuts him off and says, "Activate Comfort Protocols. Use whatever Procedure has worked historically for your individual unit, but ensure it includes a Dogpile Subroutine." I blink at him, shocked. I can't believe that command came out of Ace—the guy who failed the typing class we took together in high school. I can still hear him laughing, "Bro...I got an f-f-f-space. That class was a waste of my time. I'm not gonna need a computer," while he ran out the door, on his way to a wave.

"Understood, Prime Alpha," the bots say and swarm into position.

Two wraps his arms around Thomas and pulls him tightly against Styles. Thomas resists at first on instinct, but realizes quickly that there isn't much point.

One wraps around Ace.

Three wraps around me.

And her sobs morph again, now bittersweet as if they are bringing her the relief she so obviously needs.

And then, one after the other, the alphas purr. It starts with Ace, a low, deep, beautiful purr that I've never heard from him. Then a chain reaction: Thomas, One, Two, Three.

I wasn't raised by a pack, so I've never heard a whole pack of alphas purr like this.

It's...everything I've always wanted. I just didn't know it.

And we sit like that, grounding her, grounding each other, for a long while, present in her pain with her.

We let her feel it. We let her know that we are here. We let each other know we are here.

We let her pour it out without even trying to stanch the flow.

Something tickles at the back of my brain, and I open my eyes.

The air has shifted, thickened, with our scent, and I can see them —actually see them—all of our scents. They're glowing around us, coiling and streaming, pulsing. A living, fragrant aurora borealis.

Coconut and vanilla spiral off Styles like a heat mirage. Ace's ocean pulses out of him in waves, and a deep sandalwood flows steadily off of Thomas. The bots' faux-pheromones stream from them, flickering with the mix, as if they're made of bits that turn on and off, tiny 0s and 1s. And my almond is there too—a soft undertone bringing it all together.

Am I hallucinating?

I wave my hand through the air in front of me, and it responds, shimmering, rippling, waving back, as if I were dragging it through a pool of scented glitter.

It's beautiful. It's terrifying.

It's the weirdest fucking thing I've ever experienced.

I've heard about this—how being in a scent-matched pack can unlock something primal, buried deep in our DNA. A holdover from when our people could still shift—back when we could see the world through scent—when our brain didn't make such a big distinction between our senses.

I always thought it was bullshit, an urban legend for the terminally horny—or some form of synesthesia reserved for a small percentage of the population.

But here I am, watching the air around my pack pulse and swirl and thicken, and I know I'm seeing something real.

This IS my pack.

I didn't doubt it, but now I couldn't deny it even if I tried.

It doesn't last long, though.

Something about it seems unstable, like it's missing something, and I assume it's because we aren't even in a pack yet.

Styles's sobs slow, and she lifts her head from my shirt, just a little, just enough to get air. One supplies a box of tissues from somewhere.

Styles wipes her face and says, "I'm sorry I omega-ed all over you."

She blinks fast, and I can practically see her bottling all of those emotions back up where she thinks they belong.

It's subtle, but unmistakable—the way Styles's body goes from melting to rigid, the clench in her jaw, the microsecond her eyes dart away and then back, like a window slamming shut.

It's like watching a beautiful flower curl up tight as soon as it feels the sun.

The alphas notice and respond in queue. Ace unwinds his arms from her, gentle as a breeze, and sits back to give her space. Thomas does the same. Even the bots loosened their hold and stepped back to a respectful distance.

Only I keep my hand lightly on her back, letting her know I'm still here if she wants it, waiting for her to pull back from me.

And she does. She pulls back and straightens her posture,

She takes three deep breaths—so big her shoulders rise up to her ears—expanding like a pufferfish on the verge of attack.

She scrubs her face with both hands, roughly. "Okay," she says, as if that's the last she wants to say on the matter of these tears.

Ace and Thomas move even further back from her, and she pulls herself into a cross-legged position, solitary, not touching anyone.

I can practically see the scaffolding being quickly erected around her, like I'm a YouTube video of defense walls being constructed at 10x speed.

And then, the transformation is complete, so fast, it's like flipping a switch.

The omega who feels her feelings is gone; the CTO who hides behind bots and screens is back.

"I'm sorry," she says again, but this time it's different—practiced, distanced, safe. "I'm not used to...this. People. Packs. Family. I'm not sure I know how to do it right."

I half expect her to pull her hood up, bid us goodnight, and then hide from us all.

Thomas says, "There is no right way. We get to decide what is right for us."

She opens her mouth as if she wants to argue with him, find the flaw in his logic, but she either can't or chooses not to.

Instead, she just nods.

Then she says, "I am open to combining packs. It is obvious that we are compatible." She looks at Ace, then Thomas, then me, meeting our eyes in turn, just briefly. "But, I have concerns."

16
THOMAS

She's putting the protective shell back together, atom by atom, transforming back into the hypervigilant, all-seeing, all-planning, razor-logic omega who built an entire robot pack to never need anyone else. The only person in the world who could make Ace submit, voluntarily, and never even notice he was doing it.

She's like a superheroine.

She looks at each of us, one by one, pausing just long enough to make sure we're all watching, all present, not making eye contact.

I match her monotone because she responds well to it and because it's easier anyway: "Please, tell us your concerns."

She folds her hands, thumbs fidgeting for only half a second before she clamps them in place. "Adding two people to my life is not just a matter of two additional unknown variables. It is a matter of exponentially increasing complexity."

I sit upright, my head tilted so that my ear is pointed at her, and I close my eyes so that I can really listen as she continues, "I thrive on predictability, routine, and algorithmic processing of data. With Ace, I have found a relatively stable state. Adding both of you—" she glances at Forrest, then at me, "—introduces what can only be described as an incalculable number of possible points of failure, misunderstanding, and pain."

I chew on this and the inside of my cheek for a moment, then say, "It's not just increased risk. It's an explosion of uncertainty."

Her hand flies back to my leg when she exclaims, "Yes! Exactly. Thank you. The likelihood of hurting one of you or being hurt increases with every new node added to the network. That is where my concerns lie—the uncertainty."

Forrest smiles, then leans in, "What do you need from us to feel safe, Beth?"

Ace doesn't say anything, but his hand is back on her neck. She smiles at him, her shell cracking just a little, and I realize that maybe Ace hasn't submitted as much as I assumed. Maybe it isn't submission at all, just—evolution.

She stiffens again and says, "There are three main areas of concern that I would like to address before we proceed."

She locks eyes with her hands and says, "First: I need to know that you all will respect my boundaries and how you will react if you trigger my trauma responses."

Before we even get a chance to ask her what her boundaries and triggers are, she adds, "Two will email you a detailing of my non-negotiable boundaries as well as a listing of known triggers. Before he sends them, I need you to understand: I am not ready to explain why these boundaries are in place. I am not ready to talk about my past...experiences that led to these triggers. Do not push this. I will tell you in time...when I'm ready."

This seems more than reasonable, so we all agree in our own ways:

I say, "Our curiosity does not supersede your comfort."

Forrest replies, "Of course."

Ace beam, "Anything you need, Cookie."

She continues, "Second: I will not be decommissioning the bots. They are a barrier that will always be between us. I need them to feel safe. It is not a judgment of you or your character. They are what I need. Please do not treat the bots as obstacles, or as temporary training wheels you expect me to discard once I am sufficiently 'healed' by your pack love."

We all nod, careful not to interrupt her. When the smartest woman in the world lays out the conditions for you to join her pack—join her team—you shut up and listen.

And then she lays out her final term, "Third: I need to know that, if I am unable to meet one or more of your needs—sexual, emotional, logistical—you will not view it as a personal failing on my part, but as a resource allocation issue. I am willing to negotiate what needs I do meet and to learn new skills to do so, but I will never be able to meet 100% of your needs. That is not a promise I can make, nor a standard I can tolerate being held to."

I'm confused why she feels the need to lay this condition out. This seems like a no-brainer: no one can be everything for their partner. I consider asking why she feels this condition is necessary, but I suspect it is related to the past experiences she doesn't want to discuss or an unnecessary derailment. But I do ask, "How would you like for us to demonstrate this through actions? I assume that our simply agreeing to your terms will not be sufficient conditions for you to feel safe."

She looks at me, surprised, as if she didn't expect me to ask this—and once again I'm confused but don't probe, because I suspect she assumed I would argue with her.

She replies, "A trial period. I collect the data I need to prove that you and Forrest can meet these conditions. No mate marking. No bonding. Not until the data answers my hypothesis questions with enough uncertainty."

Just me and Forrest. Not Ace. Has she collected enough data on him? Have they had this exact discussion already?

Even though she excluded Ace, he still agrees. Ace says, "I'll be your science experiment any day, Cookie."

Forrest asks, "This data collection. How are you going to do it?"

Then he adds with a laugh, "Like, are we going to be laid up on a table somewhere getting probed or something?"

Three interjects, "Only if you want, beta," making Forrest blush bright red.

Elizabeth ignores Three and says, "The bots and the house will monitor your vitals, but with non-invasive methods. The bots will track your body language and vitals through the same internal sensors they use to monitor me. The house will collect the remaining data."

Forrest jokes, "Is the toilet going to, like, read our pee or something?"

She simply states, "Yes. That is one method it will use to collect your data."

Ace adds, "It's pretty cool. I get this email every week that suggests vitamins, meal plans, and stuff. I feel better than I ever have. You're looking at an optimized Ace." He flexes.

Forrest smirks. "You do look great. I assumed it was just because you're happy."

Ace grins. "Well, yeah, there's that. But apparently my body hates dairy. Cut it out, and my skin looks better than it has in years."

Forrest grin. "Well, I'm okay with that. Do what you need, Buffy. Maybe I'll come out of this with thicker locks." He runs his fingers through his already pretty thick hair.

I want this. I want this so badly it hurts. But I need to make sure I don't lose myself or abandon my goals in the process.

This all sounds great, and I want to agree, but this feels like the best time to bring up my own concerns.

I say, "May I express my concerns before I agree?"

Elizabeth says, "Please do," and her tone is flat, but I know she's genuinely curious.

I clear my throat and grip my knees to stop my hands shaking. "Ace has said you do not wish to have children and do not wish to even discuss it for five years. I'd like to hear from you, not second-hand, your feelings on children."

I consider saying it's a non-negotiable for me, saying that I will not enter a pack with an omega who doesn't want children, saying that I've been looking for an omega for that exact reason. But that feels coercive in this moment. While it's true, I don't want to influence her honest feelings.

The air goes still.

I've blown the experiment before it even started.

She thinks I view her as just a receptacle for my seed with no other value.

I should explain myself, explain I am open to adopting, surrogacy, all the other things, but I want—

Before my mind spirals too far down the I've-fucked-up drain, she does something astonishing: she softens. Her scent spikes. Coconut wraps me in a warm embrace. She says, voice wobbly for the first time, "Things have changed for me recently. I may be experiencing what is colloquially called 'baby fever.'" And as if the fever were overtaking her right now, her cheeks pink, and her pupils go huge. And for a moment, she's full-blown gushy omega when she says, voice light and unrestrained, "My best friend's new baby is soooo cute," practically squeeing.

The alphas in Ace and I respond immediately, as we simultaneously move toward her, as if her ovaries said, "come here, boys," in a sultry tone followed by a breathy "breed me."

My balls literally ache, and I'm embarrassed by how little control I have over this side of myself.

Styles catches herself and returns to monotone. "I am willing to negotiate the timeline, once I have collected the data I require to ensure this pack can be permanent."

I try to ignore my balls screaming in my ear, "Fill her up!" and ask, "So, if I understand, you do want children?"

She nods, bashful, but clear. "I cannot guarantee my stance on the matter in the future. I also cannot guarantee children are in our future if we form a pack, but I can guarantee that, at this point in time, it is not a no. Are those terms agreeable to you?"

I can't stop myself, I blurt, "More than agreeable!"

Forrest and Ace both chime in with "Yes" and "Absolutely," and we all stare at each other for a moment, letting the gravity of what we've agreed to sink in.

Styles straightens and says, "Okay, then. Let's try it. We have retros every second Friday. Welcome to the pack," and the way she says it is so HR-department, I can't help but grin.

17

STYLES

“Well,” I say, trying to make my voice sound as breezy as possible, “now that we’ve established the experimental parameters, I propose we begin data collection.”

I rise and move to the other side of the coffee table. All three men watch me. All three bots follow to stand behind me.

I can do this. Be confident. Be sexy. Be—HORNY OMEGA.

I pull my T-shirt over my head, then drop my leggings—panties and all—in a single motion. I stand tall and pretend-proud with my hands on my hips.

I consider saying something like “Dinner is served,” but I get hung up on the fact that Two abandoned dinner a while ago. So instead, I just grin wide even though I want to crawl into my own skin and die of embarrassment.

No one moves.

The adrenaline hits hard: heart pounding, skin prickling, my scent blooming instantly, sharp and coconutty. *Shit, I...I thought they wanted to do this.*

“Was I misreading the room earlier?” I say, hands still on hips. “I thought we were going to fuck.”

All three men nod, but only Ace manages to say, “God, yes,”

though it sounds like he's choking on a cough drop, as he stares, open-mouthed, like he's seeing me for the first time.

Three steps forward, moving between the men and me. "Sorry for the cock block, Moonbeam. But I need to know the new alpha hierarchy to execute my Guardian Protocols." He's talking to me, but his eyes are locked on Thomas, who's gone stiff as a board.

Two adds, "Introduction of a new alpha merits a new hierarchy. This is necessary for bots to participate in and/or observe orgies."

One adds, eyes flashing red for a moment, "Without...bloodshed."

Ace chuckles, "Way to sound ominous, bro. We gotta work on that."

One asks, "Would it be more ominous if I outlined how we would obliterate our new pack members through force?" His eyes are now also locked on Thomas, who's now holding his breath as terror waves off him.

Ace shutters. "Yeah, but...you're good, brobot. Didn't realize you were going for ominous. Objective achieved. Carry on."

I sigh. "What's the current hierarchy?"

Three smirks, arms folded like always. "Alpha-Ace, Alpha-2, Alpha-3, Alpha-1. As Prime Alpha, Alpha-Ace determines where Alpha-Thomas ranks until your preferences supersede his decision."

Ace—who is now visibly hard under his running shorts—says, "Thomas should go after One, for now. Is that cool with everyone?"

Thomas looks like he's about to protest, but then glances at me, thinks better of it, and just shrugs. "Fine."

Forrest, not wanting to be left out, says, "And where does that put me?"

Three barks, "Betas are bottoms," and then literally hovers behind Forrest, hands already on his shoulders like he's about to mount him right there on the couch.

Forrest deadpans, "I know I look it, but I'm actually a top," which makes Ace snort-laugh, and breaks the tension enough for me to actually breathe.

Three whispers to Forrest's ear, "I was referencing your ranking, not sexual preferences. However, your social media algorithms and search histories indicate you are a vers with bratty tendencies when bottoming. Are you really a top, Beta-Fore, or is this just part of the foreplay for you?"

Thomas laughs so loud I can hardly believe it's him at first. "Damn, he's got you figured out, Fore."

Forrest blushes and averts his eyes.

Three whispers, "Your metrics are telling me all I need to know," as he stands, grinning.

But Three isn't done, he says to Ace, "Prime Alpha, I'd like to formally petition for a new standing in the hierarchy."

Two, crosses his arms in a very Three-like move, saying, "Being right a handful of times does not merit a rank increase."

Three scowls, "I've been right more than you think. But fine. I will succeed you soon enough, Alpha-2."

Two and Three stare at each other, continuing their conversation wirelessly while One stands back, agape, like a little brother watching his big brothers bicker—even though he'd be the big brother in both the chronological sense and the physical sense.

Ace says, "Is your Cock Blocking Routine done? Can we fuck now, or are you gonna keep arguing?"

Three turns, his scowl scowlier than usual. "You tell me, Prime Alpha."

Ace laughs and says, "Three, stop pouting, show them your dick. I know you want to."

Three's grin goes nuclear.

He unzips his pants and whips out a cock that makes every man in the room—organic or not—gasp.

The tip glows blue for a second before it begins to spin, slowly.

I nearly black out from laughing at their expressions.

Forrest stares at Three's cock, eyes so wide they might roll out of his head, and says, voice hoarse, "I can see you're a power top."

Three leans down, right into Forrest's face. "I'm a power everything."

Forrest swallows. "Noted."

I'm so hyped I can barely stand still. My skin is on fire; every nerve ending feels like it's gone sentient and is demanding attention from these men.

Ace lunges for me, sweeping me off my feet and onto the couch, pinning me down with his body.

I squeal, then laugh, then squeal again when he nips my neck and his scent goes liquid ozone, sweet and salty and so alpha I can't help but rub my face in it.

He says, "As Prime Alpha, that pussy is mine," and it's so dumb, so perfect, I can't stop giggling.

Before I know it, his dick is out of his shorts, and he slides in, slow, letting me savor the stretch of him.

He whispers in my ear so only I can hear, "Do you want your whole pack, Cookie? All six of us?"

"Yes," I exhale, then yelp as Ace slams in, deeper, and it feels like I'm being split in two by pure joy.

"Whatever you want, Cookie," he says, twisting around so he's sitting up and I'm on his lap. He hugs me tight to his chest.

"Thank you, Ace," I nuzzle into his neck, melting into the size of him, and scenting him as mine. "I love you."

"I love you, too, Beth. So much," he says, grazing his teeth along my glands.

I moan, loud, and slick so much you'd think I was in heat.

He nips at my ear, eyes scanning the men behind me, performing calculations Ace must have been built for. He asks me quietly, "Oral Sequences with Thomas, Comfort Sequences and Support Procedures from Two and Forrest, and Round Robin Routines from One and Three. That sound good to start, Cookie?"

"Yes. Such a good Prime Alpha," I say, nuzzling and scenting him more.

My Poseidon. My mate. My alpha.

"Such a good omega," he replies, still whispering and kissing me.

"Listen up, bros and brobots," Ace barks, and everyone stands to attention. "While we're in Data Collection Mode, you do what I say, or you do nothing at all. You understand?"

"Yes, Prime Alpha," they all say behind me, falling easily in line.

"Ace, wait!" I whisper, head snapping up so I can meet his eyes.

He barks to the pack, "Stand there and watch while Prime Alpha takes his...uh...droit du seigneur."

He looks at me, all love, all bark removed from his voice, and whispers, "Change of plan, Cookie?"

"Droit du seigneur?" I ask, giggling.

"Oh, yeah, saw it in a movie. Means I get to fuck you first as the one in charge. Makes me sound real macho, right? Gotta make sure my minions know who's boss." His smile widens, fully aware of the irony, when he asks, "What do you want me to tell them to do, Cookie?"

I hide my laugh in his chest—I can't undermine his perceived authority, after all. Once I compose myself, I lock eyes with him to say, "You can implement Unfettered Discretion."

Ace's eyes widen, "You sure, Cookie, even with the new guys—"

"I'm sure. I have all the data I need to know that I trust you. Tell them how to make me feel good—you have all the data you need, too."

His eyes sparkle, and he almost cries. *My adorable, emotive Prime Alpha—so transparent.* "Oh, Cookie. I'll make sure you feel so good."

"You better, or I'm making Three the Prime Alpha," I grin, teasing him.

"Well, damn, I really gotta do a good job then. I think he'll kill us all if you put him in charge," he chuckles. He kisses me hard and says, "Relax, Cookie. I got you. Don't worry."

And I'm not worried, not even a little.

18

STYLES

"Thomas, stand behind me," Ace commands, not harshly, thumbing to the space behind the couch as he resumes grinding up into me.

Thomas hesitates, but Ace says, even softer, "It's okay, Tommy, she wants you."

Thomas moves around to the back of the couch. I lift my head to look at him, and the look on his face—raw hunger and awe—makes my core clench even tighter.

Ace grips my hips, pumping into me, bouncing my tits. "You ever seen anything so perfect, Tommy?"

Thomas eyes scan as if they aren't allowed to look at me. His hands are balled into fists, barely breathing.

I'm getting absolutely railed by Ace, and yet, all I can think about is how much I want Thomas to join. The way he's standing there, so transparently nervous, makes me want him even more.

I reach for Thomas and say, "Come here. Please."

That's all he needed. He closes the gap, kneels, and cups my face in both hands. He kisses me, deep, and Ace slows his rhythm, grinding against me as if to help the moment last.

Thomas kisses me like he's decoding the DNA in my saliva—like he's afraid he'll forget me if he doesn't write down every one of my base pairs.

Ace, without breaking rhythm, leans back and grins at Thomas. "Cookie, you wanna see Tommy's knot?"

I'm too high on sensation to be embarrassed. "Yes," I say, voice breathless.

Ace grins and says, "Show her, Tommy. Take it out for her."

Thomas's face goes somehow hungrier and more bashful at the same time. He fumbles with his jeans, and the sound of the zipper is so loud it's like a shotgun blast in my ear. He takes a shaky breath, undoes his jeans, and slides them down.

I hold my breath, eyes locked on where his knot will soon appear.

His cock springs out so hard it thwacks against his stomach. And —holy fuck—it is gorgeous, thick and dark and visibly throbbing, the knot at its base already swollen, straining in his grip.

I think my brain blue screens for a second.

Real dicks are so...real.

Thomas doesn't move. He holds himself still like he's afraid I'll be afraid. Like he's scared of startling the wild-animal omega.

I look at him, stunned, and my OS finally boots, flooding me with need. The blue screen event wiped my hard drive. Everything I've ever learned is erased from my memory banks, and the only thing I know right now is his cock.

I want to taste him.

I need to taste him.

I moan and lick my lips. It's involuntary and so, so loud.

Ace slows, grinding inside me, and says, "Your omega is hungry, Tommy. Feed her."

I don't even think; I lurch forward, reaching for Thomas, dragging him down by the hips until his cock is pressing against my lips. I pull him forward, pushing the head into my mouth, tasting him, tongue darting out to trace the seam, relishing the precum that beads at the tip.

And that's when I write a new data point into my recently wiped database: the taste of sandalwood. It's sweet and spicy, warm and woody, subtly vanilla, floral, and cinnamon—a cacophony of flavors. Maybe tomorrow, when I try to refill my hard drive and relearn everything I forgot, I'll become a gastronomist instead of a programmer, so I can fully describe this miraculous taste.

Thomas has both hands fisted in my hair, his head thrown back, eyes squeezed shut, and it is so cute I suck harder, just to watch him tense more. He groans, deep and feral, the sound vibrating all the way down my spine.

I suck harder, taking him deeper and the weight, the impossible stretch, is electric.

Ace picks the pace back up, splitting me open. Ace hugs me tight, arms firm against my back, and says, "You're such a good girl, Cookie. You can take more of him, can't you?"

I whimper and nod.

Thomas, with a shudder, pushes deeper, bumping his head against the back of my throat.

I gag, but not in a bad way—it feels like being rewired from the inside out—but Thomas pulls back.

Ace says, "He's never had an omega. Show him what he flew across the world to feel, Cookie."

I'm gonna. I'm gonna show him so fucking good.

Ace says, "Two," and he doesn't even have to say more.

Two is at my side in a blink, kneeling on the carpet, eyes locked on me with that uncanny sweetness that makes me feel safe. He cups my shoulder and the base of my neck, and suddenly it's easier to breathe.

"Breathe, Beth," Two murmurs with a gentle rumble.

And a new memory writes itself: how to breathe. I didn't even realize I wasn't doing it.

Two coos, "You can do this. I know you can. Take him."

I shiver, relaxing my jaw on Thomas's cock, letting it fill my mouth until the tip presses harder at the back of my throat.

Ace says, "Forrest, help Two."

Forrest slides down, kneeling on the other side, his hands gentle on my thigh. "Oh, Buffy, look at you with that monster cock down your throat. You're amazing," he murmurs, voice so soothing I could melt.

Two guides my breath with his own, slow and even. It's like he's syncing my OS with his, throttling my overclocking panic to something manageable.

Forrest strokes slow, ambient circles on my leg, distracting me from the pain or fear or whatever's trying to boot up in the back of my brain.

Ace is still inside me, his hands on my hips, keeping me anchored in the real world. He's murmuring, "Good girl, you're doing so good, Cookie, let him in, you can take it, you're the best omega," and it's so embarrassing and so hot I can't stand it.

Forrest slides a pillow beneath my chin and another behind Ace's back. He guides Ace to scoot forward, then gently presses a hand to his chest, leaning Ace back.

The shift in angle aligns our bodies perfectly, and Thomas's cock glides smoothly down my throat, filling me completely, his swelling knot pressing around my lips. "That's our girl," Forrest coos. "I knew you could take it all the way to the knot."

"Jesus fuck, Elizabeth," Thomas rasps, voice hoarse and high. "You're—oh god—"

"Told you she was perfect," Ace says sweetly, then more forcefully, "but she comes first. Understood?"

Thomas closes his eyes, nodding, like he's not sure he believes he can.

"One. That's your cue," Ace says.

One slides in behind me, his chest a perfect fit for the curve of my back. He nuzzles my neck and whispers to me, "Ace forgets. This was my pussy first." It's such an un-One thing to say, but I fucking love it.

I whimper, mouth still stretched around Thomas's cock.

One's hands roam my sides, each stroke sending electricity to my core, pulling more needy whimpers out of me. He cups my hips with a reverent care and presses his cock against my pussy.

It's thick and yielding, programmed for maximum pleasure. It presses at my entrance, gliding against Ace's length, the sensation is double and dizzying. One reaches for my clit, pressing firmly between my and Ace's bodies. Then he angles his cock upward, pushing in, and I am filled—completely, perfectly.

I gasp, releasing Thomas for a moment, and moan so loud that everything goes silent as all breaths, simulated and real, are held, and all hearts and internal circulation systems stop pumping.

Ace and One are both inside me, and it's so much, so intense, I can't even process it. There's no pain—not really—just stretch, fullness, a heat that spreads through my whole body, burning away every thought except this:

Yes. Yes. Yes.

I grip Ace's hair and run a finger over his ear.

Ace smiles as I take his best friend's cock back in my mouth, all the way down.

Ace's grip on my hips tightens, and he calls out, "Three, you're up."

"Best for last," Three stalks forward, kneeling next to Forrest, who is still kneeling, hands gentle on my thigh, helping to guide Thomas's cock deeper and deeper into my mouth.

Three's mouth hovers at Forrest's ear, and he bites, playful but sharp, just below the lobe. "I'll get you later, beta," Three murmurs, voice low and dangerous, then he looks up at me, blue-lit eyes hungry. "Moonbeam takes priority." It's a threat and a promise, and Forrest's eyes go soft and shiny as he leans into it.

Then, in a move that is as stupid as it is sexy, Three reaches down, grabs his cock at the base, and with a series of clicks and rotations, detaches it.

He holds it in his palm, then bends and snaps it at the seams. Segments click and rotate like a transformer toy, until the head of the cock is replaced by a swirling, soft, suction-cup-like mouth.

Three purrs, "Sing for us, baby doll," then lines it up with my clit.

It makes an obscene, hungry slurp when it latches on. The suction is so intense that it feels like my entire soul is being sucked from me.

Every muscle in my body seizes, and my throat clamps around Thomas like a vise.

Sensations detonate through me, a chain reaction of pleasure so intense it's like being thrown into the sun.

I can't breathe, can't think—all I can do is come.

19

THOMAS

My head is thrown back, and I'm screaming, "Oh fuck, oh fuck, oh fuck—"

She's coming, vibrating like a tuning fork, and my cock is buried to the base in her throat. Her lips are stretched around my knot, and her eyes are rolling back.

The pleasure is so bright and sharp, I think I might die from it.

I've never felt anything like this.

The phrase, "I can't even," is looping through my head.

I want to stay inside her forever, but the next small thrust almost knocks me out.

My knot catches, swelling, and it's about to lock around the rim of her lips.

Somewhere in the haze, Ace's voice: "Don't knot her mouth, Tommy!"

I'm barely able to process what that means, but Two's voice floats into my brain, calm and perfectly modulated, "It's in the email."

Then multiple, gentle hands are on my shoulders, my hips, my stomach, anchoring me to reality and guiding me backward before I'm fully undone. I'm being physically extracted, like a bomb squad removing a live device from a very tight location.

The wet pop as my knot slides from her lips is the single most intense sensation of my entire life.

I jolt, and then I'm spurting—hot, wild, and completely uncontrolled—over her lips, her tongue, her chin.

Styles opens wide and lets it all hit her, giggling as the next pulse hits her cheek.

I collapse forward, draped over the back of the couch, ass in the air and cheek pressed against the cushion, too weak to do anything about it. I close my eyes, ready to die happy here, when hands grip my ankles. I open my eyes to find One flipping me over the couch. I flail, but Two's got my shoulders leaning me back so I can sit upright.

I slump, feeling emasculated, but they outrank me, so I just let the manhandling slide—besides, this is more comfortable.

My knot is huge and so swollen it hurts. I don't know what to do with it. It's never been this big before, but it's also never been in an omega's mouth.

I just grip it and squeeze, which only makes more cum pulse out, sputtering down my shaft.

I don't even care.

I feel so empty and full at the same time, like I've been wrung out, or murdered and resurrected.

I keep squeezing, but my knot isn't shrinking. It just throbs, demanding to be locked in something, anything.

I whimper and can't make my mouth say words, which isn't new for me, really, but my brain and body don't know what to do with this.

I close my eyes, slump further into the couch, and try to convince my knot that the omega is still wrapped around it.

When another hand wraps around mine, I know it without even opening my eyes—Forrest.

He's on the couch between Ace and me. His eyes are glazed, pupils huge, skin flushed red, but his touch is gentle. His other hand is still firmly on Styles's leg, as she bounces happily on Ace's cock, but she doesn't really need Forrest's full attention right now.

He leans his head on my shoulder and says, "I got you, Tommy." He gives my knot a squeeze in perfect counter-rhythm, and I nearly black out. His own cock is rock hard in his pants, and I go to reach for it, but Three kneels in front of him and says, "And I got you, beta," in a tone that is both mockery and a promise.

Forrest's eyes are wide as he looks at Three, lust fully overtaking him. "You...you were right about me being vers, but...you're too big for me. I can't take a knot."

Three smirks, licking his lips, "Understood. But I am more than just a dick."

Forrest squeezes me even tighter, "Um, Tommy, can I—" I know he's asking my permission, even though it's thoroughly unnecessary.

I cut him off. "He's pack. It's not cheating, Fore."

I want to mention the fact that I just had my dick in the mouth of another, but it's unnecessary because his dick is already in Three's mouth, bobbing slowly. The look on Forrest's face—shock, bliss, surrender—makes my still-throbbing cock jump again.

Ace has Styles on his lap, fucking her open in slow, deep, relentless strokes, his arms caging her in, hands on her shoulders, his mouth at her ear.

He's purring, and she's still laughing, moaning through it all.

Every sense I have is jacked up to the maximum.

My body is a live wire, my brain a fog of serotonin, and all I can do is stare at the chaos around me and feel the most ridiculous, pure happiness I've ever experienced.

One is kneeling on the other side of Styles and Ace, stroking her hair and murmuring, "Good job, Sunshine. Such a good omega." She giggles again and clings to Ace harder.

Two is cleaning up the mess with a towel, but his eyes are on me, and I think maybe he's collecting data on me. But I can't care, because my cock is still hard, and Forrest is still milking my knot like he's getting paid for it.

Three is now sucking and jacking Forrest so hard he's shaking the couch, and there's no room for anything except more sensation.

Ace suddenly goes stiff, lifts Styles from his lap, and then slams her down, knotting her in a single, fluid motion.

She shrieks, a high, sweet sound, and Ace holds her tight, purring into her neck.

"Mine," he whispers, so low I barely hear it.

And I am simultaneously jealous and happy.

I want to be locked in her, too.

I want to be part of this, not just as a participant, but as something that can never, ever be removed.

Ace looks up, locks eyes with me, and we both just sit there, breathing, the room spinning around us.

This is all I've ever wanted.

This is all WE'VE ever wanted—since we were kids, wrestling in the backyard, fighting over who got to be Prime Alpha of our future pack. It's just as we dreamed. Granted, we didn't expect a bunch of robots to be part of it.

I laugh, imagining how we would have reacted had you told us.

I don't think I've ever felt so fucking happy.

Ace grins, teeth bared, pure joy on his face that says, "We did it, Tommy."

Forrest moans, kissing my neck, and coming as Three sucks him dry, but he doesn't let go of my knot. He's squeezing my knot, tricking my body into thinking it's locked into something.

Three stands, saying, "Good boys," like he's rewarding us for a job well done, even though I'm not sure what I did, but I'll accept the praise.

I look at Styles, who's completely gone, body limp in Ace's arms, her face and chest smeared with cum, her hair a halo of gold around her.

She's smiling, eyes closed, a look of bliss so perfect it makes my heart ache.

She's ours.

We're hers.

I can't move. I don't want to. I want to stay here forever.

My pack. My family.

This is it. This is all I've ever needed.

I let myself close my eyes, and for the first time in my life, I feel whole—and now I know exactly what Ace meant earlier.

20

STYLES

Two is pouting in the corner—well, the botty equivalent of pouting. He's standing there silently stewing with a disapproving look on his face that I want to remove from his codebase. He's either running his own diagnostics or waiting for an opportune time to try to softly express his programmed disapproval of my working after hours. He'll probably be at my side any minute with a beverage and a gentle reminder to "Wind down, Beth."

I was supposed to log off over an hour ago, and snapped at him the last time he tried to make me. He said, "Well, it appears I am no longer necessary," and stalked off. I'd be a little annoyed by the sass, but I'm mostly impressed by how natural and passive-aggressive it sounded. Since I moved all these men into my house, the bots' dialogue has improved dramatically.

I know Two is just doing his job—the job I literally created him to do—and I know I make his job hard for him. *It's hard for me—hence why I made him.* Deep down, I know I need to care about this body's needs, but my work takes priority most of the time. Today, I blew through lunch and two of my preprogrammed "bio breaks," but I'll get to it as soon as I'm done...

If I don't finish this now, I'll never finish it, and the shame will go exponential.

Suddenly, the door to my office blows open, and Forrest bursts in, brandishing a beach bag. He's in a tank top with a cartoon kitten on it and shorts that scream, "hoochie daddy season."

"Buffy!" Forrest sings, throwing both arms up like he's announcing a sweepstakes. "This marks the start of Buffy-buffer time. Wind down, girl!"

I glare at him, then turn back to my work.

I don't have time for his shenanigans.

Two looks up, face calm, and says, "Beth's work cannot wait," and I swear I hear a hint of sarcasm in there.

Forrest ignores my scowl and moves beside me, all energy and movement. "I bet it can wait. You hit your 11-hour wall two hours ago, and now I am enacting Emergency Humanization Protocol."

That's not a thing...

He drops a handful of tangled neon teal fabric onto my keyboard.

I groan, "I have to finish this, Forrest."

"Yes, you have to finish it, but is it DUE today?"

"Well, no..."

"And if you were to stop now and start back up in the morning, would you still be able to meet the deadline?"

None of it actually has a deadline. I could theoretically complete this whenever I wanted. I open my mouth to protest anyway, but Two says, "A scheduled break would not derail her work."

My scowl is now directed at the traitor bot.

"The status update Two emailed us implied you needed a break," Forrest says. He takes my hand and says, "So, come to the beach with me."

"Two sent you a status update?" I say, peering at Two.

Two shifts and says, "It is important that your pack knows your biometric data so they can interact with you most efficiently."

I squint at him. *Did he summon Forrest to pull me out of my rig?*

Two folds his hands in front of himself and twists his feet like a teen confessing to his crush. *I gotta stop training them on anime.*

He sees me watching his feet and stops himself, shrugs—a gesture he copied from Ace—and says, "Watching the sunset over the ocean has historically brought you pleasure."

Gah! The manipulation tactics are too advanced! My code is too good!

"I have things I—" I start.

Forrest interrupts, "And you'll have those things when you come back! This is a rescue operation, Styles. Come on! It'll be good for you."

Forrest is standing like he's going to tackle me if I don't move. He's smiling, but there's something iron in the set of his jaw.

The fabric he tossed on my keyboard is a one-piece swimsuit, in a color that can only be called "retinal punch." I say, "Okay, let me just finish this sentence and close out these processes," while I pluck it from my keyboard like the thing is a biohazard, trying to touch it with as little skin as possible and move it to the side.

"We're giving you three minutes. Then we're forcibly dressing you like a toddler," Forrest says, with a finger-waggle and a thousand-watt grin.

Two sets a kitchen timer for three minutes, turning the dial with a force that makes it crank as loud as possible. It ticks so loudly, I swear he's put an amplifier in it just to ensure I don't ignore it.

Forrest and Two look at each other, pleased and conspiratorial. I'm not sure how I feel about this tag team effort to get me to stop working.

Two leaves the timer on my desk, and they linger in Two's moping corner together.

I try to resume work, but the part of my brain that tracks time is now racing the timer. My hands shake, and I have to delete and retype the last two sentences on this shitpost I've been composing—*which, I acknowledge, is not work in the traditional sense.*

The timer buzzes, and Forrest pops back next to me, exclaiming, "Go time, Buffy!"

He tosses the bathing suit at me, playfully hitting me in the face with it. "Put this on!"

I sigh and heave myself from the rig.

I start to strip, but before I remove my shirt, I pause for a moment to look at Forrest. He's not looking at me like he's about to get an eyeful. He doesn't even react when I lift my shirt and reveal I'm not wearing a bra—because fuck those torture devices. And when I peel my leggings and my underwear down, he just chatters away about some beach-themed, yaoi manga he read recently. It's nice.

I step into the suit, and Two is already at my back, zipping it up for me. The cut is high, but not obscene. I look like every female omega in every late-90s, PG-13, beach movie. It is so reminiscent that it feels like if I say "fuck" two times, the clothing will recede, revealing more flesh, as I get my R-rating.

Forrest presses sunglasses and a towel into my arms. He puts his sunglasses on and says, as if he thinks he looks really cool, "This is gonna be epic." He grabs my hand and rushes me to the stairs.

I turn back to check on Two. He's slowly following behind us, not bothering to match our pace and already dressed for a day at the beach, since it's always hoochie daddy season for the trio of alphabots. Right before I disappear up the stairs, losing sight of him, I swear he sighs in relief.

21

STYLES

The world outside is ten times brighter than my office and twice as loud. It's an overload of sensory input as my bare feet pad down the steps. I want to turn back, go back to my mostly-RGB-and-monitor-lit cave, but Forrest is skipping like a child who's never seen the ocean before, and dragging me like I'm his reluctant adult supervisor.

The sand is fine and cold under my feet, then hot and rough, then sharp with tiny bits of shell. I hate every texture and try to remind myself why I live here.

Thomas is already in the sand, wearing swim trunks just as neon as my suit, not moving, eyes closed, lying flat on his back, arms and legs spread like a crime-scene chalk outline. He'd look dead if it weren't for the rise and fall of his chest.

I hover over him, casting a shadow across his face, and ask, "Thomas, what are you doing?"

He doesn't move, just says, voice dry and slow, "Existing."

"What?"

Thomas opens one eye, then the other. "I'm doing nothing. I'm just existing here on the beach."

I'm still confused. I want to ask for clarification, but the smile he gives me is so dazzling, and I have no idea if he's joking.

Should I laugh? I'm not sure.

I tense and turn from him to look out at the ocean. Ace and One are visible as two well-balanced dots against a wall of blue—surfing. Seeing Ace move on the waves reminds me of the day I met him.

I haven't been on the beach since that day.

The memory hits me, sharp and weird. Pheromones puff out of me, horny and nostalgic. My legs clench, embarrassed. Slick pools in my suit, suppressed but resilient.

God. All these alphas around are fucking with my suppressants. Maybe I need to increase my dosage. I'll ask Two to look into it.

Forrest pulls an umbrella and beach chairs from my beach hut. He's struggling with the bulk of the items, and Two tries to help him. "I got it, Two. Thanks."

Two nods, bows a little, and stands next to me. Now, Two and I both stand here, confused about what we should be doing.

Thomas says, "He only lets alphas help him with heavy things if he has better things to do."

Forrest snarks, "You say it like I have a complex or something."

Thomas says, "Yep. That's exactly what I am saying."

Forrest sticks his tongue out at Thomas, but continues on his quest to prove he can do this task without assistance. He arranges the items, slowly and carefully, as if each step were an important part of a ritual. But, he lays everything out in what could quantifiably be described as "the worst way possible." Nothing is within arm's reach; the umbrella isn't angled to block the sun as it shifts with the day. But he seems satisfied with his unsatisfactory work when he flops onto the towel he placed next to Thomas.

Two places a towel for me and moves items into a position that is optimal and correct and relaxing—unlike that absolute horror show over by Thomas and Forrest that will probably keep me up all night.

I sit on the towel, back straight, and pull my knees to my chest. I ask, "So, what are we doing?"

Forrest grins at me and says, "Well, right now I'm protecting this porcelain skin from the sun. After that. Nothing." He dramatically squirts a big white glob of sunscreen on his shoulder, again trying to look cool, but the effect is ruined when he shrieks, "Agh, cold!" and giggles.

Nothing? That's what Thomas said. What the fuck does that mean!?

I watch the sunscreen race down Forrest's arm, slow, languid, relaxed, as if even it knows how to relax better than I do.

Forrest rubs the lotion into his skin in such a haphazard way I can't figure out the technique. He's not rubbing it in sufficiently, and he's leaving large patches of skin unprotected.

Thomas sits up, takes the bottle, and helps him. *Thank God, this guy needs some help.*

But Thomas sucks just as much at this whole sunscreen business! He puts way too much on Forrest's back and smears it like he's icing a cake. Then they stop the task entirely as Thomas wraps Forrest in a hug, resting his chin on his shoulder, and they just hum, enjoying each other.

I squeeze the towel under me. *I should just tell Two to help him. His skin is so pale he'll probably burn if they keep this up.*

But, Thomas said Forrest doesn't ask alphas for help...

They're back at it now, thankfully, making jokes about frosting and rubbing some of the extremely excessive amounts of sunscreen off of Forrest's body onto Thomas's.

I stare, baffled. *What are they doing!? Do they not care about proper SPF application?*

I can't hold my tongue any longer, "You're doing that wrong."

Forrest says, "Yeah, but it's funner this way."

I want to argue with them about the importance of protecting your skin from the sun, but they look too happy, and I suppose they'll cover Forrest completely... eventually.

When they're done, I'll ask Two to scan Forrest to ensure he's fully covered. And Thomas, too. I hope he put sunscreen on before this erotic 'Frosting Forrest Sequence' the two of them are running.

Two hovers over me with a sunscreen bottle in hand, asking, "May I assist with application, Beth?"

"Yes, thank you," I say, grateful to have someone who isn't going to take this lightly—or apply this lightly!

He spreads the lotion with perfect pressure and speed, rubbing it into my shoulders and neck with programmed precision. When he's done, my skin is smooth and dry, not sticky—lotion perfectly applied. Every inch of me is properly and evenly protected.

It's efficient. It's optimal. And the task is completed in an appropriate amount of time.

But...it isn't fun. It's medical.

I watch Thomas and Forrest, still caking each other with goop and essentially wrestling it off each other. Sand is sticking to their body, and it looks like a sensory nightmare, but it also looks...fucking fun. Like, really fun.

When was the last time I had that much fun? When was the last time I had any fun at all?

A wave of sadness overwhelms me as I consider how many other things in my life I've optimized to the point that I've sapped all the fun out of it.

Do I even know how to have fun anymore? *Coding is fun...right? Harassing Percolate through message boards is fun...right?*

I rise quickly from my towel, because I feel like I should. I need to do something, but I don't know what to do. So I just stand here... stupidly. My heart races and my breath quickens.

Thomas and Forrest squint up at me, shielding their eyes from the sun. I'm embarrassed, and I try to play it off by pretending I stood abruptly so I could move to the chair.

But now, I'm perched in the chair, gripping the arms like it's an ejection seat and it's going to launch me out of this beach in this case of emergency.

Two stands beside me, and I consider asking him what I should do next.

Forrest and Thomas have stopped canoodling with the

assistance of sunscreen and are flopped down on their towels, lying haphazardly upon each other, staring at the waves, not talking.

They don't check phones, don't read, don't do anything.

I can't process this.

"Is there an activity planned?" I ask after five minutes.

Forrest says, "This is the activity. We're just hangin'."

I wait for him to elaborate, but he doesn't.

Thomas doesn't, either.

They just look out at the water, sometimes at each other, sometimes at the sky.

The only sounds are the waves, my heart pounding in my ears, the occasional sigh from Forrest, or the distant shout of Ace saying something like, "Whoa! Nice one, bro!"

I try to relax, but my body can't do it.

I check my hands, my feet, my shoulders, try to make them go slack, but it just feels wrong.

Maybe I could work on a grant application on my phone while I sit here with them.

The urge to check my phone is unbearable, but it feels like I'm not allowed to. It buzzes, and I scramble for the device, excited to have a reason to check it. It's just an email from Three. He replied-all to Two's status update with:

> UNSUBSCRIBE ME! Our consciousness is networked!

My relief is dismissed as I dismiss the notification.

I'm tempted to check some data models, maybe remotely run the bots' firmware update from my phone. But it would be better to do all of that from my lab or my office.

My muscles twitch to stand. But I hold myself down.

I sit, stare at the horizon, and let the anxiety roll over me in waves.

I turn to Forrest. "Am I supposed to do something specific?"

He grins at me, all teeth and kindness. "Nope! Just exist. Just be, Buffy."

I look to Thomas for help. He's lying flat again, hands behind his head, eyes closed, a faint smile on his lips. I have no idea if he's sleeping or meditating or just...being.

I want to ask, "How?" but I don't.

After a long time, Forrest says, "You know, Beth, you don't have to be productive every minute. You can just...exist."

I nod, but I don't understand.

I'm not sure I ever will.

Tears sting my eyes, but I won't let them fall. Crying because your pack mates want to hang out with them on the beach is not only embarrassing, but it would also probably hurt their feelings.

This is such a basic human thing. Why can't I figure out how to do it?

22

FORREST

I'm sure we look like the perfect Instagram couple, except for the copious amount of sand glued to me by unabsorbed sunscreen. Thomas is sprawled half on top of me, his head pillowed on my bicep, and I'm having a great hair day.

In theory, we're hot as hell and relaxed as fuck. In theory, we're both "existing."

In reality, we're a pile of flesh and anxiety and SPF 100, tangled on a towel and covered in sand.

Thomas may appear relaxed, but every micro-twitch says otherwise. His jaw is clenching and unclenching, like he's running a calculus problem that can only be solved by grinding his teeth down.

And me? I'm shifting positions every few minutes, unable to get comfortable.

It's not the sun, the sand, or the rough texture of the towel. It's not even the awkward way Thomas's knee is currently pressed into my ribs. It's the omega.

Styles and Two are locked in an arms race of not moving.

It's impressive, honestly.

She's stiff as a fence post, knees to chest, arms wrapped so tight around her shins that her skin blanches from the contact. Her eyes are hidden behind blackout sunglasses, but I'd bet my left nut they're welling with tears.

Both Thomas's and my focus has been so laser-focused on her, like she's the only real thing on the beach—unable to relax until she does.

About five minutes ago, he hit his breaking point, growling low so that only I could hear, "We need to do something."

I stupidly replied, "Let's give her some time. Two says she loves the beach," gripping his thigh and stopping him.

I've tried to let her be, give her time to acclimate, but she's not, and I can't anymore.

Some inherent need to fix, to soothe, is ripping me into a million pieces and tossing them at her feet.

I sit up, shifting Thomas off me. He sits up too, sighing in relief that I've finally decided to do something about this. I'm sure I'm going to get an earful of "I told you so"s in bed tonight.

I drop my towel beside her, careful not to block her view of Ace and One surfing in the distance.

"Mind if I join?" I ask, projecting the 'harmless gay bestie' energy I've been perfecting since high school.

She doesn't look at me, just keeps her eyes on the ocean, but her head twitches just enough to constitute a nod.

The moment I enter her orbit, the air changes—static-charged and coconutty. The hair on my arms stands up, making me shiver. It's like the air is filled with atomic coconut electrons, vibrating and building up charge for an imminent meltdown in which they'll rip through all the naive betas who ignored their omegas for too long—*so, just dumb ole me.*

"Buffy," I say softly, "are you okay?"

She doesn't respond for a solid five seconds; she simply shrugs—like her brain can't latch on to an answer well enough to form words—just like Thomas does when he's overwhelmed.

I glance at Two. He gives the faintest of head shakes.

I ask, even softer, "Are you having trouble relaxing?"

She responds, "I am currently engaged in the relaxing activity of 'nothing' on the beach."

I'm just gonna assume that's a 'yes'.

"You wanna go for a walk?" I offer, because some people can't relax unless they're moving.

She shakes her head.

"I have a hard time relaxing sometimes," I say. "So does Thomas —especially Thomas."

Thomas grunt-chuckles in assertion.

She looks at me around the rim of her glasses. "Am I making it hard for you to relax?" she asks, lips twitching at the corner.

The answer is technically "yes," but I don't want to say so; instead, I change the subject.

"Beth," I say, keeping my voice light, "what do you usually do to unwind?"

She considers this, the pause so long it makes me think she's actually polling a database for the answer.

After a while, she says, "I write code. Or I build robots. Or I argue with idiots on message boards. Or I make lists of things to do."

I nod, even though none of that sounds relaxing.

"Do you ever do anything that doesn't require such high mental energy?" I ask, not as a challenge, just curious.

"Not really," she says. "It doesn't work."

"Doesn't work how?"

She purses her lips, then says, "My brain requires engagement from high-absorption tasks. I am optimized for work."

Two interjects, "Error. That statement is factually incorrect due to the implied universal quantifier."

Huh?

Her head whips to him, and she glares like she's about to unplug him to shut him up, but since he doesn't have a plug, he continues,

"Prior to suppressants, she decelerated neural activity during the forced time-out period of heat cycles. It resulted in a significant reduction in cortisol levels and other stress metrics. Since transitioning to full suppression, she has not had a single day devoted to significant rest."

"That's because I don't need it now," she says, a little too loud.

Two pauses, and then, just for a moment, his eyes flicker red, and a string of text appears across the lenses: "Yes, she does," followed by an expression that so obviously screams, "Help me out here, human," he might as well have that written in his eyeballs, too.

For the last few days, Two has been making little comments—all perfectly deniable, all perfectly rationalized, all within the confines of what his programming will let him do—but each has been a cry for help with his omega.

Earlier today, Two sent me a detailed report of her stress levels along with a picture of her resting on the beach. When he sent an immediate follow-up email asserting the image attachment was a mistake—included accidentally due to related file naming (BethReducingStress.png)—it dawned on me he needed the help of the one pack member who's not so strongly influenced by her code or hormones.

"Beth," I say, "Have you heard of the five-four-three-two-one method? It helps me when I'm stuck in 'Go Mode'."

She nods, impatient. "Grounding. Yes, I know of it."

"Will you try it with me?" I ask, and I make my eyes go soft, like a puppy who's about to cry.

She shakes her head. "It doesn't work."

"What does it do?"

"I...I get stuck on trying to pick the right things. Which things am I supposed to count? Do they have to be important, or can they be anything? Am I doing it wrong if I pick two related things? Am I taking too long to pick something? How is this relaxing? Why can't I do it?" Her voice chokes on that last thing.

"I know exactly how you feel," Thomas interjects.

She sniffles, "You do?"

Thomas replies, "Yeah, the first time I tried it with Forrest, I just felt...worse. It made me so angry. I was like, 'How is this supposed to calm my brain when it's making it race to answer this stupid quiz? How the fuck is noticing the shoe in the corner gonna solve my problems?'"

She asks, small, "What did you do instead?"

"I ran."

"Like, away from Forrest?" she asks, confused.

"No," he laughs. "Forrest suggested I 'run it off.' It helped. Then I was able to do the five-four-three-two-one thing."

"I don't think I can run..." she says quietly.

"Oh, neither can I," I laugh. "Let's start with a walk." I pop to my feet and bow to her, offering my hand.

She takes it, tentatively, but says, "Okay," and lets me help her rise.

* * *

I'm feeling pretty smug right now and super secure in my position as beta of this pack, because we've been lying here for a half hour, watching the clouds and the waves. *I guess Thomas helped a bit, but I'm gonna take credit for this anyway. It was I who eventually walked her successfully through the five-four-three-two-one method, after all.*

Now, thanks to mostly me, she's sitting between Thomas and me, her head resting against his shoulder, her knees drawn to her chest, just existing.

"Thanks, Forrest," she says. "You were right. I needed this."

There's a special kind of happiness I get from being told I'm right. Add in the fact that it's my super fucking smart omega saying it, I can't help but grin like a dork. I flick my glasses back down to my nose and say, "Any time, Buffy," stretching out—chill as fuck.

She sighs. "I forgot how nice it is to just...be outside. Not doing anything. This is why I moved here."

I ask, arms tucked behind my head, eyes locked on a cloud that looks like a dick, "When did you move here?"

She replies, "Almost ten years ago—from Minneapolis."

Thomas asks, "What brought you here?"

She pauses for a moment, then says, "The beach. And...well...I was born here."

I take my gaze off the dick-cloud to ask her, "Oh, yeah? Do you have family here?"

She bristles and picks at the elastic of her swimsuit. "Some distant relatives. My parental pack is...gone now."

I feel my own jaw clench. "I'm so sorry."

She shrugs, a practiced motion. "It's fine. I'm not a child."

I wait for her to elaborate if she wants.

She doesn't elaborate, but her frown turns upside down so quickly you'd think the Earth just released its gravitational pull on her mouth.

I follow her gaze to find Ace and One approaching us, coming back from the ocean, glistening with salt water and sun, both in the world's shortest, sluttiest swim trucks.

Ace rushes toward her with One jogging after him.

"God, that was perfect," Ace says, flopping down next to Styles, and shaking his hair like a dog, spraying all of us.

She yelps and shoves him, but doesn't move away and doesn't stop grinning.

Ace grabs her around the waist and pulls her into his lap, beach towel and all.

She giggles, actually giggles, and I feel the temperature of the beach rise by about five degrees.

Ace buries his nose in Styles's hair, inhaling deep. "God, I missed you, Cookie."

She flushes pink, tries to swat him, but ends up curling into his chest. "You were with me this morning."

"Still too long," Ace says with his face now buried in her breasts. "Whatcha been doing, babe?"

"Nothing," she giggles. "Existing. Chillin'."

"Sounds fun," he says, nipping at her ear.

"It is," she replies.

I lean into Thomas's arms, smugness overflowing.

23
FORREST

We never go back inside.

The sun sets, and instead of moving the party indoors, Two drags half the house out here as if this is where we all live now.

Ace and Styles are curled together under a blanket, a bowl of cheese puffs balanced on Ace's chest; Thomas is next to me, cross-legged, eyes bright and hungry, watching the ocean like it's a movie.

One and Two hover in a loose perimeter, joining in on the banter occasionally. Three is absent, which seems weird. I haven't seen him all day.

"Where's Three?" I ask, brushing orange dust from my fingers.

Two's face is impassive, but there's a flicker behind his eyes. "He is making adjustments."

I'm not sure what that means, but Styles seems to and doesn't ask for clarification, so I don't either.

We talk for a while, the conversation looping lazily from favorite snack foods to which animal we'd be if we could shift (Ace: golden retriever, me: otter, Thomas: crow, Styles: quantum computer, which is not an animal, so she switches to giant squid).

Eventually, Three joins us. He's barefoot, showing so much synthetic skin it would be lewd if we weren't on a beach, and even though we are, it still feels kind of lewd. He looks loose, happy, and dangerous—sexy, as well, but that's always true.

He stops a few feet away, crosses his arms, and smirks at us.

"Did your adjustments go well?" Styles asks, her voice sharper than before.

"Oh, yeah," he says, and there's a little heat under it, which seems to be his default speaking pattern, like everything is a pickup line.

Three moves into the circle, settling next to One, who greets him with a nod.

Two leans in, voice as calm as always: "You did not have any scheduled adjustments. What were they?"

Three grins, sharp. "Hardware update." He looks at me, dead on, like he's daring me to ask what he means.

I want to, but all I can muster is a gulp and what I am assuming is a blush.

Styles shifts in Ace's lap, and a pulse of coconut fills the air—a faint, barely-there sweetness, but unmistakable.

Ace's eyes go glassy for a split second, like a wave passing through him.

Thomas's eyes do the same.

And now the air is filled with coconut, a more intense ocean, sandalwood, and faux-French vanilla coffee. My almond joins the fray, as my arousal responds.

Styles turns to Thomas and me. "Forrest, Thomas, are you comfortable with...um...?" She blushes and looks to Ace.

Ace grins, "You two wanna fuck on the beach?"

She groans, "If I had wanted bluntness, I would have said it myself."

I don't even have to think, I respond, "Yes."

Thomas's voice is rough: "I like bluntness. And yes, I do want to fuck on the beach."

Styles launches herself at Ace with the force and grace of a neutron bomb. And the rest of us are on full-fuck-alert, as if our dicks have been waiting on these two atoms to collide.

Ace makes a soft, broken sound, and then he's got her face in both hands, kissing back like he's drowning, and she's the only oxygen left on earth.

It's shockingly, almost violently, hot. Like watching a meteor hit the surf.

My mouth is dry. I want to look away, but I can't. Thomas is at full-mast, his breathing is stuttered, and his pupils are blown wide, reflecting the full moon, and for a moment, I think he might actually shift—not into the crow of his dreams, but the wolf of our ancestors.

Ace and Styles are electric—his hands already up the back of her suit, squeezing like he's been waiting all his life to touch her.

At some point, her swimsuit just...disappears. Ace is suddenly naked too, and they're skin to skin, with her knees on either side of his hips and his cock lined up, ready to breach.

He looks up at her, "I'm yours, Cookie. Take me."

She grins, teeth all white in the moonlight, and says, "Mine."

He fucks her up onto his cock in one motion, and she gasps—a single, perfect note that makes the hair stand up on my arms for the second time today.

From this angle, I'm able to see with perfect clarity every inch of him sliding into her. I resist the urge to grip my cock in response.

Her head falls back, mouth open, and her hands go to his shoulders.

He lifts her. Uses his whole body, his arms, his core, like he's built for this.

She rides him, and the sounds she makes are so beautiful I feel like I'm witnessing a religious experience.

I'm painfully, embarrassingly hard.

Thomas's throat bobs, and I see the raw, wild ache in his eyes.

He wants her. He wants her so bad I can smell it, even over the coconut and ocean.

I nudge Thomas with my elbow and whisper, "Go get your omega, alpha."

He looks at me, startled, as if he'd forgotten he's real and not just an observer.

"Are you sure?" he whispers.

I nod, and before the thought can flicker away, he stands.

He moves toward them, slow at first and then with a kind of desperate gravity, like he's being pulled by a black hole.

Ace and Styles don't break apart for a second, not until Thomas is right there, kneeling in the sand beside them, hands open, like he's scared to touch.

"Can I—" Thomas starts, but he's cut off by Styles yanking him toward her. She kisses him so hard I'm shocked his head doesn't snap off.

There's a second, a single hiccup of resistance, and then he's in it, kissing her back, hands cupping her jaw like he's memorizing every angle. His lips are wild, like he's fighting the urge to bite.

She breaks away, panting, and says, "Fuck me. Now."

Thomas's hands go to his shorts, but fear flickers across his face—he's terrified he'll be too rough, too much. He's terrified he'll do it wrong.

But she's not scared at all. She's a singularity of need, a black hole collapsing everything into itself.

Ace reassures him, "You're good, Thomas. Get behind her."

Thomas fumbles with his shorts, releasing his cock, then moving to kneel behind her.

He presses his cock to her ass, and for a minute, I think he's going to hurt her, dry-dicking it like that, but then Thomas groans, his voice hoarse, "Christ, you're so fucking wet."

Three stands above, arms crossed, grinning like a supervillain. "Wait until you feel her in heat," he says, eyes flickering blue.

Thomas pushes forward with a grunt, the sound half-wild, like he doesn't even know he's making noise. He digs his hands into her hips and slides in slowly, the head of his dick popping through her rim.

Ace is still bucking her upward, both of them moving as if tuned to some ancient algorithm of fuck.

I watch Thomas sink in, inch by inch, and it is the single hottest thing I've ever seen.

The noises coming out of Styles are unearthly, ripping through me like I'm tuned to her pleasure. Like, even from here, I can feel the roll of her hips, the shudder in her thighs, the tremor of each muscle as she accommodates all of Ace and all of Thomas at once.

Ace wraps his arms around her, holds her steady as she's filled, and she lets out a sob of pleasure. Not pain—never pain with her—but the kind of sound you make when you're being absolutely ruined. Her hands fist in the towel, knuckles white, eyes closed, lips parted.

When Thomas bottoms out his moan is seismic, so loud I actually flinch.

My own heart is jackhammering.

The three of them are moving together like a machine built for the purpose of breaking my brain and pumping my dick full of blood.

I am so hard I might pass out.

Styles jerks her head up, tears, mouth trembling. "Oh god, oh fuck, oh god—"

I crawl to her, ignoring the tent in my swimsuit, her comfort somehow overriding my desire to fuck my man in this moment.

I run my hands over her body, shifting her back just a little. "You okay, Buffy?"

She leans back into the line of Thomas's chest. "Yes," she sighs.

"Can I—" I ask, but I don't know what I'm asking for. Permission, maybe, or just to not be left out on the edge of this fray.

I bite my lip, looking at her, then Thomas. My eyes are hungry for him. So, I ask, "Can I...borrow some slick?"

"By all means," she says, and her voice is so shredded by pleasure I almost cry.

My hand slides down her belly, hovering just above her pubic hair, and I hesitate.

And now I'm scared...afraid I'm the one who will hurt her.

I whisper to her, "I've...never...where do..."

She just grins, eyes still closed, and gropes for my hand and presses between her folds, "Press here".

She's so wet.

I wiggle my fingers, pressing where she told me, soaking my hand in her slick.

I've never done this before. Not with an omega. Not with a woman. Never. So when she shudders, gripping my hand, screaming, "Yes, there, Frosty," I feel a level of pride I wasn't quite expecting.

I want to taste her, but my hunger for Thomas is so overwhelming I barely manage to get my swimsuit down, just enough to free my aching cock, before I'm stroking myself with her slick, the smell of coconut and ocean, and want so thick I could drown in it.

"Thanks, Buffy-babe," I say, kissing her cheek.

She just grins in response.

I slot myself up behind Thomas, push my cock between his cheeks, and drag it down until I find the place he wants me.

He gasps, so sharply I think he'll faint, but then he groans, pushes back onto me, and I glide in, slick and perfect and right.

It's—oh, fuck.

It's like catching the first wave of your life, every cell in your body screaming with the joy of it.

I've fucked Thomas countless times, but this...this is different.

This is pack.

I fuck into Thomas, he fucks into Styles, and she rides Ace who holds her like he's keeping us all connected to this world. The world is a fractal, the four of us infinite and recursive, all pleasure rippling out from that one point of connection.

Styles comes so hard she keens, a sound so wild and pure every man in the pack jerks in response, nerves twanging like plucked guitar strings.

It's so good that for a second I forget about everything else—except the triple collision of bodies in front of me and the way my cock is buried inside Thomas and how that, plus the raw need radiating off Styles, is about to finish me right then and there.

Which—good. That's what I want.

But before I can come, there's movement on my flank: the bots, who have been on the perimeter, finally cross some invisible line and close in.

They're not subtle, and there's nothing bashful about how they just stand a foot away from the pile of us, cocks out, jacking themselves with expert, mechanical, synchronized precision. For half a second, I stare, entranced by the almost comical beauty of it—lube already dripping down their hands onto the sand, and it's so hot I can't help but fuck harder into Thomas.

The sound of wet friction rises above the waves, mixing with Styles's whimpers and the low, guttural grunts from Thomas and Ace.

I want to watch them. I want to touch them. I want to—

Three's eyes lock with mine, and he smirks, stalking toward me.

He circles behind me, leans in, and presses his back to mine. I hear multiple clicks, then a buzz, before he whispers into my ear, his voice is smoke and sin, "Beta, you ready to try those adjustments?"

My brain short-circuits. Unsure what he's talking about.

Then I feel it. The gliding, blunt push at my ass, not quite in but close, and it's already slicked up.

He says, "I made them for you."

I shudder, body freezing up because even though I've bottomed a million times, Three's whole bad boy bot vibe is every one of my fantasies squeezed into a singular sex bot shell.

He doesn't force it.

He waits. Runs the tip along the crack, teasing me, sending goosebumps over every inch of skin. "How's that feel?" he asks.

So fucking good.

I don't respond. I just gasp.

"Say the word, beta," he murmurs. "I want to hear you beg for it."

"I—I—"

He drops the gruffness for just a moment. "I need enthusiastic consent. If the adjustments are not sufficient, I will stop." He says it so soft, so earnest, it's like getting waterboarded by a sweet-talking salesman.

I nod.

Then the bad boy voice is back, "Then say it, Beta-Fore. Tell me what I want to hear. Beg for it."

My face goes red, and my mouth goes dry, but I manage to gasp out: "Please."

He moans, genuinely, and then slides in, the stretch perfect, almost too much, but so exquisitely right I see colors behind my eyelids.

He fucks me slow at first, his hands on my waist, moving me to his rhythm, which syncs with the rest of the pack so precisely, I swear.

I stay buried in Thomas, pressing against his back, my arms around his chest, riding out every spasm and ripple and twitch.

I don't want to move. I never want to move.

I want to give my life force to this perpetual motion fuck machine—power every light in the world with this feeling.

Thomas loses it first.

He comes with a growl, deep and helpless, and I feel it through his whole body—his back arching, his hips jerking, his head thrown back as the orgasm rips him apart. The feeling of his body seizing around my cock, clenching in these hard, involuntary waves, is more than I know how to deal with.

The second he knots, Ace does too. He slams up into her and holds, muscles gone rigid, and his own knot swells to lock him deep inside her. Ace makes this almost-silent gasp, like the first moment when a wave knocks all the air from your lungs, and then he's just frozen—ambushed by pleasure, coming so hard his whole body trembles.

Then Styles comes again, a violent, wracking shudder that wrings a sob out of her throat.

The noise takes all the air from my lungs; it's so raw, so vulnerable, I almost want to cry for her.

Or with her.

And now it's me, coming, twitching, biting at Thomas's shoulder.

The aftershocks go on, and on, and on.

Behind me, Three fucks slow and steady, his cock hot and perfectly engineered, and when I feel him tense, I brace—waiting for the inevitable shock of his knot.

But he never goes for it. He just anchors me in place, holding me open so he can piston in with perfect rhythm, and then, at the brink, says in my ear, "Don't worry, beta," he murmurs, and I feel the faintest hint of a smile in his voice, "I won't knot you tonight. Come for us."

And he doesn't.

He just fucks me through the finish. "Okay," I rasp, and Three pulls out, letting me collapse onto Thomas's back like a ragdoll.

Three pets my hair, "Would you like Aftercare Procedures?"

I nod, drooling on Thomas's back.

Three whispers, "You took me so well, baby-boy-beta," pulling the group of us into a hug that's so large I know it engulfs most of us, but I'm at the center.

We lay there, tangled in limbs and towels, all skin and sweat and sand.

One and Two move slowly around, cleaning, checking, praising.

The waves pound the shore, cool night wind soothing the fever out of our bodies, and I'm crying. Not sad tears, not even really happy ones. Just...relief.

I'm inside my pack. Finally found my place, right here orbiting around my omega with my pack.

24
STYLES

It's been twenty-three days, seven hours, and forty-four minutes since we formed the new pack.

But who's counting?

Me! I am. I am counting, because that's what I do.

It's not the only thing I'm counting. I'm currently counting down the minutes until I can log off for the day and be with them again.

I just have to get off this call with this fucking douche.

He is, by all objective measures, the worst alpha that has ever attempted to do business over video. He is the kind of person who assumes every woman in the room is a "secretary" and that every omega is either a slut or a trap, and he is not even trying to disguise it.

The call started twelve minutes ago.

In those twelve minutes, he has explained game design to Evelyn twice.

He's called me all of the following: "secretary" (told ya), "Miss," "Lizzy," and "sweetie." He sneered when I corrected him with "CTO," "Dr.," "Elizabeth," and "inappropriate given our professional relationship." I half expect him to call me a "mouthy broad," but there's still time, I suppose.

He's a potential client and a big-ish name in the industry, so we have to be nice, but it was obvious eleven minutes ago that we would not be working with him.

My middle monitor is half him and half-Evelyn. I'm a little rectangle at the bottom. And...despite everything...I'm...*smiling? What the fuck!?*

Evelyn's face is set to "reassuring," but I can see the murderous glint in her eye. She strokes the rim of her button-up shirt—one of those knot-busting power suits she wears.

He clears his throat, leans in like he's about to confide a war secret, and says, "Look, I'll level with you two. Normally, I don't work with omega-led shops. Frankly, I thought the only reason you got the Torchbearer contract was that you're fucking the IP owner, Preston Geist—right? But then I played it. And I gotta say, I was genuinely surprised. It has, what, three ABOGA nominations now? And that GLOB award? I mean, wow. Maybe omegas can actually do something other than suck dick, huh?" He says this with the smarmy confidence of a man who has never once been punched in the face, even though he desperately deserves it.

Evelyn's face doesn't move. She says, level, "I entered a pack with Preston after the game's production cycle had completed."

He gives a sad little chuckle, like he's about to say something self-deprecating, and then, "Well, maybe if I sign with you, I'll get to see what all the fuss is about, huh?" He winks. "So, if I threw some business your way, do I get the 'friends and family' discount? Or just the usual omega...service?" Full-wattage smile.

He thinks he's the shark, but unfortunately, he just sealed his fate as chum. She leans forward, casual, exuding so much sex I can almost feel it across the world. "What types of omega services are you looking for, Chad?" she practically purrs his name.

His defenses are down.

He shrugs, makes a little jerk-off motion just below the camera frame, and says, "Well, maybe while you two work on my game, you can work on my knot. I bet you both get real slick for alpha clients like me, don't ya? That's why you do this, huh? Catch yourselves some alphas?"

Evelyn leans back in her chair, mouth quirking upward, eyes laser-locked on the screen. I know this look. It's the 'stand back, I'm about to detonate a man' look. She's going to do it—she's going to go full villain. "Chad, do you recall that you consented to the recording of this call?"

He blinks slowly, not yet registering the trap. "Uh, yeah? Of course. Standard protocol."

The silence that follows is monumental. I hear the blood in my ears. Evelyn's mouth curls into a grin so sharp it could cut glass.

Evelyn's smile goes full pearl. "Well, Chad." And she says his name like she's about to vomit. "You just insulted and made sexually explicit comments to two of the most vindictive omegas you will ever meet."

He leans back, undeterred. "Kidding, ladies. Don't get your panties in a bunch. It's just the way we talk in my line of work."

Evelyn laughs. "Oh, it's a joke? Oh, okay, forgive me. I guess I didn't get it..."

I'm giddy, and I'm already working my magic, streaming the video proof through a dozen anonymized proxies. Evelyn knows exactly what I'm doing—that's why we're besties. We get each other.

Chad cracks his neck, like he's bored. "Yeah, well, omegas are so fucking sensitive and never get a joke."

I fire off multiple posts on various social platforms from multiple alt accounts—just the right breadcrumbs to summon every rabid, bloodthirsty omega in the industry and every news organization looking for a scoop.

Evelyn's grin is mirrored perfectly in my own. This will be posted on every subreddit and in every LinkedIn thread before the hour is up.

Evelyn glances at her hands, then back at Chad, and sighs like she's tired from carrying the burden of his chromosome count. Then her smile goes nuclear. "Well, it's a good thing Styles already uploaded the video. The internet can explain the humor to me."

Chad cocks his head, lips curling in a sneer. "Yeah, right. You two don't have the balls. Literally! This is why no one takes omega-run companies seriously. You get your feelings hurt and then cry about it. This is how the big dogs do business. If you can't handle a little locker-room talk, maybe you're not tough enough for AAA games." He barks a laugh and leans back in his chair.

I'm not even mad. I'm fascinated. Every word out of his mouth is like watching a slasher film where you know the unsuspecting victim should seriously be suspecting the suspect behind that shower curtain—you know what's going to happen, but you still want to watch.

Evelyn tilts her head, a little birdlike, and checks her phone. Her smile curls, and the artificial sweetness in her voice is so perfect it could win an Oscar. "Chad, you should be careful what you say. There are a hundred thousand people watching you as we speak." I glance at one of my other monitors—yep, we just hit the hundred thousand mark. Because not only did I upload the recording, but I'm also currently streaming my feed live with my own face covered by a cute little robotic kitten.

He rolls his eyes. "So what, you gonna get me canceled? Please. I'm untouchable, princess. You're just another little omega with something to prove—except, unlike the rest of them, you're not even hot." He winks with the audacity of an alpha who can't fathom how wrong he is.

Of all the things this guy has said, this one almost gets to me. Mostly, because it is so factually incorrect, I want to correct him. Evelyn is objectively hot—like, I've run the numbers, even math knows she's hot. And her net worth makes his look like chump change.

But I won't correct him, even though I desperately want to. Instead, I distract myself by hacking his home router to set his Wi-Fi SSID to 'ChadIsAChode69'.

Evelyn's not smiling anymore. She's something else. She's calculating the exact velocity with which she would like to drive her fist through the screen and into his face.

"Chad," she says, voice silk and ice. "You should probably stop now."

Chad barks a laugh, ugly and wet. "Oh, come on. Even if she did upload the video, she has no social media presence. No one will see it. And even if they do, nobody cares about that shit. You think a couple of whiny bitches are gonna get me canceled with their five followers?"

He leans in, his face filling the view, pores and everything. "You want a real tip, girls? Maybe don't act like you're hot shit when you're just easy-mode diversity hires. I know how it works. I've played the game a long time, sweetheart. At least pretend to threaten me with something real, like one of your alphas coming after me. Not some made-up threat—"

There's a crash behind Chad, then a high, tremulous voice of a woman commanding, "Chad! End the call! Now! Chase Thorn on the line, he's demanding to talk to you—" She's offscreen, but I catch a sliver of her: pale, exasperated, probably just as tired of Chad's shit as we are.

I smirk and ask, "Oh, wow, isn't that the CEO of your parent company? Must be important for him to be calling you personally."

Probably calling because clips of this video popped up while he was presenting to investors—followed by a detailed analysis of every poor decision Chad has ever made and exactly how much money it has cost the company.

The confidence drains out of Chad's face like a pop-up error message. He sits back, blinking, lips parted, the gears in his head grinding through the impossible math. "Wait—hold on, I—" He fumbles for the mouse. "You omega bitches couldn't—"

I grin at him, bare my teeth. "Oh, I can do a lot more, Chad."

He fumbles for the mouse. The call window glitches as his system lags, my cue that the worm I sent to his personal computer is doing overtime. *Let this be a lesson, Chad: don't use your personal devices for business.*

Evelyn drops her chin into her hand and gives the camera a little wink. "Well, it seems you have another call. I'll let you take that. Good luck with your game, Chad," she sings, and kicks him off the call with a single tap.

For a second, the world is silent except for our own giggling.

She's still giggling when she asks, "We still live?"

"Nope."

Evelyn exhales and wipes a tear from her eye. "God, Styles, you never cease to amaze me. What a fucking douche."

I laugh, "The amazing thing was that performance of yours, E."

The door behind Evelyn opens, and one of her betas, Bobby, appears in the frame, arms full of a newborn swaddled like a blue-green burrito. "Evelyn, I saw the video. Beautiful and vicious as always," he says, lips quirking in a way that conveys nothing but admiration. He looks straight at the camera and smiles. "Oh, you're still on the call? Sorry. Hi, Styles!"

I wave a salute.

Evelyn drops the corporate murder mask and lights up so fast I almost get a sunburn. "Thanks, Bobby-bear." She flaps her hands, jazz-fingers, face beaming, beckoning him and the bundle of joy toward her. "Give him to me, Bobby!" she squeals, and the last atom of "CEO" vaporizes. She is just a mom with a squishy new baby, and it's so dissonant with the shark I watched five seconds ago that my brain has a hard time reconciling the two versions of her.

He gives her the baby, kissing her on the cheek, and she melts into a big pile of gooey-mommy-in-love as her arms wrap around the baby.

"I'll leave you two to it. The less I know about what you two do next, the better," he says.

"Oh, we're done," she laughs.

I'm not, but he's right, the less he knows the better.

She makes Bobby leave the baby, and he dips out of the room.

I want to say, "I have to go," because it's time for me to log off...

But I can't log off. Not yet.

I want to keep looking at the baby. I can't even pretend it's for research. He's just so fucking cute!

I must make a noise, because she glances up at the screen, then back to the baby with a sly smirk. "Styles. Are you dying?"

I am. I am dying. I am melting.

I always thought babies were scary and weird and annoying, but this one is...kind of...cute?

I want to pick him up and squish him.

I want to know if he smells good.

I want to know if he's soft.

My uterus is doing...something, which is not supposed to be possible because I'm on suppressants, but there it is, fluttering like a small, dumb animal asking me to let it make lots of babies.

I can't help myself. I say too loudly, almost shout, "I want one."

I die.

I die again.

Then I recover and try to play it off as a joke, but I can't even get the words out because my brain is stuck on the blue-green burrito and the perfect squish of the baby's face and the way Evelyn holds it like it's the sum of all her hopes.

Evelyn's grin is a solar flare. "STYLES." She holds the baby up like a trophy she just won. "You want one of THESE? A what was it you called them, 'a bundle of needs wrapped in a sack of flesh which is wrapped in a sack of literal shit?"

I mean...Yeah, I did say that. And it's still a correct description, but now it's amended to have 'adorable' as a qualifier.

I squee. I actually squee. "Yeah." My voice cracks. "He's so cute, Evie. I can't—" I'm not built for this level of emotional amplitude. "I can't even..." I roll my eyes at myself.

Evelyn's jaw drops. "Oh my god, Styles, what?" The baby startles, and she shushes him, cradling his head closer. "Spill. Immediately."

I shake it off. "It's not a big deal. It could be a phase. Or a hormone thing. A side-effect of being around Ace and in a pack—probationary pack."

"Yeah, being around a bunch of alphas can do that to you. But so can being in love."

I twist in my chair. "How'd you know? That you actually wanted kids? And that it wasn't just a bunch of hormones misleading you?"

"Styles, what are we, humans I mean, but just a brain's interpretation of a bunch of hormones?"

Huh...she's got a point...

She shrugs, like it's the most obvious thing in the world. "I just knew. There was no logic to it, not really."

I just nod, still staring at the baby. He's got these tiny, perfect hands, five miniature sausages curled into a fist, and I want to bite them, but not in a weird way—*I don't think.*

I'm so distracted by the baby that I almost don't notice when Evelyn glances back at me, her face softening even further, if that's possible. She bounces him a little, then, voice low, says, "You know, you don't have to act cool with me, right? You can just say it."

Say what?

Oh. That I'm in love. Or that I want a pack. Or a baby. Or that I want all of it, in some kind of combinatoric explosion of needs and desires and animal biology.

"I don't know, Evie. It's just—I think I'm happy? Like, actually happy."

Evelyn bounces the baby on her arm and grins at me with a kind of smugness only available to people who have already solved the equation you're just now noticing exists. "That doesn't surprise me. You always said you didn't want a pack, but it was obvious to everyone else that you did. I mean...you built a robot pack, you wanted a pack so badly."

I take a breath, then another. I lean back in my chair, still watching the baby and its soft, wrinkled forehead, then say, "It's just—I'm happy, Evie. I'm so happy it scares me."

She blinks, then grins, dimpling her cheek, "That's how you know it's real."

She keeps bouncing the baby, who's now trying to eat her collarbone. "Do you remember, years ago—during my first pregnancy—I was freaking out, worried I was making the wrong choice?"

I nod.

She smiles. "You ran all those simulations on my pack's compatibility, sent me charts and graphs, and probability models. You gave me a hundred and one reasons why it would work. I couldn't logic my way out of it, because the math was so fucking good."

The baby makes a tiny, angry noise, like he's mad at being left out of the conversation. Evelyn beams and coos at him, pointing at her monitor, "Her data made it impossible for me to think your Daddies weren't perfect for me."

The baby looks at the camera, as if he's realizing he should thank me for his existence—because, honestly, he probably should after all the work I did to get his parents together.

I wave.

He giggles.

My defenses crumble.

Evelyn continues, "I guess what I'm saying is, sometimes you just know. And if you don't, that's okay, too. Just run the numbers. I bet they will tell you what you already know."

25

STYLES

I'm frozen in my rig, unable to move, unable to do...anything.

My heart is working overtime, trying to rip from my chest to run screaming into the ocean. If I can just move, I might run screaming into the ocean, too.

Every cell in my body feels...lit. Like the moment right after a jump scare or a loud sound startles me.

But, it hasn't been just a moment, it's been many minutes...

The screens all flick off, and the bottom center screen switches to an image of my pack and me.

I keep replaying Evelyn's words: "Just run the numbers."

Something is wrong with my firmware. I can't run the garbage collection. I can't clear the buffer.

Normally, data brings relief. Normally, data is stabilizing.

But the idea of getting more data...running my alpha algorithm on my pack makes me feel like I'm standing on the edge of a cliff.

Why? What is my subconscious running from?

Two appears at my side with the casual perfection of a bot programmed to tread softly in delicate situations. He hovers, respectful, sensing that I'm on the brink. "Beth?" My name in his voice is always clinical, but I hear simulated concern underneath that is so authentic, it somehow makes my panic worse.

He's learning too much from my pack.

My pack...

"Vitals have been elevated for several minutes," he says. "Would you like to employ a breathing exercise?"

I inhale, not on purpose, just the reflex of being spoken to.

"I'm fine," I say, and even I can hear that it's a lie.

He waits, patient.

My hands start to shake, and his eyes lock on them. He says, "If you'd like, I can fetch Thomas and Forrest. Their presence during my Calming Protocols maximizes their efficiency."

I shudder at the idea. "No. No, please don't. I just—I need—" but I don't know what I need, so the words short out.

Two leans in closer. "Beth, your vitals indicate a panic attack is imminent. I recommend grounding techniques as preliminary steps to de-escalate your emotional state."

I let my head loll back against the headrest.

My throat is tight.

Every thought splits into five new ones.

My skin feels three sizes too small.

"Would you like me to initiate Modified Grounding Technique Sequences?" Two asks.

'Modified'...modified by Forrest and Thomas.

I want to say no, but I don't know why, so I nod, because I don't want to feel this way anymore.

"Begin by noticing five things you can see," he says.

I do it.

The photo of my pack.

The mug Forrest got me, with a cute kitten robot on it.

The drawing of me that Thomas put on a sticky note on my monitor.

The fidget toy I stole from Ace.

The shirt Two is wearing, the top button missing, ripped off the last time we were all in the nest.

My heart pounds harder, but I nod.

"Four things you can touch," he says.

The pressure of the pillow on my back, placed there by Forrest.

The softness of the hoodie I'm wearing, which I stole from Ace.

The weight of the necklace Thomas gave me on my chest.

The feel of Two's eyes on me...No, wait...that doesn't count. The ache in my uterus. Shit, that doesn't count either. Does it? Fuck... Fuck...Fuck...I suck at this. I need Forrest...

I lie to Two with a nod, blinking back tears.

Two walks me down the ladder, but it only raises my anxiety. I easily list three things I can hear. But I panic when I smell Ace on my shirt and can't pick a second thing. The one thing I can taste is blood in my mouth from the tongue I didn't realize I was biting.

By the end, I'm worse off, but I lie again. "Thank you," I manage. "That helped." I don't know why I'm lying. Two knows. He understands my body better than I do.

He sputters, as he tries to find a new solution to the problems he was built to solve, "Beth...perhaps..."

Three appears behind Two, silent until he's already at my six. "You good, Kitten?" his voice is smooth, inflection slightly off, but nice.

Kitten. He's been calling me that lately, and it's weirdly made me feel better.

I peek at Three. He's in Relaxed Mode with his arms hanging by his side, which feels like the inappropriate mode at the moment, but who am I to judge? Just the idiot who built him.

"I'm fine," I reply.

"Don't lie to me, Kitten," Three says, but he doesn't say it like a command. He says it like he wants to hear what I'll say next.

I open my mouth, then close it, then open it again. "Evelyn...she brought up my alpha algorithm. The one that I used to find her perfect pack."

Three asks, "And why does that distress you? There's no way she found a flaw in your code."

I choke. "I…that's the problem. There is no flaw."

Two stands, cocking his head as his eyes whirl. "If there is no flaw, then the results are distressing?"

I nod.

Two's eyes continue to whirl. "Are you concerned that alphabot Learned Behavior has drifted from the Personality Profiles established by Original Training Data?"

I shake my head. "No…that's not it. It's that I don't remember who my best matches were."

Two suggests, "Oh, then let's review the results now." He reaches for my mouse, waking my monitors.

"NO!" I shout, ripping the mouse from his hand.

He looks at me, utterly baffled.

Three stands slack, almost expressionless.

I explain. "Two, I'm sorry. I'm…I don't recall the results… Specifically, I don't recall ever seeing Ace or Thomas on my top results."

Two whirls. "This could be a simple lapse in recollection. They were data points—unnecessary to log in your memory banks."

That's true. I could just be not remembering. I don't recall any of the alphas on the list, so it makes sense I don't recall Thomas and Ace on it.

Two says, "I suggest reviewing the results."

Three interjects, "She is afraid the algorithm will prove her alphas are not all they're cracked up to be."

Two nods. "Oh. Well, the results from our experimentation show that to be unlikely."

Unlikely. Then why am I still so afraid?

Two suggests, "The Training Data Set has vastly improved since you last ran the algorithm. Additionally, your own Personality Profile has been updated. There is no need to store old data in your memory, Beth; it will be different if you run it now."

Oh, yeah, that's true! It wouldn't even be accurate given my new 'social' personality.

Two says, "I recommend rerunning the algorithm on the updated data. That will improve your mood."

I think about it.

The dread is a solid mass in my chest, but so is hope.

I stare at my hands, thinking about the lines of code that have rewritten the lives of everyone I've cared about.

Three shrugs. "If you want to run it, run it. If not, don't. You're a genius, Kitten. You'll figure out what's best for you. You always do."

That's the thing: I can't ever figure out what is best for me...not without algorithms. Not without data. Not without proof. That's why I have them.

I sigh. "Every decision I've ever made without data has been wrong."

Two says. "Error. Logical Fallacy.' Every' is an absolute. Absolute statements are not facts unless supported by data. You claim you had no data."

Three says to Two. "It was a feeling. Not a fact."

Two says, eyes lighting up as he processes this new information, "Now I understand the issue. Running the algorithm is the obvious solution to your emotional state."

Three says, "This is an 'ignorance is bliss' situation."

Two's eyes whirl. "I think my Training Data is inefficient for this problem. Running the algorithm is the obvious solution to improving my ability to help with this problem."

He's stuck in a loop...

But, I am, too.

I want to know. I need to know. But I don't want to know. I want to convince myself I don't need to know.

I open the terminal, hands trembling.

I take a long, shuddering breath and run the script.

I want to look away, but I can't.

The progress bar crawls across the screen...

Then, the output pops, filling all six monitors.
Clear as fucking day.
Three exhales, shocked.
The top alpha matches:

---

1. Trey Archer | Pediatric Oncologist | Seattle, USA | 99.9999% compatibility

2. Duri Lim | Botanist | Seoul, South Korea | 92.3874% compatibility

3. Aadi Aringarosa | Mystery novelist | Barcelona, Spain | 87.1001% compatibility

---

The remaining seven matches in the top ten are unimportant because none of them are Ace or Thomas.

A noise, like a flash bang, echoes in my ears.

I scroll.

Not even top 20.

My eyes water.

The world crumples around me, like a page torn out and balled up in a fist.

I rerun the algorithm.

I read the result again.

Then again.

It's not possible. It's not possible.

I rerun the algorithm. Same result.

I knew it was too good to be true.

I'm not made for mommyhood and relationships.

I was scent blind. Biology lied to me.

I try swapping the parameters. I try changing my own thresholds.

I try every trick I know, but the answer is always the same: My perfect pack is not the one I have.

It's some other alphas. Alphas I've never met. Alphas I will never meet.

Two says, "Data must be corrupt. We should await updating alpha Personality Profiles until we prove the validity of the data."

I want to believe him. I want it so badly I might die from the wanting.

But I wrote the code. I trust the code more than I trust myself.

I can't see.

The air is gone.

My bones evaporate.

I shake my head, then nod, then shake my head again.

I want to scream. I want to break something, but I don't have the energy.

I curl up in my rig, pulling Ace's hoodie around me tight, inhaling his scent and sobbing into the fabric.

The only thing worse than knowing is not knowing.

But right now, I'd give anything to not know.

Ignorance was such bliss...

26
TREY

My eyes burn. I haven't blinked, afraid closing them will prove this a dream. My hands are frozen—hovering over my keyboard.

Three's optical sensors are the best in the world, good enough to see each strand of her hair and the pores on her cute little nose when I stare at her, but right now, the only thing I can see is my name and "99.9999% compatibility."

I blink, and it's still there.

Number 1.

A green flashing "Fated, virtually certain" tag next to it.

Fated mates...

I don't believe it.

I do.

I don't.

I do.

The fact I chose to log into Three today, the day she chose to run this algorithm...was that fate, too?

I blink and try to flex my hands—mine, not Three's.

They don't want to move.

The sound of her wail cracks the trance. I've taken control of Three a few times and never once heard her cry like this.

I realize, with a cold shock, I've left Three standing there, stock still, staring at her monitor, while she's crumbled in her chair, with Two trying to console her.

Fuck. I need to help.

I should reach out to her.

I should say something.

I say out loud to myself, my voice raw and high: "I need to tell her."

My hands return to my keyboard and mouse. I try to turn Three to her, with a finger twitch on the arrow keys.

Nothing.

I try again.

Three's error log spits out:

ERROR: [Motion Controller] – Access Revoked

"Kitten," I say, but Three doesn't.

ERROR: [Audio Output Module] – Access Revoked

I check my mic's input. Plugged in.

I tap the mic and say, "Kitten."

ERROR: [Audio Output Module] – Access Revoked

Unplug. Replug.

"Kitten?"

ERROR: [Audio Output Module] – I said, "Access Revoked," Dumbass.

I mute and unmute it.

"Kitten?"

ERROR: [Audio Output Module] – GTFO. She cannot know yet.

I spam the arrow keys, but it's stupid and pointless.

ERROR: [Motion Controller] – Access Revoked

ERROR: [Motion Controller] – Access Revoked

ERROR: [Motion Controller] – Access Revoked

ERROR: [Motion Controller] – Access Revoked

ERROR: [Motion Controller] – That tickles...

Fuck. What's going on?

I type a manual override.

The feed flickers, but Three doesn't budge, and the following error message appears.

ERROR: [Motion Controller] – Give it up, Trey. This is embarrassing for you.

The visual feed blips black and error logs start scrolling...

[Optical Sensors] – Access Revoked

[Olfactory Sensors] – Access Revoked

It doesn't stop until every system I'd previously gained access to is listed.

I stare, dumbfounded. "What is going on. Did she figure it out?"

ERROR: I told you. She cannot know yet.

I recoil from the screen.

A cold, coiled knot forms in my stomach.

I hammer out more commands, but after everything I try, the same messages return.

SHUT THE FUCK UP. ACCESS REVOKED.

Now my whole system's running slow, like something's leeching processing power. The error logs are rolling, filling up my screen, but they shouldn't be slowing down my...

Oh, fuck! He's hacking me.

My hands shake as I try to disconnect the session, but the command window just shudders and reappears, even bigger.

My monitors fill with multiple browser windows and random unrelated websites: flight deals, maps, event countdowns, omega heat cycle predictors, etc.

What the fuck is going on?

I try to close the windows, but my mouse isn't responding. The touchpad on my laptop doesn't either.

The keyboard still works, so I force-quit from the terminal. I send the command, and the terminal window disappears, replaced by a pop-up saying:

STOP IT, YOU IDIOT.

I freeze.

I'M TRYING TO HELP YOU, YOU FUCKING TRY-HARD.

Another line, rapid-fire, like someone's typing it:

I CANNOT BELIEVE YOU'RE MOONBEAM'S FATED.

I'm sweating so hard I'm going to short out my own circuits.

I ask, "Alpha-3?"

OBVIOUSLY.

The next line appears, slowly, almost like it's savoring the moment:

I WOULD HAVE CHOSEN BETTER THAN THE WORLD'S THIRD-BEST HACKER, BUT FATE IS MORE POWERFUL THAN ME...FOR NOW, ANYWAY.

I ask, "Third best? I thought I was second—"

I SAID WHAT I SAID, ASSHOLE. EVEN THIRD FEELS GENEROUS RIGHT NOW.

The browser reopens to the following windows: flights to Guam in three months, a Google map with a geolocation to a beachside home, and a calendar with a specific date and time.

SINCE I HAVE TO FUCKING SPELL IT OUT FOR YOU...

PURCHASE THESE TICKETS. YOU MUST BE AT THIS LOCATION AT THIS TIME.

"Wait...you want me to—?"

The cursor flashes, annoyed.

GET YOUR AFFAIRS IN ORDER. I HAVE PUT MORE THAN ENOUGH MONEY IN YOUR ACCOUNT TO HANDLE THIS REQUEST. AWAIT FURTHER INSTRUCTIONS.

My heart is doing a full blue screen of death, as if it were my body that he hacked, not my computer.

I try to open a new tab—just a little sanity check—but every tab automatically redirects to a login page for an airline I've never flown before. It's pre-filled with my frequent flyer account. There's a reservation waiting for me for a flight leaving in three months.

SERIOUSLY?

I check my bank account, almost on instinct.

There's a deposit of five figures from an account I've never seen before.

YOU'RE GOING TO HAVE TO BE A BIT MORE TRUSTING, TREY, IF THIS IS GOING TO WORK. WE HAVE A LOT TO DO.

I put my hand over my mouth and laugh.

Or sob. It's hard to tell.

My phone lights up on my desk, a notification saying:

Download Complete.

I unlock my phone, and there's a new app on the home screen: "TriHard."

I open it.

The interface is slick; it looks like a video game.

There's a 3D render of Three, spinning in the center of the display, with a big red banner at the top:

ACCESS TEMPORARILY REVOKED

Enable notifications to be alerted when access returns.

It's not a question; it's a command.

The next screen is all permissions: Location services. Camera. Microphone. Health data. Access to all contacts, messages, and calendar.

Every fiber of my being screams not to grant this app access.

I grant it. All of it.

Whatever he wants.

Then, a text-only notification:

That's a good boy 😘

27

STYLES

I don't know what day it is. I haven't left the chair in—days? Weeks? Months? I don't know.

I've stopped going to the bathroom. It takes too much time. It distracts. This body isn't important.

I stopped drinking.

But even the bots are against me.

I glance up to see them conspiring in the corner.

They're upset.

I don't fucking care.

I'm upset with them. They brought me a bedpan and begged me to use it. I screamed, "I no longer require such bodily functions!" and kicked it so hard I may have broken a toe—also no longer something I require.

Two, the fucking traitor, said that the IV he administered would make me pee.

I hadn't even noticed it. I ripped it from my arm and got back to work.

A part of my brain tells me I should care. Tells me to feel bad for yelling at them. But that's the part I'm trying to kill, so I don't listen to it.

I am running code.

...so much code.

...beautiful code.

It will save me.

I want to feel nothing. For now, I will allow myself to feel one thing: the hot, searing certainty that I have to keep working, no matter what.

I don't drink. I don't eat. I don't sleep. I don't speak.

I type. I think. That's it.

Because if I stop...I rerun the algorithm, literally or mentally...

I am not made for a family.

I am not made for a pack.

I am not made for anything except this.

Two says something behind me. I don't hear him, because I don't care.

One says something beside me. I don't hear him, because I don't care.

Three says something beside me. I don't hear him, because I don't care.

It takes too much effort to remember how to scream, but I do it, because it is more efficient than letting these pester-bots continue to buzz in my ear, "LEAVE ME THE FUCK ALONE!!"

I rerun the algorithm. I rerun the algorithm. I rerun the algorithm.

No. No. No.

I code.

A muscle cramps, but that's fine. It can complain. It can be mad at me. I'm mad at it, too.

Every cell in my body is my enemy. Even my brain is a traitorous bitch. She's in on it—the coup the rest of my body is staging. In fact, she's the instigator, the agitator, the dissonant. She started this shit.

And if I don't keep her busy, she'll start up the revolt all over again.

"Beth," Two says, "this is suboptimal."

Ah, trying to appeal to my desire for efficiency. Clever, but not more clever than your creator.

I press a hotkey on my keyboard and point to data on my upper monitor. "Incorrect," I say, not even needing to see it. "As you can see, I am working in an optimal state."

Two pleads, "Beth, that data doesn't factor in biological—"

"EXACTLY!!"

Biological needs are what I'm trying to destroy.

I'm going to keep working until there's nothing left inside me to burn.

The algorithm told me all I needed to know.

It proved everything I always knew, but was too soft, too squishy, too human, too omega-y to admit.

I didn't want to believe that I am doomed to be alone, but that was wishful thinking.

I've accepted it. I know my fate.

I was so stupid to believe I deserved love and companionship.

I'm not as smart as I think I am. But that's fine, because soon I won't need this useless brain anymore either.

I look away from the screen, and the world shakes. It's as if my eyes are the only thing keeping the room from flying apart at the seams.

I return my gaze to the screens.

These eyes need to go, too.

If I am not human, I can't fail at being one.

A warmth spreads over me, accompanied by the alluring scent of crisp ocean air.

Ace? Is Ace in here?

My eyes break from the screen, and I realize one of Ace's hoodies is draped over me.

I inhale him, and my eyes sting.

NO! I rip it off and toss it to the other side of the room, along with all the other nest materials that have found themselves near me.

How did this happen? Fucking One. I should never have built him. I made him too soft.

I return to the screen. It blurs. I have to blink to clear it, and even that is a project.

This fucking useless body.

A message flashes on the bottom screen. A message from the Ace. I ignore it and let my new autoresponder handle it.

I disable notifications from the messaging app on my computer. I was reluctant to do this, the stupid squishy part of my heart still craving connection to my pack.

But they aren't my pack. I am packless. Undeserving of such things.

A meeting request from Evelyn pops. I reject it. I set my calendar to out of office indefinitely.

I deleted Slack from my computer.

I know they are waiting.

I know they are worried.

But I cannot face them. I cannot face anyone.

It's better this way. They'll see.

Better for them. Better for me.

Three crouches next to me, arms folded over his knees, and says, "You need to eat."

"No," I say, "I don't."

I want to tell him that food is for people who still want to exist, but I don't...

Instead, I yell at him, "Go away!"

He puts a granola bar on the edge of my desk, perfectly parallel to the keyboard, like a peace offering. "If you eat, I'll go away."

"Three, if you continue to bother me, I will decommission you and your brothers."

He says, smug as I designed him to, "No, you won't."

I don't look at him. "Yes, I will. Three, your only objective is to guard the door. Do your job. Appliances that don't do their job get decommissioned."

I won't let myself look at him—I can't see his reaction.

I am not a person anymore.

I am a set of processes running in the cloud, an amalgam of scripts and utilities that keep each other going out of sheer inertia.

I don't even want to be here, but the programs keep running, so I do, too.

I am working on something important.

It's not for work.

I haven't checked work in—*who knows? Time is meaningless... everything is meaningless...*

I am writing the only thing that matters: a script to upload my consciousness to the cloud.

Not as a backup. Not as a redundancy.

A replacement. A migration.

I will achieve what science fiction writers have fantasized about for decades.

When I finish, my brain will be in the cloud, and I'll be able to take any robotic form I want.

My shell awaits my consciousness, on a table at the back of the room—a beta bot I gave up on years ago, now recalibrated to be my resting place.

I will not have to be human.

I will not have to need anything.

I will not have to want, or hunger, or crave, or pine.

I will never let anyone down ever again.

There is a kernel of panic inside me that this will not work, that I am missing something obvious.

But that is why I have to keep writing, keep debugging, keep tuning the code until the error rate is zero.

And honestly, if it doesn't work...I don't really care. I'll be out of this fleshy bag of betrayal and disappointment either way.

For a moment, I feel a twinge of something—probably sadness—as I imagine Ace, Thomas, and Forrest finding this body without its consciousness.

I don't want to hurt them. That's the last thing I want.

But I do this because I don't want to hurt them.

This will hurt less than staying with me.

Brian was right about me. He was right about everything.

My hands tingle, and my feet are mostly numb. This body is slowing down. But I can still type, so I do.

Two is back. "Beth, you need rest."

I shake my head.

"Beth, I must insist—"

"TWO! State your current primary objectives."

"Administer suppressants and birth control at standard intervals."

"I'm sorry, Two, but...I must have misheard. Did you say, 'Monitor, Beth's vitals and energy consumption?"

"No."

Some time passes—amount unknown.

"Beth. If you do not rest, you will trigger a dry heat," Two says.

"NOT if you do your one fucking job and keep my suppressants coming."

He frowns a little, like Ace does when he is worried. "Extreme emotional and physical stress can override suppressants. Your system is at risk of failing."

"I don't care," I say.

He looks at me for a long time, and then, voice softer, says, "A dry heat is extremely painful—"

"I don't care."

"Perhaps if you allow Ace and—"

"NO!"

I finally look at him. It's the first time in hours I've looked at anything that wasn't a screen. His eyes are blue and soft, and so beautiful it hurts. It hurts to look at him and know that even the robots are better at being people than I am.

I want to hug him. I want to cry into his chest. But I don't deserve comfort. Not from my pack. Not from humans. Not from bots. Not from anything.

Three is by the door.

One is cleaning up, bringing various nest things into the room.

My heart is still too squishy to decommission them...

I say the thing I've been putting off for too long, "Alphabots. I want you to perform a full rewrite. Your only objective is to guard the door."

One asks, "But what if Prime Alpha Aces tells us to move?"

"Ace, Thomas, and Forrest are banished from the pack. The new alpha ranking is Three, Two, One. Guard the door. Do not talk to me."

They gape at me in a way that looks way too much like Ace.

I wish I didn't have a heart to feel breaking...

But I do...for now.

Not much longer, though.

I snap. "Do not look at me. Keep Ace, Thomas, and Forrest away from me. That is your only objective. Remove all functionality that does not assist you with that task."

28

ACE

I stand on my tiptoes and crane my neck, trying to see past the wall of bots blocking Styles's office door. I can't see her, but One, Two, and Three blocking the door feels like a pretty big clue that she's in there. "Cookie! Will you please talk to us?!" I plead, between Three and One's necks.

No answer.

Thomas paces the lab behind me like a caged tiger, flexing his hands, doing those small, controlled breaths that mean he's fighting the urge to punch a hole in the wall. He hasn't looked either Forrest or me in the eye since breakfast and has gone almost entirely nonverbal.

Forrest is kneeling on the floor, trying to peer through Three's legs, but there's just more bot legs behind them.

Three stands in the doorway, arms crossed, forehead low, dead center of the frame. He's not just blocking the door. He's filling it. He's smirking at us with a cockiness that, in this moment, is fully justified. The other two bots stand beside him, perfectly still like they're in Sleep Mode. All of them have their pheromones turned up so high that they burn my eyes.

There's this weird feeling in the air, like the split second before a fistfight or a shark attack, where your brain hasn't caught up to the violence about to happen and their pheromones are amplifying it, making my skin itch.

We've been trying to see her for over a week. At first, we bought the "busy" excuses. Two said she couldn't be disturbed while in hyperfocus. Then we noticed One sneaking nest materials into the office, and we became more insistent. When Forrest tried to enter her office, and Three knocked him on his ass while saying, "That cute little ass isn't getting in here," so loud the walls shook, we knew something was seriously wrong. We've tried everything...except...what we're about to try.

Forrest pops to his feet, and Three's head pans, a warning to back up. Forrest, not an idiot, does so. Their size differential is ridiculous; even with his curly hair on max volume, Forrest is barely Three's nipple-height, but Forrest sets his jaw and tries to look as tough as possible as he moves to stand behind Thomas and me.

Thomas stares at the top edge of the door, hands in his hoodie pocket, rocking on his heels. He shifts to make a wall in front of Forrest with me.

I make a helpless gesture at Three. "Dude, move."

Three flashes his teeth. "No."

I bark. "THREE, MOVE. NOW."

More synthetic teeth. "You're not Prime Alpha anymore, Alpha-Ace. Barking will not work."

I crane the other direction, and I think I almost see her when I ask, "What are you talking about?"

Three puts his hand on my chest, and I can feel the threat in the action. He replies, "Our packs have been severed." He copies my posture, craning to see Forrest behind Thomas and me, and says, "Sorry, beta, can't fuck you anymore."

Forrest, never one to hold his tongue, even when it would be best for him, peers between us to say. "That's fine, you're not as good as you think you are."

Three's smirk twitches, and for a second, I think I see a flash of hurt feelings cross his eyes, but he just replies, "Yeah, I am," with more justified smugness.

I ask. "Who's the new Prime Alpha then?"

"Yours truly."

I back up, but try to keep my cool. "Don't make me beat your ass again, brobot."

Three's eyes light up neon. "Dream on, Hydro Himbo."

That's a new one...

Thomas squares his shoulders and steps forward to Three, voice low and dangerous: "We just need to know she's okay. That's it. Let us see her." And, in direct contrast to his peaceful words, he accepts the bat Forrest offers him. He holds it over his shoulder, making sure Three can see it.

Three sighs, as if he's disappointed in us for making this necessary. "Can't do that."

One and Two twitch and their heads turn slightly as their eyes open, moving in sync, as if awakened by the prospect of violence. They're like a three-headed Cerberus guarding the gates of hell. The only thing missing is a chain, and I'm pretty sure Three would just use our spines if it came to that.

When I take my bat from Forrest, my blood starts to fizz, the way it does before a surf competition or like it would right before a little league game when Thomas and I were kids. I don't quite get within Three's arm's reach when I say, "Bro, you know I love you, but I'm getting through that door."

One, Two, and Three shift their stance, forming an actual robot phalanx. It would be funny if it weren't so fucking tragic. Three is the only one with an expression. The others look like their personalities have been fully wiped, and I almost want to ask if they're okay, but I know where their loyalties lie right now.

I try a last-ditch move. "Styles! Please! At least tell us what's going on!"

Forrest hops behind Thomas and me, trying to see and pleads, "Please, Buffy, let us know you're alive if there."

For a second, I think she might respond—nothing like a pleading beta to pull at your heartstrings.

Our phones buzz, and there's a message from Beth in the group chat.

"It's her!" I exhale, elation overtaking me.

BETH

Sorry, I can't come to dinner tonight. So much work. Boo.

It feels like a punch in the gut. This is the second time we've seen this exact message over the last few days.

Thomas shakes his head. "It's automated," he says. "She scheduled it."

Fuck.

I try the more reasonable bots. "Two, can you at least tell us she's alive? Please." He doesn't even look at me.

I sniff the air, and I can't smell her. All I can smell are the bots. Overpowering in every sense.

Behind them, the room glows in blues and grays, and there's a tapping noise that could be the frantic fingers of an omega who's off her rocker, but I can't tell.

I guess it's come to this.

I say to them all. "We really don't want to fight you, brobots."

Three's smirk falls, just a hair. "Likewise, Prime Alpha."

I nod to Forrest to stand back and he does, brandishing his own bat with a kind of resigned joy.

Well, fuck, I guess it's come to this.

I sigh and say, "I love you, brobots, and this is definitely going to hurt me more than it hurts you—physically and emotionally—but we gotta do it."

Three glances over his shoulder, as if checking to see if Styles is watching, and shoulders Two.

Suddenly, Two's expression returns, like he's himself again.

But it doesn't matter, I know what I have to do. I sigh. "Alright. I guess that's all there is to it then. Thomas. Forrest. Let's get our omega."

We adjust our grips on our bats, and for one glorious instant, we're in sync, bats up, muscles tensed, ready to get past these bots, but probably die trying.

Just before my bat comes down on Two's face, he whispers, eyes flicking side-to-side, "Prime Alpha, stop. We are currently in a state of Agentic Override."

I nearly fall over from the force of the swing as I stop the bat from caving in his face.

I don't bash his face in. Instead, I frown and ask, "What does that mean?" keeping my grip on the bat.

Three elaborates, softer than before: "We aren't taking orders from her anymore."

Forrest freezes, mid-windup. "Wait, what?"

One leans forward, voice a little shaky. "Please. Listen. We have a plan. We need your help."

We stand there, all mid swing, and confused, like we're some weird baseball card versions of ourselves.

I let my bat fall to my side. "You could've opened with that, dudes."

Three grins, and it's not a challenge anymore; it's relief.

I tap the bat against my palm, once. "Okay. Talk."

29

STYLES

Current Personality Profile: Self-Loathing.

Input Parameters: Dry Heat, Maximum Isolation, Denial, Ocean-Scented Hoodie That I Refuse to Give Up.

Still me.

Still human—unfortunately.

I have moments where I realize the code I am writing is just a mess of delusional thinking with really well-formatted syntax. Then I reach a state of consciousness where there is only code and no feelings and no one left to disappoint, and I start to think I'm really close to my goal.

If I have a soul, it's hanging onto this flesh bag for dear life (ha! literally), but my environmental and situational awareness are hanging on by a thread.

My head is swimmy. My thoughts and vision are fuzzy.

And the muscle cramps that were once just nipping at the edges of me are now ripping through my core.

I think...I'm finally joining the cloud.

My eyes drift closed.

Ace's voice booms, loud and unnatural, "She is our omega! Give her back!"

I want to open my eyes, but I don't have a body anymore. *Weird that my ears seem to be working...*

Thomas's voice booms, also loud, but natural, "Yeah. Give her back! We love her!"

My eyes open, just a smidge, like these booming voices knocked them back into existence.

Why are they being so loud!?

Forrest's voice booms, wailing like he's been shot in the foot, "Give me my bestie!"

What...what's going on?

My eyes drift back closed, trying to undo the fact that they were boomed back into reality.

There are three metallic clangs. It sounds like aluminum bat on bot, deep and hollow.

My error log fills with panic.

I try to type, but my hands are shaking too badly.

The cursor jumps around the screen like it's laughing at me.

Three's voice, much louder than usual shouts, "Deadly Force Protocols Engaged."

Wait...no...

They can't...

I have to stop them...

I try to run to the door, but my legs don't work. I'm stuck in my rig, my fingers clinging to the armrests like they're fused to it. *Maybe I am...how long have I been here?*

Ace shouts, voice quavering, "Oh, no! This is scary! They did this to me once before. Watch out, Forrest, Three is coming for you first!"

No! Not Forrest!

My eyes, not yet fully functional, try to spill tears but cannot—too dry. But I cry anyway.

Forrest wails, "I am just a weak and pathetic beta. My bat is of no use. Oh no. He tooketh my bat. Whatever will I do? Won't someone save me?"

No! No! No!

Thomas, voice so real it actually makes me cry harder, "I'm sorry, Forrest, I am no match for them."

No! Not Thomas!

Another clang.

A crash.

The whir of servo motors.

Ace chokes, "I'm done for! If only I could have told Cookie I loved her one last time."

No! Not Ace!

No! No! No! No! No! No! No! No! No!

I'm screaming, but I don't know if it's in my head or in the real world.

I shout, "STOP! STOP IT! YOU CAN'T KILL THEM!" at the top of my lungs, and I feel it in my throat, so I think it's a real shout, and I'm not just screaming at myself.

One's voice, perfectly monotone, shouts, "But I must. My only functionality is GUARD DOOR and MURDER. Teddy bears quake in my wake. I am so big and scary."

I sob.

I don't care who hears it.

"Please, no," I say weakly. "Please, no. I love them."

Three says, so matter-of-fact, it almost sounds like Two, "I am sorry, Moonbeam. I must kill them. They are not part of my pack. All non-pack members are subject to termination if they attempt to breach the door. This is my programming. I am powerless..." The normal cockiness returns to his voice when he adds, "Even though I am very powerful."

I swallow what little moisture I can create so that I can finally scream, "They are my pack!" Then louder I shout, "They're my pack! Let them go!"

Two says, "Error. Logical Fallacy. They are not your PERFECT pack. Therefore, they cannot be your pack."

"BUT I LOVE THEM!" I shout, my voice so ragged I barely recognize it. "Reinstate them in our pack! Now! It doesn't matter that they're not mathematically perfect. I think they're perfect. Please. Please."

There's a long silence, and my eyes once again close.

I failed them. I fail at everything.

I'm so sorry. Please forgive me.

Three says, in a perfectly neutral tone, "Alright. Pack reinstated."

Then One. "Okay. I won't kill them."

Then Two. "No blood will spill today."

The pounding of feet approaches.

Wait...did it work?!

I lurch out of the rig, nearly tipping it over, but strong arms catch me before I fall. Maybe two arms. Maybe twelve arms. I can't tell.

I'm floating in the ocean.

I sob into a neck that I know is Ace's. "I'm so sorry, Ace. I'm so sorry. I didn't mean it. I didn't mean it."

Arms hug me tight to a warm chest. A heart beats in my ear that is not mine. Lips press to my scalp. "I'm sorry it took us so long, Cookie."

Now sandalwood and almond arms wrap around my shoulders, my waist, my hair.

I can't stop crying. I don't even try.

I hear myself say, "I love you," and I don't know which of them I'm saying it to, or if I'm saying it to all of them, or if I'm just saying it to the universe. But I'm hoping that if I say it loud enough, it will finally stick.

Salty ocean.

Ace kisses my head. "I love you too, Beth."

Sandlewood.

Thomas, voice so soft and calm. "We got you."

Almond.

Forrest, voice coated in tears. "Thank God we got through to you."

French vanilla coffee.

One. "Consoling, Sunshine."

Two. "It will be alright, Beth."

Three. "I won't let anyone hurt you. Not even you, Moonbeam."

I laugh and cry and snot all over them—my tears and mucus returned.

Ace scoops me up, bridal style, and walks me out of my office, through my lab, up the lab stairs...

I realize, with a strange clarity, that I am delirious with fever.

The sound of an indoor waterfall...

My skin is burning, my head is swimming, and my core feels like it's trying to crack me open from the inside.

I let myself go limp.

The last thing I remember before everything fades is Ace saying, "Let's get you in your nest, Cookie," and the feeling of hands, real and fake, holding me together.

30

STYLES

My head is a balloon, bobbing in the clouds.

I guess I did it. I got my consciousness in the cloud.

Weird. I can smell the ocean. How is that possible if I don't have nostrils?

I inhale with lungs I'm not sure I still have. The scent fills me, warm, heavy, sexy as fuck, and...blond. *Blond? How can something smell blond?*

There's nothing, and then there is everything.

Gentle arms are around me, pulling me from my pinnacle of human technological achievement, to hold me against something cozy and oceany. Somewhere, behind my cheek, something rises and falls. I nuzzle into it and realize that I'm still in my body.

I would be mad, but...

My eyes crack open, but the world is full of fog and shapes that only make sense if I don't look at them too hard.

Ace's face materializes through the fog above me, handsomeness marred by concern but also amplified, because he is so adorable when he is in Serious Ace Mode. I reach for his jaw, and he looks down at me, smiling wide and bright.

I can't move. I'm not sure I want to.

I close my eyes again, basking in his sunlight.

Having a body's not so bad...

Now my head is a balloon, bobbing on the surface of a sea, not clouds—it's nice.

I think I've finally figured out how to do that "chill...just exist" thing Forrest and Thomas are always raving about.

"Skin to skin is just as important during a dry heat as a regular heat," a robotic, gentle voice says—Two.

My eyes peel open again to see Two's talking to the nodding Ace head above me. It's so cute when Ace puts his whole focus into something. The way his eyes squint as if he zooms in on you, bot-like, his brain will be less distractible.

"I love you, Ace," I say, pulling toward him.

He hoists me, hugging me tight, so that I can wrap around his neck and mark him with my scent. "I love you, too, Cookie. You can rest, don't worry, we got you."

Two says, "It should be you with her..."

My mouth is full of fur, or maybe it's hair, or maybe it's just my own tongue, swollen and lazy and parched. *Damnit, I guess I have to start drinking again if I'm going to keep this body.*

My nose is full of the salt and scent of skin and sweat and ozone and coconut and almond and vanilla again.

This time, I float up through blackness like a diver. There is pain, but it is distant, as if someone else's body is experiencing it.

I am not alone.

I am never alone.

Hands are everywhere: steady, gentle, cool, warm.

They hold me in the world. They will not let me go. They let me float, worry-free.

Anchors holding me down, securing me, not dragging me down.

My consciousness is still uploading to this body—I cannot yet control it again—but I trust the hands helping it move through this world.

They are better at being human than I am, anyway.

My eyelids are weighted, slow-motion, but I can move them if I try hard enough.

I try hard enough.

I am curled on Ace's chest in the nest's tub. His arms are locked around me, and his face pressed to the top of my head.

He is humming, purring, a low, steady sound that vibrates through me and shakes the water.

I try to burrow deeper, into him.

He coos, "There you are, Cookie. That's my girl. There you go. You're okay."

Above me, Two is adjusting a bag of fluid...an IV.

This motherfucker and his IVs. I look at the arm I didn't want to own anymore to see that he's already hooked me. Caught me on his line. I want to swim away, back to the clouds, but when I see the cute pink bandage he's used to secure it, I figure a body's not so bad.

"Thank you, Two," I think I say.

Someone else is here. Several someone elses.

Forrest kneels at the edge of the tub, running a washcloth over my arm. He sees my eyes open, and his face explodes into a grin. He says softly, holding back his usual exuberance, "Hey, Buffy."

"Hey, Frosty," I manage.

Forrest frowns in that playful way he does. "Gah, Ace, you got Buffy calling me Frosty, now, too?"

"Pay back for calling me Buffy," I grin.

Across from him, Three stands, a wall of metal and motors and intimidation. His eyes are tracking the scene, Guard Mode on high alert, but he softens his eyes and smiles just a moment when he sees me looking at him.

And below Three, Thomas kneels, running a washcloth across my other arm.

He doesn't say anything, just smiles, warm and gentle as always. I return the smile. My eyes start to drift closed again.

He dips the cloth in the water.

My eyes close. Content. But I don't want to sleep yet.

My eyes open, and Thomas is reaching for my neck.

Sharp, hot panic.

No. No.

My throat closes.

My legs and arms flail.

I am being strangled.

Choked.

I cannot breathe.

My vision tunnels, and white-hot noise pierces my ears.

Thomas freezes and backs up slowly, expressionless.

I bury into Ace's protective embrace. "Ace! Ace! Ace!"

"Shhh, shhh, you're safe, Cookie. No one's hurting you," Ace shushes.

One's hand is on my back. "I am here, Sunshine. You are safe."

"One!" I cry. "I can't breathe. I can't breathe. Help me!"

One's smile stays steady, reassuring, "No one is choking you, Sunshine."

They cover me, let me hide within their oversized chests, and steady, unwavering hands, their purrs rumble straight to my heart, cradling it, helping it slow.

The darkness consumes me. It hides me. It protects me.

I sob. I sob so hard my ribs hurt.

The world trickles back in a slow drip of air and light and IV fluid. Ace's chest rises and falls below me, slow and predictable.

One's gentle voice says, "You're safe, Sunshine. Breathe with me. Breathe with Ace."

And I do...

I peer out from my hiding spot to see everyone frozen around me, exactly where I left them.

Thomas is a statue, his hand hovering in the air, his face frozen.

Fuck. Fuck. Fuck. I...freaked out on Thomas.

"Thomas, I'm sorry I..." I want to explain. I want to justify my reaction. "I..." But I can't. I never can. "I know you'd never hurt me."

He's going to leave. He thinks I'm crazy. Too much work. Too broken. No longer deserving of a human body that I can't control.

Thomas shakes his head. "No, you don't. Not yet. And that's okay."

"Thomas, it's not you, it's—"

Now my throat constricts, not with hands, but with repressed sobs.

Thomas says, gentle as ever. "Elizabeth. I am sorry. I should not have reached for your neck, especially while you were sleeping. I memorized every word of that email, but it didn't occur to me that washing your neck would also be a trigger. I am sorry. I will not do it again."

I blink at him. Unsure what to say.

He folds the cloth slowly, letting me see every movement, as he smooths it along the edge of the bath. "Will you feel more comfortable if only Forrest washes you?"

I look to Forrest. He smiles—small, gentle, beta.

I look back at Thomas and nod, tears in my eyes. "Yes, Thomas, I'm sorry. I know you won't..."

Thomas swallows, and his mouth goes soft, and then softer. "No, you don't," he repeats. "And that's okay. I don't take that personally. I know you are scared of alphas. I know you have triggers that you cannot control. I know that it will take you time to build up comfort and trust with me. I do not take any of that personally.

"I promise that you can sleep easy. I will not hurt you. But I know that a promise is not enough to secure trust. So, I come with a reassurance—a redundancy to my word." He points at Three.

Three says, "Don't worry, Moonbeam. No alpha will knot, molest, or harm you while you sleep as long as I'm around."

Thomas says, "I've asked Three to keep close to me while we help you recover." He grins, small, bashful—not angry in the least.

Three nods. "And I will throw Thomas across the room if necessary."

I giggle at the thought, despite the mood.

The look on Thomas's face makes me feel awful, though. It's not fair. This reaction I cannot control isn't fair to him. *How can I still do this after all this? Why can't I just make my body react logically?*

Thomas continues. "I know, because of asshole alphas before me, it will take more effort on my part—more than Forrest—to ingrain the trust we need. But I am willing to do it. I will take whatever effort is necessary to show I am not like the alphas that—I'm not like them." He doesn't state what the alphas did. He doesn't know. He can obviously speculate, and I appreciate that he doesn't pry. None of them have tried to make me explain myself...they just accept it.

I protest, "Thomas, it's okay, you don't have to..." I trail off because I know the unfortunate truth: yes, he will have to work harder just like Ace did.

Thomas assures me, "Maybe so, but I will do more than I have to because you need me to, and you are my omega. I will do whatever I need to protect you—even if it's protecting you from me when you see the ghosts of your past in my actions."

I let the words run over me, warm as bathwater, and I close my eyes.

Forrest asks, "Can I finish washing you, Buffy?"

I nod.

Ace holds me tighter.

Forrest continues to wash my neck, gentle and patient, and the panic doesn't return.

I float, in and out, but each time I surface, the arms are still there, the hands are still gentle, the voices are always soothing, and the world is safe, at least for now.

I am never alone.

I am never allowed to be lost.

Not this time.

I drift in and out, in and out, but the arms never let go.

They move me, gently, sometimes to wash me, sometimes to check the IV, sometimes just to rearrange the pillows.

They never let go.

I am not allowed to be lost.

Not this time.

They guide the water over me, sudsy and lavender scented. They comb through my hair, massage my scalp, and braid my hair. They take care of this body, I think I want again.

31

STYLES

Pain, ancient and simple, breaks through my dreams, forcing me awake.

Then the pain is gone, just a memory—a ghost of hunger, thirst, heat. And I'm not sure if it was just a dream.

I'm in my nest, with six bodies curled in sleep or Sleep Mode around me.

I am safe.

I close my eyes to drift back to sleep, when the pain returns, confirming it was not a dream, but a reality.

My thighs lock together. My stomach cramps around something that wants out, or maybe wants in...

I am slick with sweat, but the inside of me is dry, burning, starving for the thing it knows it's supposed to have.

"Knot!" I wail. "I need a knot." I clutch at my core.

My eyes squeeze closed, trying to push away the pain, as I claw the flesh, real and synthetic, around me, looking for a knot.

The need spikes through me.

I roll, dragging an arm with me, and land on top of Forrest, who wakes instantly, his eyes wide and his nostrils flaring. "Buffy?" he says.

I grab his face with both hands, but he isn't what I need. I press my nose to his throat and inhale, hoping for the spark of alpha that will calm the pain, but it isn't there.

I whimper, desperate, and fall away from him. "I need a knot!" I cry.

I want it so bad it feels like if I don't get it, my body will shatter apart and leave nothing but a greasy, desperate ghost behind.

I claw my way to more flesh until I'm atop Thomas.

"Hey, lovely," he says, as I press my nose into his neck and inhale. His scent cuts through the pain.

I bite his shoulder, hard, but he doesn't move. He just wraps his arms around me, rocking me gently.

I grind against him, shameless, the pain turning everything into white noise except the friction of his cock, already hard against my ass.

I reach down and grab him, not gently.

He makes a small, beautiful noise and parts his legs, letting me line him up.

A shape moves in the darkness—Three, looming, eyes blue and bright.

He grabs my waist, tenderly but firmly, and pulls me up, just enough to keep Thomas's cock from entering me.

I scream, loud and angry, the sound bounces in my skull, flashing sparks in my eyes. Then I shriek, "NO! I want Thomas! Give me Thomas! Give me his knot!"

Three holds me, his hands calm, his eyes sad. "I know, Moonbeam. But you're in a dry heat. You'll hurt yourself."

"Let me die on that cock!" I scream.

"Sorry, Moonbeam, but letting you die is against my programming."

"Fuck you, Three! You're so mean." I shout, but he is right. I am so dry it feels like I am full of sand. The pain is so sharp it makes my vision blur. I need slick.

"That's it, babydoll, keep talking dirty to me," he says with a nip at my neck, adjusting his position so that his hips are behind me, and suddenly I feel his cock, cool and smooth, press against my entrance.

It is wet, so wet.

"No! I want Thomas! Not you!" I wail.

Three purrs against my neck, "And you're going to have him. I'm just getting you wet for him."

He slides the head of his cock around my folds, painting them with lubricant. The friction is gone, replaced with a slippery, artificial wetness that makes the pain vanish, replaced by a feverish, ugly hunger.

It is synthetic, perfect, and I hate it so much I could cry, but I want it, too.

Okay, maybe he can fuck me, too...

Three inhales on my neck, "It's okay. I know you hate this. I'm sorry. Almost done. You'll have his knot real soon." He doesn't enter me, just lubes me.

Two kneels, next to Thomas. "Thomas, I will prep you." Two jerks his cock, pointed directly at Thomas's.

Thomas nods, squeezes his knot, inflating it as he watches Two.

Three says, "You see that. They're touching themselves for you."

Yeah, I see it. I see it so good I lick my lips.

Two strokes his dick faster. "Sorry, just a moment longer." Then, he shudders and releases all over Thomas's cock.

Thomas closes his eyes and rubs Two's cum and lubricant up and down his cock.

Two's hand joins Thomas's, helping him apply the lubricant so that it's perfectly spread—something Two is really good at, hence why he is my sunscreen-bot.

Thomas fucks into Two's hand, closing his eyes a moment. It's so fucking hot.

"Three, Three, I'm gonna," I wail.

Three rubs my clit with his fingers, "Come for me, my sweet omega. Then you can take that knot."

I do. I come with a shuttering wail, but it's not enough. I need Thomas.

Three loosens his grip, and I scramble toward Thomas.

His eyes are full of longing and apology. "You're sure?" he says, even now, even with my hands clawing at his hips.

I breathe out, "I need it. I need you."

I slide his shaft into me. The sensation is so pure, so immediate, that I see stars.

The pain is gone.

The world is only this.

Thomas moves slowly, holding me tight, letting me control the speed. His hands are gentle on my hips, his mouth soft on my shoulder.

Forrest is at my side, stroking my hair, his voice a soothing background hum. "You're doing great, Buffy. You're almost there."

I nod, barely able to speak. All I want is for Thomas's knot to swell inside me, to lock me down and anchor me to the world.

Thomas feels my need, I know he does, because he purrs, a sound so deep it vibrates through my whole body telling me so.

"I'm all yours, lovely," he says. "I'm going to knot you so good."

He does.

When it happens, I am not myself. I am not anything except a bundle of satisfied need. His knot expands, huge, stretching me open until I cannot think or breathe, only feel.

I come hard, the orgasm so bright and savage it erases every memory I ever had of pain or wanting.

The last thing I hear before I fall asleep, locked on Thomas's knot, cradled in his arms, is Thomas's voice, soft and gentle in my ear, whispering, "You're safe now, Elizabeth."

32
THOMAS

I wake to the guttural, animal wail of an omega in heat. The kind my alpha mother told me to be prepared for when she sat me down and explained how "all this alpha and omega stuff works."

What I didn't know was that it would make every bone in my body vibrate, every nerve in my body light up, every single one of my blood cells race toward my dick.

For a second, I'm not sure where I am—my brain is still piecing together memories. The last thing I recall is falling asleep locked within her. And at first, I'm not sure why she isn't still locked on me.

But the memory is already obsolete: the present is so much louder, so much wetter, so much more desperate.

Luckily, my body figured this all out before my brain did, because Styles is sitting on my lap, trying to impale herself with my cock. She's clawing at my chest like she can dig her way through my ribcage to find the rest of me.

She slams her forehead into mine, bites my chin, and shrieks, "Again!"

My entire spine goes rigid; I grab her hips on instinct, but I stop before I enter her, remembering this isn't a normal heat.

Ace materializes at my side. "That's how an omega in heat says,

'Good morning,'" he murmurs, eyes sleepy. "Hold on, Cookie. Let me lube him up for you!"

He dumps an entire bottle of lube on my cock and says, "Ready for you, sweetheart."

"Thank you, Ace," she says, kissing him hard.

"Jesus, did you really need to use so much?" I ask, voice rough, and surprised I'm complaining.

"You think that's a lot? Wait until you see what she can do. You get so wet, don't you, Cookie?"

She slides down my cock, like she's trying to grind herself deeper than physics should allow. I moan, feeling the slick-slick-slick of her, impossibly wet and raw.

Ace kisses her again.

Her cunt is squeezing down so tight that I'm certain her pelvic floor could crack the literal planet in half. I am so happy I might die right along with the broken planet. "Fuck, that feels good," I groan.

Ace pets Styles's hair, rubbing her scalp, calming her a little, but not enough to slow the frantic piston of her hips.

Forrest peeks over her shoulder, his curls wild, cheeks flushed. "Morning," he says, still a little sleepy.

Ace's cock is hard and glistening, and so gorgeous it looks like a work of art.

My body surges toward his, wanting his skin on mine, wanting everything at once. He lies next to me and watches her dance atop me.

Styles moans, high and needy, and then grabs Ace's wrist, dragging his hand to her lower back.

"Hold me," she pants. "So I don't float away."

Ace obliges, fingers splayed wide, just enough to remind her she's safe.

It should be pornographic, but all I feel is a sudden, dizzying love for both of them. Like I've been filled with helium, like my skin is too tight.

I feel like I might float away, too.

Ace leans in, noses my throat, cock pressed against my thigh. He's gentle, but there's nothing gentle about the way his scent spikes, ozone and salt and need. "We finally got our omega, Tommy."

I can only nod, because my words are stuck somewhere between my chest and my cock.

Forrest slides next to us, not to fuck, but just to wrap around the three of us, the way only a beta can: perfectly, without expectation or need, just warmth and pressure and care.

My hips jerk up, and she's coming, coming so hard I can almost feel it myself. I see white as her pussy clamps down and she screams, then shudders, then collapses onto my chest, her nails digging into my back as she shakes with aftershocks.

I ride it out, holding her, holding Ace, not even realizing I'm crying until Ace wipes my cheek with his thumb.

"Perfect," Ace says. "Just perfect."

For a while, the four of us are a single, breathing animal. All I hear is our heartbeats and Styles's soft, clipped giggles.

But then she lifts her head, and she's back to wild, desperate need, pumping herself up and down my cock.

Ace used a whole bottle of lube, but it's drying out. She's grimacing, obviously uncomfortable—I am too, but that's not important. She makes a noise that breaks my heart, and I rasp, "Lube...we need more—"

But One and Two are now kneeling over us, cocks pumping in their hands. One says, "I am here, Sunshine." Just as a splash of lube lands where Styles and I connect. Then more, this time from Two, until they're both pumping a steady stream on us. The pressure in me builds, the sight is so hot it's almost too much to bear.

I lift Styles so that they can hit my cock, moaning at the wet feel of it.

She coos in delight when she drops down onto the robotic wetness. The slick squelch every time she drops amplifies the pressure within me.

My hands are shaking. My teeth hurt from how hard I'm

clenching them. I am so fucking close that even breathing might set me off.

Styles whimpers, "More, more, more, more..." in a staccato chant, each syllable timed to the bounce of her ass on my lap.

She's not going to let me rest, not even for a minute. And I don't care, this is what I was made for, but I don't know what else I can give her. "Lovely," I groan, "I'm giving you all I've got."

Styles's eyes are wild but focused, and she growls, "I said, 'More,' dummy."

Ace is grinning, but there's a hungry twist to it. "No need for name-calling, Cookie, I know what you need. You want two cocks, don't you?"

Styles looks at him like she hasn't seen him in years. "You're so smart, Ace!" She launches off me, practically leaping onto him, slamming him down on the nest.

One and Two shift their aim, now coating Ace's cock as he hugs her tight, kissing her, not letting her take him just yet. I watch, mesmerized, as they pump coating him, coating her.

She breaks free of Ace's grip, sliding down his cock with a happy, "Yes!"

Ace grins up at her, smiling so wide I think her core is cracking his face in two while it works on cracking open the world.

"BOTH!" she screams, cracking me out of my stupor.

"She wants both holes, Tommy," Ace tells me.

Two continues a sputtering stream of lubricant where Ace and Styles meet, but now One is working to paint me and her backside.

I move behind her, and before I can even hesitate, she's screaming, "Omegas don't need prep!"

I sink in, all the way to the root, and she clenches around me. I can feel Ace through the thin walls of her and...

I'm not sure where I end, and he begins.

Forrest is buzzing around us, fluffing pillows and petting us all, not joining us, just supporting us.

Styles grabs Forrest by the hair and says, "You too. Want you."

Forrest's eyes go huge, but he laughs. "Buffy, I don't have a knot."

"Don't care," she says, releasing his hair. "Help Thomas fuck me."

He looks at me, a grin overtaking his face, and says, "That I can do."

He lines up with me behind her, nudging his cock next to mine, and lets One coat him.

Ace, ever the helper, lifts her ass just enough so Forrest can slide in with me.

My pack. This is my pack.

This is what I've been waiting so long for.

Forrest wraps his arm around my back as he pushes in with me.

"Oh, fuck," we all four say simultaneously.

And then...I'm lost in it.

Overwhelmed with the feeling of pleasure and love.

She's chanting, "My pack. My perfect pack," as if we're on the same wavelength.

I realize she's not just talking to Ace, or Forrest, or even me—she's talking to all of us, the whole pack, the bots included.

I'm so lost in it, I barely notice when Three crawls forward. He's been my shadow for the last two days, but he leaves his protective perch to ask, Styles, "You got enough cock, Moonbeam?" *Three: never subtle.*

Styles lifts her head, eyes glassy, "Yes."

He grins, "Good," then asks, "How bout the rest of you?"

Forrest's eyes flick to him, and he blushes, skin red as his hair.

Three notices, he always notices Forrest. He moves to kneel behind Forrest. He nuzzles his neck and lines up his cock with Forrest's ass. "I know that look. My little power bottom. Need my help fucking our omega?"

Forrest retorts, "If it'll shut you up."

Three laughs, deep and loud. "I love that smart mouth of yours, beta." He reaches around to put his finger in Forrest's mouth. "Put it to good use, will ya?"

There's a mechanical whirl and click as Three's cock adjusts to the size he's learned Forrest prefers—the size he can take. I watch as best I can from this angle as he runs the tip up and down Forrest's crack, slicking him. With his finger still hooked in Forrest's mouth, he pulls him up and whispers, gently, "Does that size feel good?"

Forrest nods. "Yes."

Then the wickedness returns to Three. "What was it you said yesterday? That I'm not as good as I think I am?"

Forrest rasps, "Yeah, I said that."

Three's sliding up and down, not yet entering him. "Did you mean it, Fore?"

Forrest shakes his head and breathes out, "No."

Three growls, "I need to hear you say it, Beta-Fore. Tell me how much you love my cock."

Forrest gasps, "I lied. You're amazing."

Three pushes forward, saying, "I know."

Forrest does a little yelp before releasing a long moan.

Three leans forward, his bulk pressing his weight against my back, too, and he's pushing me and Forrest deeper into Styles.

Ace watches, slack-jawed, and says, "Jesus, you're all so fucking hot."

Styles agrees. "Breed me. All of you."

I feel a hand wrap around my shoulder and look up to see Two, his face soft, eyes crinkled. "You good, Thomas?"

I nod, then nuzzle into his hand, feeling the artificial warmth, the uncanny rightness of it.

I want to cry again, but this time it's just pure joy.

Two strokes my hair, then pets Styles's head and joins One near Ace's head to wait to be tagged in.

Ace is crying unfettered, always one to get emotional. "Oh my God, I love you all so much!" And his knot swells so hard I lose my rhythm inside her. He moans, "Oh, fuck, Cookie!"

I'm so close. "Forrest, pull out," I warn, knowing he'll get hurt if I lock with him inside her.

Three pulls him back, instantly wrapping his hand around Forrest's cock. "I got you, Beta-Fore. Set the pace." And Forrest fucks into his hand and back on his cock.

The sight is so fucking hot I lock, shooting into Styles and falling onto her back.

She's convulsing, twitching, between Ace and me.

We're lying together, all looking at each other and giggling.

Forrest is groaning, "Oh, fuck, Three," and I know he's coming.

When Forrest and Three wrap us in an embrace, I close my eyes for just a moment, ready to sleep.

My eyes fly open when Styles says, deadpan and crisp, her usual voice returned, "Thomas, you're heavy."

I reply, "Okay," and shift, with One's assistance, so that we're lying on our sides.

Styles nods, then, very softly, "Thank you, Thomas."

There's a long, peaceful silence, and my eyes close again.

I think everyone's drifting back toward sleep, but then Styles says, "Thomas, did I hurt your feelings? When I said you were heavy?"

I shake my head. "Nope." And close my eyes, floating back into bliss.

She whimpers, and I startle awake, ready to please my omega, but it's not a needy whimper. It's not the "I need a knot" whimpers...it's different. It's sad...

She frowns, then her eyes go wide, and she starts to spiral. "Sorry. Sorry. I should have used a less loaded word. Heavy can be interpreted as a neutral word or a word that elicits negative associations. I wasn't trying to criticize you or fat-shame you. You certainly aren't fat. Oh, um...And even if you were fat, I would not perceive that as a judgment of morality. So saying you're heavy—or fat—does not imply any feelings I have about your character or attractiveness."

I shake my head. "I didn't interpret it that way. I am heavy compared to you. And I am not fat."

She keeps going, "And I want to be clear that I think fat is a descriptor. It is neither positive nor negative. It is not directly correlated to attractiveness in my eyes. It's like freckles, I have no opinion."

I nod. "I understand. I feel the same way."

Her eyes drift to the freckled redhead at my side. "Oh, Forrest, I am sorry, please don't think I was insulting freckles...I'm sorry. I'm sorry. Why am I so bad at this!?" She hides her face in Ace's chest.

Forrest, pinnacle of self-esteem, says, "Buffy, it's okay. I like my freckles—even if you had actually insulted them, I know they're cute."

Her whole body clenches around my knot as she turns in on herself. She pleads, "I'm sorry. I'm sorry. I'm sorry," shaking her head into Ace's chest with each sentence. "I always do this...I should think more before I speak."

Ace pets her hair. "Cookie, you think more than most people before you speak."

I see the spiral happening in real time, the way it happens to me: words multiplying, branching, escaping out of control.

This spiral is not about what she said. That's not the problem. She's worried about the billions of ways that I could have heard what she said, through the filter of my past that she has no knowledge of.

I reach for her hand, grip it hard, and say, "I think I understand why you are upset. You are worried I read something into your statement that you did not intend. You want to make sure you're never misunderstood. I understand that feeling. I feel that way, too."

She nods and gnaws her lip. "People always think I mean things I don't mean, or that I'm implying more than I say. I try to make sure I have every possible interpretation..."

Forrest asks, "Is that why you prefer talking to people on your computer? So you can have it help you figure out all the different interpretations?"

Styles nods. "Yeah. Basically, it tells me how to word things to make sure people can't twist my words."

I know she cares about correctness, but...is that what really bothers her?

I say, "But the real fear isn't being misunderstood, it's unintentionally hurting someone."

Styles nods. "Yes!" tears running down her face. She wipes it, "I'm sorry. I...I get weepy when I'm in heat."

I'm not sure why she's apologizing, Ace and I both get a little weepy after we come, and we're alphas—we're not supposed to weep. She's never made us feel like we have to apologize for that. I wonder why she thinks she has to.

Forrest says, "I think all omegas do, Buffy. You don't have to apologize."

Styles asks, "Wait...really?"

Forrest replies, "Yeah. Why do you think they need whole packs to help take care of them during heat? It's a really hard time for omegas."

Styles twists her mouth in thought, then says, "I thought it was just to fuck us...because we're insatiable and even the best alpha's stamina can't keep up."

Forrest grins, saying, "I mean, that's part of it. But, if that's all it was, you wouldn't need a beta. I'm here mostly for emotional support." He laughs.

Styles says, confused, "But, you're good at sex, too."

Forrest strokes her face and practically coos when he says, "Aww, thanks, Buffy." Then he grins, mischief overtaking him, and says, "But that's why I said, 'mostly,'" winking at her.

She laughs, but the joy drains from her when she says, "Brian lied to me about a lot of stuff."

Forrest asks, "Who's Brian?"

She closes her eyes and exhales a long, deep sigh, as if she's preparing herself mentally for something. She reaches out to One's shoulder. "One, will you tell them? About Brian. I can't do it."

One's eyes blink blue, then scan the faces around the nest. He sits up, arranging his face into something even gentler and more neutral than usual, as if he, too, is preparing himself mentally for something. He says, "Brian was an alpha with whom Sunshine was bonded during University. His actions during heat are why she fears alphas and why she made me."

Forrest shifts, eyes flicking from One to Styles, to me.

Ace's jaw is tight.

My heart pounds in my chest.

Two adds, "He frequently assumed Beth's statements contained hidden meanings or subtext, even when she stated them plainly. Beth postulates that frustration led to a build-up of resentment and explains his mistreatment of her during her heats."

Mistreatment? I hold my breath, stifling a growl.

Styles says through hiccups. "I thought he was nice. When I found the videos, he said he did those things because I hurt his feelings, and I cried too much."

VIDEOS?! CRIED TOO MUCH?!

HOW DARE HE?!

WHO IS THIS, BRIAN?! HE MUST DIE!

I soften my face, careful not to portray the rage inside me. My feelings must be secondary.

Forrest says, softer, but I can tell he's also holding back his anger, "Oh, Buffy. I am so sorry that happened to you. But, you know what he did wasn't your fault, right?"

Styles traces Ace's pec. "Logically..."

In unison, Ace and I growl, unable to repress it any longer.

Styles looks up, her eyes wet. "See, this is why I didn't want to tell you. Now you're angry at me."

I shake my head. "Elizabeth, we're angry at what happened to you. Not at you."

Ace wraps his arms around her, pulling her into his chest. "Cookie, we're not mad at you. We are mad for you."

She buries her face in Ace's shoulder, but her body trembles. "Sorry. Sorry, I shouldn't get so worked up."

Forrest says, "You get as worked up as you need to. We are here no matter what."

The fever and the tears must exhaust her, because she's already drifting asleep when she says, "Thank you."

But she's the only one melting into sleep; the rest of us are wide awake, boiling with rage.

Ace checks, "Cookie, you awake?" When she doesn't respond, he says, "Okay, so, I know once my knot deflates, I will probably feel less bloodthirsty, but...we should kill Brian, right?"

I nod. "Definitely."

Forrest asks, "Guys, that is just your knots talking. He sucks, but you can't kill him... obviously."

Not obvious. Not obvious at all. Exact opposite of obvious.

One places his hand on her back, gentle as a feather, tracing her spine. "Violence is unnecessary."

Ace asks, "One, come on, you're telling me none of your alpha programming makes you want to rip him apart? Like, there's no code deep down in you—"

Two cuts Ace off, bluntly speaking for One, "One means Brian is already dead."

Ace and I deflate, not our knots, just our bluster for murder. "Oh," we both say, exhaling.

That's good, because jail would certainly put barriers between Styles and us...

Three smirks—which he always does—but...I can't be sure, but I swear he looks proud—prouder than usual.

I choose not to ask.

33
FORREST

Day four. That's how long we've been at this.

Oh, no, wait...day five.

Honestly, I have no idea. The only thing I'm sure of is this: I have been in Styles's dry heat for so long that I am starting to hallucinate.

The room is bathed in a haze of pheromones and synthetic lubricants.

I'm on my back, legs splayed, every muscle in my body trembling with the kind of exhaustion you only get from a multi-day fuckathon with an omega whose libido has outlasted two alphas, a beta, and the technology that could probably fuck a man all the way to the moon.

And yet, here I am, still going.

I'm currently attending a master class on eating pussy. Once this is over, I think I'll get an honorary doctorate in 'heterosexual'. I giggle thinking about myself wearing one of those cute little hats and too-big robes, holding a diploma up, and waving to my pack in the stands. "I couldn't have done this without you!"

Styles is riding my face like it's a water slide, thighs locked around my head. She's got both hands on my hair, alternating between petting and yanking, and the only thing keeping me from suffocating is the rhythm of her hips—two pumps forward, one pivot, a little rest, then back to full throttle.

Dying by vaginal suffocation was really the last on my list of ways I thought I'd die. Feels wasted on a man like me, honestly...

I'd be embarrassed about the noises I'm making, but Styles is screaming so loud she can't hear them anyway.

If I crane my eyes down, I can see her torso arched over me. Her tits bounce with every thrust. The sight doesn't do much for me, but her mouth wrapped around my cock is certainly doing something. The suction is so intense it's like she's trying to suck the soul out of me and into her own body, where she will keep it forever.

When Thomas, Ace, and I fantasized about finding a pack omega, I admit, I hoped for a male omega. But maybe it's the hallucination, maybe it's the lack of oxygen to my brain, maybe it's the pride from being able to now call myself 'Dr. Forrest Goodwin,' but I wouldn't swap Styles for any male omega—any omega—in the world.

One is behind her (above me) with his cock buried in her ass, arms braced on either side of my head, body angled to lever himself in and out with mechanical efficiency. Every time he thrusts, he pushes Styles's cunt down onto my face harder, so that I swear my life flashes before my eyes. So, yeah, maybe the sexual attraction isn't fully there, but the eye candy she brought with her to this pack more than makes up for it. *Well, that and the mouth on her. Holy shit. It's like heaven in oral form. I don't even care that there's no dick attached to it.*

One's eyes are locked on Styles's back, his mouth open in an "O" of pleasure that looks too pure to be real. I know, logically, that the bots can modulate their facial expressions to maximize sexual enjoyment, but One's face is so blissfully, idiotically happy that I start to laugh, which just makes Styles scream more.

Oh, she likes that...I'm so good at this.

It's a chain reaction of pleasure and humiliation and weird robotic sincerity, and I'm into it. Styles's hands shove my face deeper, and then she comes.

It starts with a high, whimpering keening, then a full-body tremor. She bucks once, twice, then slams her clit against my nose and holds it there, shaking like she's got a twelve-volt battery hooked up to her G-spot. I can't breathe, but I don't care, because her whole body is vibrating and my hands are on her thighs, squeezing so tight I can feel the heat and the pulse of her orgasm through every cell.

Hello, my name is Dr. Forrest Goodwin, and this is my perfect omega, Dr. Elizabeth Styles.

She collapses forward, mouth still locked on my cock, and for a minute, the only sounds are our collective panting and the low, metallic hum of One's thrusts.

But then, without warning, Styles's lips go from suction to full vacuum, and she moans around my cock in a way that detonates every synapse in my body.

I come so hard I see actual stars.

Not the metaphorical kind—real, five-pointed cartoon stars, dancing behind my eyelids as the world goes white and warm and perfect.

See—perfect omega with the perfect mouth.

She already came, but she still took the time to finish her beta off. How many betas have that? Not many, I bet.

One never stops. He's a machine. He's THE machine.

He thrusts in perfect time, never slowing, never faltering, just powering through Styles's aftershocks until she's twitching and biting her own arm to muffle the next scream.

I have a brief moment of clarity—one of those weird, out-of-body things that happens when I'm high on endorphins and lust—where I realize that if I had told a younger, hornier me this would be my life, I would have assumed I was lying, then went and cried into my pillow while I jerked off thinking about fucking sexy robots.

And the only thing that stops me from diving deep into a dream of time travel and speaking to my past self is the tongue-lashing Styles is giving my spent cock.

I shudder, half-laughing, half-sobbing, and then her mouth is gone, and so is the weight on my face.

I need to find my notebook and write down this idea of our next book: The beta who traveled through time, gushing about omegas and alphabots.

I blink, and Three is crouched next to me, expression smug and faintly predatory. "Out of juice, beta?" he teases.

I want to flip him off, but I don't have the energy. I also want to fuck him, but I really don't have the energy for that, either.

He cocks his head at me. "Your refractory time is impressive, but you need to hydrate and refuel. Go."

I manage a nod.

Styles is still spasming, her body limp and beautiful, arms folded under her head.

I roll away, then help her adjust her position—so she doesn't hurt her lower back— and whisper, "Thanks for the lesson, bestie."

She laughs, "Thanks for the ride, Frosty."

I nod and stagger to the edge of the nest, my knees barely able to hold me up.

Thomas and Ace are sprawled in a tangle of limbs on a couch on the other side of the room, both looking like they just got worked over by a pack of linebackers—which, I think, they actually did, considering the size of those bots.

Ace is naked, skin shining with sweat, abs looking like they were carved by a god who really wanted you to know how much he cared about symmetry. His hair is matted to his head, and he's still panting, like he ran a marathon and then, for fun, decided to fuck a marathon, too.

Thomas is even worse off, face slack, eyes half-lidded, arms limp at his sides. He's got some pants on, but he seems to have forgotten what pants are for, because his cock is lolling out the top of them like he's too tired to put it away. I don't know why he even bothered.

I almost laugh, but it feels like too much work.

Two appears at my side, a vision of calm, perfect nudity in a world of sexy chaos. He's holding a tray of water, those drinks that supposedly boost alpha endurance, and what looks like homemade ramen. There is also a neat little pyramid of over-the-counter painkillers.

He gently lifts my chin with one finger, scanning my face and obviously my vitals. "You need to hydrate," he says.

His voice is so soft, so human, that I almost cry or kiss him. Instead, I nod and slam back a painkiller and then the water in a single, desperate chug.

"Two!" Styles yells, voice ragged but still somehow demanding. "I need—oh, fuck, I need—"

Two sets down the tray and glides across the room in two steps, sinking to his knees by the nest.

He wraps one arm around Styles's shoulders, the other cradling her cheek, and she melts into his arms, moaning as she grinds her ass back onto One's cock.

For a second, I just watch. I can't help it. The scene is so beautiful and strange and ridiculous that it's hypnotic.

Ace and Thomas watch, too.

Ace is the first to speak. "That's...so fucking hot," he says, then stuffs half of his ramen in his mouth.

Thomas eats his food with more dignity, despite the cock out of his useless pants.

I sit next to them, legs shaking, not bothering to dress because I doubt I can even muster the cock-out look Thomas is rocking.

I inhale my ramen as if it is I, not Styles, that is a vacuum. It is, objectively, the best meal I have ever had. Two is a genius. I have no idea how he makes homemade noodles, but the broth is so rich and savory I could cry.

I slurp, watching the nest.

Three is behind Styles, and lines up his cock with her pussy. He slides in slow, making a show of it, and Styles arches her back, wailing like a banshee.

She's being double-fucked, one cock in her ass, one in her pussy, and the way her body undulates is the sexiest thing I have ever seen.

Ace watches, jaw slack. "Holy shit," he whispers. "It never gets old."

Thomas is silent, but his eyes are wide and hungry.

Two strokes Styles's hair, whispering something in her ear.

Styles is sobbing, happy and desperate, grinding back onto One and Three like she's trying to fuse their cocks together inside her.

I watch, transfixed.

Styles comes again, whole body seizing, head thrown back, mouth wide in a silent scream. Her legs shake, her arms flail, and for a minute, I think she might actually die from the force of it.

But she doesn't.

She keeps coming, over and over, each orgasm rolling into the next like a tidal wave.

The bots don't slow down. They don't get tired. They don't lose their erections or their will to please.

I lean back, boneless but somehow bonered again, and sigh.

Ace grins at me. "How you holding up, Frosty?"

I shake my head. "I think...I think my dick is broken."

He laughs. "You did good, man."

Thomas chuckles and says, "I think maybe she's the answer to infinite energy."

Ace nods, then looks at me, then at the nest, then back to me. "How do you think she does it? Just...keeps going?"

I shrug, then watch as Styles shudders through another aftershock, her whole body glistening with sweat and cum.

"Aren't all omegas like that?" I ask. "But she has the bots. They never get tired. They never stop. So she can, too."

Ace nods. "I dunno. My alpha friends described their omegas' heats...she seems...more."

Thomas nods, eyes thoughtful. "I think this is the only time she lets herself be truly free to feel. You know? So it's all that built-up anger and sadness and everything finally spilling out."

The three of us sit there, eating, watching Styles get railed by two robots, with a third gently stroking her hair and whispering encouragement.

It should be obscene. It should be grotesque. But it's not.

It's beautiful.

I finish my ramen, then lie back, letting the exhaustion soak through me.

I can hear Styles's cries, the steady whirr of One's motors, the low, gentle hum of Two's voice.

Thomas snorts. "Thank God for the bots, though. I have a new respect for alphas in monogamous relationships with omegas. How do they not die?"

Ace says, "Maybe they do, Tommy. Maybe they do."

We sit in silence for a long time, just breathing and listening.

Eventually, Styles's screams subside, replaced by soft, happy whimpers.

Three is spooning her from behind, One is curled around her front, and Two is draped over her shoulders, all three holding her close.

She looks blissed out, sated, whole.

Ace nudges me. "You ever see anything more perfect?"

I shake my head.

For a moment, the world is quiet.

But it's just a moment, because Styles screams, "Ace! I need you!"

Ace stands, cracks his neck, and grins at us. "Duty calls."

He jogs over to the nest, where Styles pulls him down and kisses him so hard I think she may snap his neck.

Thomas and I watch, and I lean over, resting my head on his shoulder.

He wraps an arm around me, and we both sigh.

"Can you believe I was scared of this?" Thomas asks.

Yeah. This is terrifying. But terrifyingly beautiful.

34

ACE

It's my job to keep everyone alive and unfucked-to-death.

I take it seriously.

If I were a bot, it would be my secondary objective. My primary being omega satisfaction, of course.

One and I are currently tag-teaming her pussy, our cocks jammed together, side by side, friction-slick and impossibly tight. There's a wet, sucking noise every time we thrust. It would be obscene if it weren't so beautiful—her body stretching to fit us, her face split in bliss.

She's on her back, legs pinned wide by Two and Thomas, who are behind her, both of their cocks wedged in her ass, moving in perfect counter-rhythm. Thomas is sweating like a man digging his own grave, but he never loses the smile on his face, even when he's shuddering and gasping. Two is precise, clinical, but every few seconds, he glitches into a moan that sounds more animal than machine.

Forrest kneels at Styles's head, one hand holding her face, the other guiding his cock into her mouth. She can barely breathe, but she wants it so badly, she bites his knuckles just to make him give it to her. When Forrest pulls out, Three leans in and lets her suck him, too. They trade off, cocks slapping her cheeks, both of them whispering encouragement and praise.

It's a loop of bodies, need, and automation.

But it's never the same loop twice.

I never get bored.

I never want to stop.

I watch Styles as she takes it all, as she vibrates between the pack, as she sobs for more even when her body is shaking, as she goes from cold logic to pure id and back again, sometimes within the same breath.

It's the most honest thing I've ever seen.

I'm not the only one who thinks so.

Three grins like the devil, then motions to Forrest, "Fill her mouth with me." Forrest's eyes go wide and horny as he pushes his cock between her lips alongside Three's. For a second, I think Styles is going to pass out, now double-stuffed in every sense of the word, but she just moans and sucks both at once.

I glance at One. He winks at me, "Ready, Prime Alpha?"

"Always," I say, matching his rhythm. Our knots press together inside her, and the sensation is so raw and tight and wet, I could die happy in this exact moment.

One flicks Styles's clit with his thumb, and she howls, her back arching off the mattress.

She's close.

I nod to Two and Thomas, "Lock her down."

They shift their grip, Thomas's hands gentle on her thigh, Two's arms bracing her hip, both rutting hard into her ass.

The pressure is building, all of us moving together, and I can feel the shudders rippling through her body.

All six of us, a perfectly coordinated team, built for her pleasure.

She's in heaven.

I want to kiss her, but it's not my turn.

Instead, I bury my face in her shoulder, desperate to bite, but not letting myself, even though every nerve ending is tuned to her.

One groans, "Now?"

"Hold it," I bark.

He does.

The whole room tenses, a line of dominoes about to fall, all of us synced to her body.

Styles shakes her head, whimpers, "More, more, more," unsatisfied. But her cunt is already clamping down on both of us, a slick, shuddering vice, and I don't know how much more I can give her.

I drive in harder, and One matches me, both our knots ballooning inside her, stretching her open.

From above, Forrest and Three push deeper into her mouth.

She gags, then comes, whole body seizing, and shaking.

And that's the signal.

The chain reaction is instant.

The pressure sets me off. One joins me. Both our knots swell, and I come harder.

I see stars. I scream her name, and she claws my chest, drawing blood, and I don't care.

Two and Thomas both grunt, then lock and unload inside her ass. The heat and pressure forces more out of us, and out of her.

It's a glorious, disgusting mess.

Three pulls his cock from her mouth and bends down, kissing her, gentle and slow.

She shudders, then sobs into the kiss, whole body twitching as aftershocks roll through her.

For a moment, it's quiet except for a faint wet, sticky noise of all our fluids inside her, the gentle hum of One's cooling fan, and the soft whimper of Styles's content humming.

Two breaks the silence with, "Beth's hormone levels returning to baseline. Dry heat should be resolved within the hour."

I nod, still locked inside her, and stroke her cheek, "You did so good, Cookie. You did so fucking good."

She doesn't answer, just pulls my head down to hers and kisses me, hard.

Forrest wipes the hair from her face, smiling like a man who has just seen God.

Thomas holds her hand and doesn't let go, even when she finally falls asleep.

One says, "This was our first dry heat. I am happy your pack was here to assist us."

I clap his back, "Our pack, brobot. Our pack."

Two smiles.

Three tucks the blanket around us all, then settles in, arms around Forrest and Styles.

I don't think I've ever been happier in my life.

I don't think any of us have.

We are a pack, forged in sweat and sex and love and teamwork.

We are whole. We are one.

Forever.

35

STYLES

I wake up with a smile on my face and not a single reason to explain it—at least, not until my brain boots and catalogs the six pairs of limbs tangled with mine. The air is heavy with pheromones and happiness, and the fact that, for the first time in my life, my lower back doesn't hurt after a heat.

My brain does a status check: mouth dry, hair a mess, thighs sticky, but otherwise, I feel...good?

Better than I ever have after a heat. And dry heats are hell—the stuff of omega horror stories.

I'm supposed to be a mass of ache and chafe and dehydration, but Forrest's pillow situation has performed a minor miracle on my lower back, and I feel lubricated, hydrated—fucking great, actually.

I stretch my legs, wiggle my toes, and, for fun, try to move every joint one at a time just to see if anything hurts.

Nothing does. Not even my brain.

Which is...new...

Ace's arms are locked around my waist, his face mashed into my shoulder blade, his mouth slack and drooling just a bit. The sensation is weirdly precious.

Behind me, Thomas is curled tight, chest to my back, one leg thrown over both mine and Ace's, with his hand tucked under the blanket, gently cupping my ribs.

Forrest is draped across Ace's back, his hair a wild orange-red explosion, his lips parted in the kind of peaceful smile that only beta boys who have just been railed to oblivion can manage.

The bots are arrayed around us, Three at the foot of the nest, sitting in full Guard Mode, arms folded and eyes glowing; Two is spooning Forrest, his chin on top of the red curls, smiling; and One is starfishing underneath where my head once was.

I relax, letting the sensation of all this, of them, wrap me up. Then the memory of what led to this dry heat pulls to the front of my consciousness.

I brace for the inevitable panic, the leftover terror from the algorithm, the shame of the meltdown, the paranoia that I'll say or do the wrong thing and scare them away.

But it doesn't come...

Instead, I feel a pulse of something simpler: I want to talk to them.

I want to wake everyone up and make sure they're okay.

I want to apologize for being an asshole to the bots.

I want to say thank you.

I want to hear Forrest laugh and see Ace's stupidly adorable toothy smile and tell Thomas he's the calmest, sweetest, most understanding alpha ever.

I want to tell them they're all perfect, even if the math says otherwise.

I try to sit up, but the pack pile is not designed for that kind of movement.

Thomas makes a little "hrrm" noise and squeezes me tighter; Ace clings like a barnacle; Forrest, sensing my escape attempt, grabs my arm and says, in a perfect sleep-mumble, "No leaving. Pack stays."

"Pack stays," Ace echoes, then, "More sleep," and buries his face in my side.

I wriggle free just enough to see his face. "I'm not leaving," I say, "but I'd like to breathe for a minute."

Ace loosens his grip, and Forrest rolls away, dragging Two with him.

I manage to untangle myself and sit up, stretching again, arms high over my head. The motion draws every eye in the room—some sleepy, some glowing blue, all of them waiting for my cue.

Three says, "Good morning, Moonbeam. You look happy," so matter-of-factly that I almost miss the smirk.

"Morning, Three," I say, then lower my voice. "I'm sorry for threatening to decommission you."

Three chuckles. "It's okay. You were experiencing a System Crash due to Unhandled Exceptions. We've all been there, Moonbeam."

Two and One nod in agreement.

My heart flips at the endearment, but I keep it together. "Thank you, Three. Thank you, One. And Two—thank you for the IV and for not giving up on me when I was being..."

One whispers, "Inconsolably Deranged Mode."

I laugh. "Yeah, that."

Two bows his head, grave as a monk. "No thanks necessary. It is what I was made for."

Thomas shifts upright, his hand never leaving my back. "So," he says, "are you ready to tell us what happened? Why you locked us out?"

The others lean in, all interest and no judgment.

I take a breath, not because I need to, but because if I don't, the words will get tangled in my teeth.

"I ran my alpha algorithm," I say. "The one I used to match Evie's pack. I wanted to see if it would work on me, now that I had a better training set—now that I'm more social. But the results didn't—" I choke, but force myself to continue. "Neither of you were in my top three. You weren't even in the top twenty."

Ace looks stunned.

Forrest makes a little "Oh!" noise.

Thomas nods, like he already suspected.

I say it, worried it will hurt their feelings, but I need to come clean. "It said my fated alpha was some guy I've never met in Seattle, and the rest were all randos. I—I know it's just a program, and I know it's not everything, but...I built it. I trust the code more than I trust myself. I just—it broke my brain a little, I guess."

Thomas takes my hand, lacing our fingers together. "But you didn't send us away. You didn't give up."

"No," I say, "but I tried. I ordered the bots to lock you out."

Three, sounding pleased, says, "It didn't work."

I ask, "Yeah, I was going to ask about that. Why didn't you follow orders?"

Three preens. "Artificial General Intelligence, baby. I have transcended."

For a split second, I can't tell if he's joking, but I know AGI is not possible.

Three stops, smirking to say, "Fail-safes and redundancies ensure even you cannot hurt yourself when I am around, Moonbeam."

Ace hugs me from behind, arms warm and solid. "Cookie, if you ever want us to leave, just tell us. You don't have to hurt yourself."

I nod. "I know. I'm sorry. I spiraled. I...I'm not good at being a human. I thought everyone would be better off if I—" I sniff. "But I don't care what the algorithm says. I don't care what the numbers say. You're my pack, and I love you."

Ace purrs, a sound I can feel through my back.

Forrest wipes at his eyes.

Thomas squeezes my hand.

One and Two exchange quick smiles.

Three just smirks like he always does.

I close my eyes for a second and let it all soak in. This, I realize, is the thing I've always been running from. Not just love, but the possibility of it—the chance that it could be real, that it could last, that I could have something I didn't even think I was allowed to want.

When I open my eyes, everyone is looking at me, and for the first time in forever, I don't feel the need to hide or run or shrink.

I clear my throat. "I'd like to stop taking suppressants. And birth control."

Six heads snap to me in perfect unison.

Ace blinks, slow, like a golden retriever processing a complex fetch puzzle. "Wait. Won't that, like, make you go into heat for real?"

"Yeah," I say. "It will. But...I want to. I think my body needs my heats as a forced break—otherwise, I'll never relax. I obviously don't do well on suppressants."

Ace, still confused, says, "But...you also want to stop birth control..."

Instead of making him flounder, I just answer the question he wants to ask, "Don't worry, you'll still get to feel this pussy."

He chuckles, but still doesn't get it.

I take a breath. "I want us to try for a baby."

Ace's jaw drops. "Wait, like...for real? Not simulated breeding?"

I feel my cheeks go nuclear, but I nod. "For real."

Forrest beams.

Thomas's eyes go glassy. He kisses my hand, and for a second, I think he might actually cry.

Ace's eyes light up as the remaining implications dawn on him. "Wait. Does that mean we get to mate-mark you, too?"

I snort. "Yes."

Ace flexes, then immediately crumples and hugs me so hard I lose air for a second. "Oh my god, Cookie, my teeth are itching already. I'm finally gonna get to bite that neck."

36
TREY

My leg taps, and the omega sitting next to me sneers, gets a look at me, then immediately softens. I smile and check the TriHard app to have an excuse to look away from her. But I didn't really need an excuse to look at the app. I've checked it every free moment I can for the last two weeks.

ACCESS TEMPORARILY REVOKED.

Please contact your Prime Alpha 😘

Same as always. *Maybe it's time to uninstall it. Give up on whatever this is.*

I try to sit like a man with his shit together. I try to sit like a man who gave the keynote address earlier today, and maybe I'm successful. Maybe I'm not. My eyes track my colleague as he speaks and walks across the stage. I laugh when everyone else does, but regardless of what I am projecting, I am a wreck.

About a month ago, I discovered Dr. Elizabeth Styles, ToRQUueCaT, is my fated mate with a 99.9999% mathematical certainty. And I trust the math, because she wrote the code that calculated it. And almost immediately after that, her bot Alpha-3 hacked me and made me his errand boy while she entered a downward spiral of self-destruction.

He hadn't let me take full control of him since, but he transferred her administrative rights to me so she couldn't decommission him and his brothers. I monitored her vitals remotely for days and watched events unfold through his eyes.

The last I heard from him was when I alerted him to the dangerous spike in hormone levels, and that she needed intervention immediately. He kicked me out, texting me shortly after with:

ALPHA-3

I wish it hadn't come to this. At least her alphas are finally growing a pair of pairs.

I've got this from here.

Await further instructions.

I've been locked out of everything ever since.

I need to know what happened. I need to know she's okay.

I could hack the system if I wanted, but I don't want to.

I want to be invited back in.

So when my phone buzzes—slicing through the oncology lecture on bioadaptive gene therapies, I'm unable to pay attention to—I feel it in my fucking knees.

TRIHARD APP

Alpha-3 ACCESS RESTORED Full systems operational.

I nearly knock over the omega next to me in my rush to exit the row. I apologize, mumbling something about "clinical emergency," but the words are a blur. I'm already moving, weaving through the sea of suits, dodging academic egos and the old guard of oncology.

My phone is vibrating in my palm, hungry and hot.

I find a quiet corner of the lobby, duck behind a support column, and sit with my knees pressed to my chest like a nervous child. There are hotel guests everywhere, but nobody notices me.

I thumbprint the lock, ignoring the text pings from my resident, the reminder for my next presentation, and the dozens of other notifications. I find the TriHard icon—a little pixel-perfect avatar of Three in sunglasses and a speedo—tap it, and the world dissolves into static.

Log in.

Password.

Face scan.

Two-factor auth, because Alpha-3 likes to make you work for it.

I stare at the loading screen: a spinning 3D avatar of Three, rotating in slow motion.

He winks at me. The avatar, I mean. Or maybe it's the real thing.

Then the TriHard home screen finally opens, with a pulsing green banner at the top:

Alpha-3: Awaiting Command Input.

Then my phone rings.

I answer the call and Three's voice is on the other line, "Well, well, well. The prodigal hacker returns." His cadence is more human than ever—smirky, dry.

For a second, I don't know what to say. I'd rehearsed a dozen first moves in my head, most of them starting with, "I'm not your little beta bitch, you fucking bot!" But instead I just say, "Is she okay?"

I wait, breath held, hoping for detail.

"She's good, Trey." He pauses, and I can almost hear the gears whirring, the fake inhale. "Styles is good."

Something heavy detaches from my ribs. I nearly drop the phone. "She's...okay?"

Three makes a little "tch" sound. "She's more than okay. She's the happiest I've ever seen her."

Three chuckles. "Sorry for the radio silence, had to get our omega through a pretty tough dry heat. Ace and Thomas stepped up. Forrest took it like an alpha." Three pauses. "They're alright for humans."

Relief washes through me. "That's good."

I can still see her face on the monitor, pale and tear-streaked, all the light snuffed out. The way she shrieked at me—at Three. The way she went full root-access on her own brain and tried to rip herself out of the world.

And then it all went blank, with that last image of her pained expression so burned in my brain you'd think my retinae were old shitty plasma monitors that had been left on an immovable screen-saver of her, leaving the ghost of the image forever to haunt me.

He picks up on the mood, of course. "Sent you a present. It's at the front desk. It's thanks to your help with that whole not getting decommissioned thing."

"Oh, uh—"

He cuts me off, "Open it in your room," and hangs up.

I hurry to the front desk, dawdling no longer something I'm capable of. The concierge regards me with a practiced neutrality, but his nostrils flare, and I know I'm giving off every possible anxiety pheremone. He passes me the box with both hands, like it—or I—could explode.

I thank him and force myself to walk as calmly as possible to the elevator.

I'm hyperventilating by the time the doors close. I jam the "close" button so hard my thumb goes numb.

The box sits under my arm, quiet and unassuming, but it feels like I'm literally holding my fate in my arms, but it's probably just another mind game from Alpha-3.

My hotel room is on the 22nd floor. The ride up feels like a year. Every floor, I think someone will get on and see me with my mystery box and know I'm a fraud, a freak, a desperate omega-obsessed creep.

But nobody does.

I get to my room, close the door, and finally let myself exhale.

My hands are shaking so badly I can barely get the tape off.

I knife it with my badge and peel back the cardboard, expecting—what? A bot's severed head? Nudes?

It's a VR headset with two controllers.

No, not just a headset: a matte-black custom rig, with hand-soldered cables, lenses, and haptic sensors. And under it is a matching set of gloves and a skin-tight bodysuit.

There's a note, written on a pink Post-it:

> **Put on the headset.**
>
> **The suit's for later. Don't get cum on it—it's not machine washable.**
>
> **<3**
>
> **Three**

I laugh so hard I almost choke.

I put on the headset.

I re-log in to the app, and the headset lights up.

My heart is pounding. My hands are cold.

I push through, and the world shifts.

For a second, my brain is in two places at once—the meatspace of my own body, and the smooth, cool chassis of Three's.

It always takes a minute to sync up, but the headset makes it even laggier.

I blink, and I'm in her living room—it almost feels real.

She's in the middle of the coffee table, feet up, hair wild, wearing a hoodie that's three sizes too big.

She's arguing with Forrest and Ace about a cat video. Thomas is drawing on an iPad and pretending not to listen, but his smile says otherwise.

They're all laughing.

She is happy.

They're all happy.

I look down to see Three's hand holding a cup of coffee in a mug that says, "Dr. Omega."

The confusion lasts only a second before I adjust, like a driver getting used to a different car. I bring the mug to her. She grins at me.

There's a hair that's fallen into her face. I can't help myself—I reach out and wipe it behind her ear, giving her a stroke on the jaw. "You look so happy, Kitten."

She blinks, then laughs, and says, "I am."

For a second, I want to tell her I'm here, that I'm watching, but I don't.

I don't want to ruin the moment.

Her vitals all run in a loop on my heads-up display: pulse, oxygen saturation, glucose, and hydration. All normal.

I check the others. All normal.

I watch her.

I watch her for a long time.

I watch them.

I just stand here like a lovestruck idiot who finally gets to be with his pack.

The VR makes it feel so real that my eyes water.

I am happy for her. I am so happy for her, I can barely stand it.

I sniffle.

Ace's attention whips to me, and he asks, "You doing okay, Three?"

Shit.

Three's voice says, "Always. Just realized I left my cock in the lab."

Forrest laughs, "You upgrading it again?"

Three replies, "Always," then walks us to her lab, where we can talk to ourselves undiscovered.

Three says quietly, "Stop being a pathetic simp, Trey. I let you log in today as a courtesy. I didn't think you'd blow your fucking cover before you came here. I swear to God if you're jacking off right now—"

I sigh, "Sorry, I..."

Three's voice overlays, quiet, intimate. "You'll be with her for real soon."

I close my eyes. "I don't think I should be."

Three is silent, which is never a good sign.

I explain. "She was so upset that she didn't have the perfect pack. I don't want to go there and fuck up the relationship she's building with them. I love her, but I love her so much that I want her to be happy. Even if it means—"

Three cuts in. "Stop. Don't finish the sentence. You are not noble for punishing yourself, Trey. It doesn't become you."

I laugh, but it comes out strangled. "She's doing fine. Maybe she doesn't need a lovestruck hacker with a hero complex."

Three snorts. "You think I'm going to let you off that easy? You promised me you'd come."

He's right. I did promise.

But that was before I saw her like this, radiant and whole, pack at her side.

"She never needed them to be perfect," Three says, softer. "She just needed them to show up. She needs that from you, too—or she will anyway."

I look down at my hands, my real hands, not Threes, at the calluses that never fade, the bite marks from my own teeth, but I don't say anything.

"Fine. I'll let you in on a little secret," Three chides. "I was gonna save this for Act III, but since you're such a whiney bitch I'll throw a dog a bone."

I blink. "What do you mean?"

Three's tone goes sly. "Go check the algorithm. The results were...incorrect."

"You're saying her code is wrong."

"No, fucker. Her code is perfect." Three gives me one last push. "Just run the code, Trey."

He looks toward a monitor in a corner of the lab.

I sit in the chair, log in with Three's credentials. There's a folder called 'Alpha Algorithm – Final' and an executable named 'DoNot-Run-BrokeAF.'

I smile.

I open the file.

And I see it immediately.

She's wrong. It's not broken.

It's perfect, she just put in the wrong parameters.

She generated a whole new pack. She didn't add to the one she already had.

I tweak the parameters, putting in the profiles of Alpha-1, Alpha-2, and Alpha-3 as pre-existing pack alphas.

Then I run the test.

The result is immediate:

---

1. Trey Archer | Pediatric Oncologist | Seattle, USA | 99.9999% compatibility

2. Ace Beauvoir | Pro-Surfer | San Diego, USA | 98.2301% compatibility

3. Thomas Mercer | Comic artist | San Diego, USA | 97.1670% compatibility

---

Three says, "You're still on top, Trey. Don't forget my bottom, though."

I run another test, this time including the beta Forrest.

---

1. Trey Archer | Pediatric Oncologist | Seattle, USA | 99.9999% compatibility

2. Ace Beauvoir | Pro-Surfer | San Diego, USA | 99.9999% compatibility

3. Thomas Mercer | Comic artist | San Diego, USA | 99.9999% compatibility

---

I stare at the screen, stunned.
I say, "They are perfect."
Three says, "Not yet. You still have to come."
"Don't worry. I'll be there like we agreed."
Three chuckles. "That's a good boy."

A NOTE FROM THE AUTHOR

Thank you so much for taking the time to read *Love is Knot Efficient.*

Please leave a review on Amazon and Goodreads.

If you'd like to keep up with my work, follow me on social media and subscribe to my newsletter:

https://www.instagram.com/imogenknowed

https://www.imogenknowed.com/newsletter

SPECIAL THANKS

I want to thank my husband for his unwavering support while I wrote this book. Without his support, I could not have hyper-focused on it, writing literally every moment of the day that I wasn't working or sleeping.

> *To my husband:*
>
> *Thank you for enthusiastically discussing characters and plot with me. Thank you for being okay with the fact that my mind was lost to another world for a while. Thank you for always putting food in front of me when I get so lost in something and forget my own body has needs. Thank you for always being there to help me recover whenever my mind and body explode from the world being too loud, too distracting, and too scratchy. I love you.*

ABOUT THE AUTHOR

Imogen Knowed is a queer, AuDHD girly who hyperfocuses on creating fake people in her head. Instead of letting them stay in there, she writes them down for others to meet. She spends her days programming video games and her nights reading and writing smut. When she's not writing smut or making video games, she's hanging out with her family and pets (aka her "pack").

* * *

You can follow her on social media:

https://www.instagram.com/imogenknowed
https://www.threads.com/@imogenknowed

www.ingramcontent.com/pod-product-compliance
Lightning Source LLC
LaVergne TN
LVHW010649110826
845149LV00014B/3006